Haven

FIVE STAR

Other Five Star Titles
by Don D'Ammassa:

Murder in Silverplate
Scarab

Haven

❋ ❋ ❋

Don D'Ammassa

Five Star • Waterville, Maine

This novel is a work of fiction. Names, characters, places and incidents are either the product of the author's imagination, or, if real, used fictitiously.

First Edition
First Printing: December 2004

Published in 2004 in conjunction with Tekno Books and Ed Gorman.

Set in 11 pt. Plantin.

Printed in the United States on permanent paper.

Library of Congress Cataloging-in-Publication Data

D'Ammassa, Don, 1946–
Haven / by Don D'Ammassa.
p. cm.
ISBN 1-59414-229-7 (hc : alk. paper)
1. Life on other planets—Fiction. 2. Science fiction.
3. Mystery fiction. I. Title.
PS3604.A46H38 2004
813′.6 22 2004056364

Haven

Chapter One

❋ ❋ ❋

It had been the most pleasant day he'd spent in a long time, right up until the moment when Wes Avery found the dead body sitting at the edge of a field of parasoy. He had felt unusually refreshed that morning, the slightly-too-large sun had been warm and welcoming, the bell vines in the nearby trees tinkled merrily as their clappers were stirred by a gentle breeze, and his sleep the night before had been undisturbed by the nightmares that had been troubling him for the past year.

There was never any doubt in his mind that the man was dead. His fixed stare was unblinking and unseeing. Avery's first reaction was to wonder if this was just another of his hallucinations. They'd become less frequent following his departure from Aragon, his bioengineered implants gradually learning to respond more quickly, but his doctors had warned him that he would remain susceptible to them, particularly if he was under stress. There was as yet no known cure for the alien virus that had infected his brain.

"We can ameliorate its effects, but you will continue to experience occasional episodes." The episodes consisted of vivid hallucinations, often flashbacks to the Lysandran war, images of which still haunted his nightmares. "The virus concentrates itself in the portion of the brain that contains long-term memory and will occasionally superimpose old data over current sensory input." Flashbacks, in other words. A neurotransmitter embedded in the back of his neck inhibited the virus, at least most of the time, but further exposure to the source of the infection was not recommended. And so Wes Avery had sold his property on Aragon, applied for citizenship on Caliban, and set out for a convalescent vacation on Meadow while his new studio and home were under construction.

Avery hadn't actually touched the body yet, but it seemed real enough, although many of his hallucinations had seemed equally authentic. The first hint of panic should have triggered the implant if this was a flashback. He waited patiently for the hallucination to waver and then fade as the virus subsided into passivity, but the body remained as vivid and sharply delineated as ever. The dead man appeared to be only slightly past his youth, although cell decay reversal techniques and other anti-agathic treatments had made it much more difficult to accurately judge an individual's actual age. After a moment or two he began to accept the possibility, no, probability that this was an objective phenomenon, not another phantom. Callous though it might be, he felt relief rather than alarm when the corpse remained solid and real.

Avery had almost literally stumbled across the man's legs, emerging from the not particularly well-traveled path he had discovered while exploring the web of narrow lanes, paved walkways, and informal woodland trails that spread westward from the cottage where he was staying. He had just emerged from a dense growth of blue-green trees, native to Meadow but closely resembling the various coniferous strains that humans had carried with them to the stars. Before emigrating to Aragon as a young man, Avery had grown up on Parchmont, a fierce and sere desert planet sprinkled with oases and small salt seas, but when his parents died during an earthquake, he had decided to find a more hospitable home. The forests of Aragon had seemed dark and oppressive to him at first, but later he had learned to appreciate their complexity and beauty.

He had been in no particular hurry, had no appointments to keep, no self-imposed schedule to maintain, no therapy sessions to prepare for. Sooner or later, he would have to learn to function without the constant attendance of medical personnel, and the resort on Meadow had seemed an ideal setting. He had only been on the planet for three local days, and had already convinced himself that he was once again in full control of his mind. Meadow's day was approximately twelve percent longer than Aragon's, and the village of Haven where he had rented his cottage was relatively close to the equator, so the daylight period was even longer. That had been a factor in his decision to come here, since most of his lingering bad moments came in the darkness, when indistinct shapes could be transformed by imagination and transient memories into images from his past. He had even begun to work again, tentatively and without the intensity of his previous bouts of composition. The marathons of creativity he'd indulged in previously were forbidden until it was clear that he had regained his mental equilibrium. Fortunately, the royalties from his previous work were sufficient to support him adequately, in fact luxuriously, if he'd been so inclined.

The wooded area was, he judged, secondary growth, a mixture of native and imported flora planted to enhance the scenic attractions of Haven, or perhaps to shield the agricultural fields beyond from seasonal winds. Meadow was one of those rare worlds where humans could actually subsist on native food sources, although he had been cautioned that if he chose to extend his visit beyond the time for which he had contracted, he would be wise to accompany his meals with an innocuous supplement that dealt with some minor deficiencies. The planet had been discovered by a commercial vessel during the early years of the Concourse, before the present protocols had been ratified for the establishment of new colonies. Intercorp's on-site team had either been sloppy or deliberately blind, however, and the first permanent settlement was well established before a Concourse inspection team pointed out that the presence of intelligent indigenes elsewhere on Meadow made the settlement legally subject to Concourse oversight. There was clear evidence that Intercorp had been aware of the indigenes almost from the outset and had failed to report that fact until the human presence was too significant to be quietly withdrawn. Although the presence of a sentient lifeform did not necessarily preclude the establishment of a colony, it imposed sharp limits on the nature of its development, and more importantly mandated a Concourse-sanctioned civil government from the outset rather than a commercial board of administration or company-appointed governor. Intercorp had avoided being prosecuted into bankruptcy because the early colonization protocols were ill-defined and self-contradictory, and had even managed to remain extensively involved in Meadow's development, but two generations later the status of Meadow remained uncertain.

When Avery had stepped out from the cool, moist darkness of the wooded area onto the rim of the cultivated field, the sudden shift to glaring, hot sunlight had startled and briefly blinded him. Blinking to clear his vision, he had raised one arm to shield his eyes as he advanced into the open, caught the toe of a hiking boot on a protruding root, and stumbled forward, just far enough that the edge of his foot tapped lightly against the man's calf. Stepping back quickly, Avery had begun to apologize.

"I'm very sorry, I didn't see you there." He had retreated hastily, while his eyes slowly adjusted. A few seconds later he realized that the man was dead, eyes open and unblinking, one corner of the mouth drooping, the shoulders slumped at an odd angle, arms hanging loosely.

Now that he was sure that this wasn't an illusion, he crouched and examined the body more closely. His pulse was elevated and he was breathing more quickly, but without panic. Avery had been in the presence of the dead in the past. He had seen friends and neighbors cut down by laser fire during the assault on the main Lysandran base back on Aragon, the attack that had finally defeated the alien invaders and re-established human control of the planet. He had volunteered to help in the makeshift hospital after the battle and had learned to ignore the smell of freshly-spilled blood. There was no blood here, no obvious sign of injury, but there wasn't the slightest doubt in his mind that the man was quite dead.

Avery licked his lips, looked nervously from side to side, then slowly turned in a circle, scanning the horizon for any signs of nearby human activity, wishing he'd brought his wrist com with him. An automatic harvesting machine was at work several fields distant, its threshing arms and internal sorters emitting a low murmur, barely audible, the upper edge of its superstructure just visible above the intervening crops. It seemed to be moving approximately in his direction, but the artificial brain that controlled it would not be sophisticated enough to assist him. The parasoy trembled slightly in the grip of a light breeze, the individual fronds brushing together in a quiet whisper, but Avery could otherwise have been alone on the planet for all the evidence of human presence he could presently discern.

Hesitantly, he crouched beside the body, gently gripped the left wrist. The flesh felt slightly cool but the arm moved readily enough, apparently not yet suffering from rigor. Recently dead, obviously. Avery leaned closer, concerned that perhaps despite all appearances the man was not actually past help, but there wasn't the slightest tremor of a pulse beneath his fingers, and no indication of breathing. The skin was rather pale, particularly for someone on a world with such pervasive sunlight, but human stock had become much more diverse following its expansion into space, and Avery was unable to decide whether the slight yellowish cast to the man's skin was a symptom of what had killed him or simply his normal coloring. In any case, he was neither a medical technician nor a security officer, and much preferred to leave such details to those who were trained and paid for the task.

Avery stood up abruptly, suddenly repelled by the proximity of death. In his mind's eye, the stranger's face had become fluid, the individual features melting and reshaping themselves, slowly evolving toward a new configuration which he knew would be the image of someone he'd known back on Aragon unless he regained control. When he'd first been infected by the virus, just before his dissociation from reality became so obvious that his friends had compelled him to seek help, Avery's phantom memories had occasionally superimposed faces of the dead onto bodies of the living. He would be discussing his latest project with a colleague one moment, and in the next he'd be sitting across a table from Mabel Hong, who'd been crushed when the Lysandran power beacon collapsed, or Ed Hoyt, who'd lingered for a terrible two hours after a laser had taken off a third of his skull.

Despite the automatic cortical implant, he felt his control slipping and quickly subvocalized the control word he'd hoped would no longer be necessary. A second implant released a calming agent into his bloodstream. Avery hated doing this; on Parchmont the introduction of chemicals into one's body was always a matter of shame, and even though he'd outgrown this inhibition intellectually he knew he'd feel irrational guilt later on. Even worse was the numbing effect of the minute electrical pulse, which left him feeling strangely distanced from the real world, an organic robot interacting mechanically with its environment. Nor was he looking forward to the blinding headache he would experience when the effect began to wear off.

He stood up, examined the scene with more composure, though less concentration. The dead man was dressed in an unremarkable fashion: light billowy blouse and pleated dark pants, no hat, his footwear a bit fancy for walking in the woods perhaps, though showing signs of wear. His hair was not cut to the local fashion, quite close to the skull, and although his clothing was of good quality, he wore neither visible jewelry nor a wrist com. The face was perfectly ordinary, with no outstanding distinguishing features.

Avery considered searching the man's clothing for identification, but upon brief reflection he decided against it. Better to let the local security people take care of that. There didn't appear to be any signs of foul play. It looked as though he'd been out walking and had suffered a stroke or other sudden ailment, then collapsed against the tree and died. Modern medical techniques could perform comparative miracles, but they couldn't bring the dead back to life, so Avery felt no sense of urgency.

He turned in a circle once again, this time more thoughtfully, trying to find landmarks by which to orient himself. Although he remembered the route he had followed since leaving his cottage, it had been very indirect, a series of small scenic lanes, footpaths, and open fields. His sense of direction was well developed, however, a survival trait back on Parchmont, and he had a pretty good idea where the village lay relative to his current location, although he had not until today ventured far from his cottage. There were at least two sizable bodies of water nearby, one natural, one artificial, and he was uncertain whether he would save time by trying a more direct route back, or waste it taking a lengthy detour around Trilby Pond.

Eventually he decided to retrace his original path. Time, after all, was not a major concern. Whoever the dead man might be, he was past help and unlikely to stray off on his own. Avery began to feel considerably better during the brisk walk back. The neuropulse was wearing off and he began to feel a vaguely pleasant excitement with only a hint of panic. Panic was his enemy; it stimulated the virus. He needed to reach a com link, call the local security office, then explain calmly and accurately what he had discovered. He rehearsed his report in his mind, concentrating on that task until it became a discrete entity, with no emotional attachments, no more significant than preparing a meal or dressing himself in the morning. The techniques he'd been taught during therapy helped, and he ran through a series of pleasant childhood memories, indulged in a creative and biologically improbable sexual fantasy, and played some simple but engrossing logic games. It was the side effect of the pulse that was most effective, however; the growing headache started in the center of his forehead and spread up to the top of his skull, distracting him from his worries.

His cottage was one of a dozen or so scattered across a series of small dips and crests of heavily but neatly wooded land bisected by a meandering rivulet of clear water, which was in turned bridged and divided by two gracefully arched walkways. Most of the foliage was native, but he recognized a couple of ubiquitous flowering plants that humans had carried with them to the stars. The balanced beauty of the setting was obviously artificial, maintained by automated gardeners programmed to control any undesirable random growth. Although his was not the first cottage in line, Avery decided not to request help from those he passed and continued until he reached his own, where he pressed his thumb to the lock scanner and stepped inside.

The com link was old fashioned but simple to use. The town of Haven advertised itself as a rational retreat from the excesses of civilization. In theory, life here proceeded at a relaxed pace, free of the more hectic aspects of the urbanized worlds of the Concourse, without sacrificing basic comforts and services. In practice, most of the local people still had access to state of the art equipment, although he suspected that few could afford the credit necessary to import such items. Meadow was small enough not to need a particularly advanced transportation system, for example, but the advertising datasquib he'd reviewed on his way out from Aragon had stressed the presence of current virtual dramas, advanced artificial intelligence systems, and the other "basic elements of an enlightened cultural life." The planet was ideal for human development, but it was a Concourse protectorate, not a self-governing world, and would not attain independence until the question of the native sentients was resolved. That would have discouraged large scale development even if the Concourse administrators were inclined to allow it, which they were not.

He had already seen evidence that the local residents chose, or were forced to settle for, less than leading edge technology. The harvesting robot he'd spotted in the fields that morning was of a type no longer in use on most agricultural worlds. It had little discretion, would have to be programmed with specific instructions each day, and would be unable to cope with anything more than very simple problems. Even Aragon, which had been cut off for several years during the Lysandran occupation, had more advanced equipment. Meadow maintained a façade of rustic simplicity for the tourists, but it also concealed a certain amount of technological poverty. Avery wondered how much longer it would be profitable to export parasoy and other crops from Meadow without making major capital expenditures.

The com link bore an array of familiar emergency and other standardized icons and Avery jabbed at the clasped hands of security, considered adding the starburst, standard symbol for a priority message, but decided against it. The connection was established almost immediately even without the urgent override.

"Lydia Hanifer here. How may I be of assistance?" There was a short pause as the woman at the opposite end of the link glanced to one side, waiting for the facial recognition system to identity him. She had a stern, businesslike face with short-cropped, black hair and thick brows. It was hard to judge scale through a com screen but she radiated strength. Her direct gaze was mildly unsettling, and Avery realized that he was feeling a twinge of quite inappropriate guilt. "Citizen Avery, isn't it?"

His first attempt to speak was a rasping, unintelligible failure. He stopped short, wet his lips, and tried again. "Sorry, I'm a bit out of breath. Yes, I'm Wes Avery. I'd like to report a death."

There was a longer pause this time, and when the woman spoke again, her voice was more professional, cool and authoritative, but her face remained professionally neutral. "A death, Citizen Avery?"

"Yes. A man. I don't know who he is. He's lying dead out there." The memory of the slumped body made his head hurt again. "I was out for a walk and I found him lying in the fields, on the edge of one actually, under some trees. I didn't realize he was dead at first, of course." He realized that he was babbling, forced himself to stop. His headache was much worse now, a persistent buzzing.

"What man is this, Citizen?"

"I told you I don't know his name!" He heard his voice growing higher and made an effort to calm himself. "I've never seen him before, but I've only been on Meadow for a few days. It looked like he died very suddenly. There was no sign of violence, and no one around that I could see. I came straight back here to call you."

"And you're certain of what you're telling me? The man was actually dead, not just sleeping?"

"Of course, I'm sure! Do you think I'm a complete fool?" He stopped again, realizing he was overreacting. He felt irrationally impatient, irritated by the woman's methodical, calm questions. "Sorry, I'm a bit on edge, Officer."

"No need to apologize, Citizen Avery. Your reaction is perfectly understandable under the circumstances."

Somewhat mollified, he forced himself to speak more calmly. "I was out for a walk and I almost literally fell over him. It was quite obvious that he was dead, but I did check for a pulse or respiration. A heart attack, I suppose, or something of that nature. He looked quite peaceful, actually."

"And where did all of this take place?"

"It's a bit difficult to describe. I don't know the local landmarks. Out west of here, west of the town center that is."

"I know your present location." Of course she would; the origin of all calls to security would be automatically displayed at the receiving terminal. "Could you be a little more specific? That covers a great deal of territory and our resources here in Haven are very limited."

"He's lying on the edge of a field of parasoy, under some trees. It's quite a way from here—the way I came—although there might be a more direct route."

Hanifer hesitated. "That doesn't narrow it down very much. Haven is completely surrounded by parasoy fields, rings of them in fact, alternating with other crops and native growth. It would be quite time consuming to search them all."

"I realize that. I think it was on the inner side of the second ring out." He had walked past open stretches of parasoy several times, however, and wasn't absolutely certain. "But some of the paths were pretty overgrown and I might have missed a set of field markers, so it might have been the third. The fields aren't always regularly shaped," he added defensively.

"Would the site be visible from the air?"

He thought she sounded a bit exasperated this time and Avery suppressed an angry response only because he realized how frustratingly imprecise he was being. "Probably not. He was sitting under some trees when I found him. Listen, I can't direct you because I don't know the area well enough, but I can retrace my route. I suppose I'll just have to lead you out there."

"Are you quite certain of that?" Hanifer made no effort to disguise her skepticism. "The fields around Haven are very irregular, as you just pointed out. It would be quite easy to become disoriented."

Avery wondered if the woman was deliberately looking for a reason not to investigate further, then dismissed the idea as nonsense. "I'm from Parchmont," he answered calmly, then realized this might not mean anything to a Havener. "That's a desert world, virtually undeveloped outside the enclaves. Children who can't memorize an intricate travel route rarely survive to be adults unless they confine themselves to the urban centers. I was born at a weather station and spent most of my childhood away from the cities. I'm quite sure that I can find my way back."

"All right. I'll accept your word for that. Stay where you are and I'll be along shortly." He started to break the connection, but she spoke again as he was raising his hand. "Have you mentioned this to anyone else?"

"No, of course not. I mean, I haven't seen another soul this morning and I'm staying here alone."

"Good. Please keep this to yourself then. If it turns out that a crime has been committed, a security investigation will be necessary, and I'd rather not raise an alarm in advance."

"Of course." He felt a growing impatience with the woman. Didn't she realize that he would know better than to discuss a security matter with casual passersby? "Just hurry, will you? This entire situation is very upsetting and I want to get it over with as quickly as possible." The thought of carrion eaters had suddenly occurred to him as well. He had no idea what form of life filled that particular ecological niche here on Meadow. Should he have done something to protect the body? But if so, what? There'd been nothing to cover it with and he certainly couldn't move it.

After the connection was broken, he treated himself to a

mild painkiller. The ache in his skull ebbed very quickly, but never completely disappeared, and he felt twinges of discomfort whenever he moved too suddenly. Although he tried to sit calmly, nervous energy drove him outside where he stared up into the eastern sky, eyes and ears alert to the approach of Hanifer's lifter.

Officer Hanifer took a good deal longer reaching him than Avery expected, and he was not a patient man under the best of conditions. He paced back and forth until there was a visible track through the carpetgrass. "Where *is* the woman?" Exasperated, Avery stormed back into the house, poured himself a cold drink from the dispenser, and was about to punch up the security icon a second time when the house AI announced a visitor.

Avery hastily ordered the door to open, wondering how he could have missed the sound of her lifter landing outside. Hanifer was even taller than he expected. She towered at least two full meters, a finger's width or two more than he, and as he'd suspected she was large boned and heavily muscled. If he'd been asked to pick a single word to describe her, it would have been "intimidating."

"I'm sorry, I didn't hear you land or I'd have come out to meet you." He was suddenly aware of the drink in his hand. "Can I offer you something?"

Hanifer shook her head. "You didn't hear me land because I didn't. I walked out from the village. The security station is less than a kilometer from here."

Avery was incredulous. "You walked? What in the world for? I assure you I can pick out my route from the air, and we can save an immense amount of time that way. To say nothing of my feet."

Hanifer sighed softly but her face remained expressionless. "I'm sorry, Citizen Avery, but this isn't Park City, I'm afraid. Security in Haven consists of two officers, of whom I am one, and a single lifter, which is at present out of service, waiting for a replacement part to be sent down from the capital. I realize this is inconvenient, but the only other vehicles presently at my disposal are some privately owned groundcars and I don't think they'd be of much use to us off the paved roads."

Even though he felt foolish, Avery allowed his voice to rise peevishly. "Well then, couldn't you have borrowed a lifter from someone else, or commandeered one? I mean, this does count as an emergency situation, doesn't it?"

Although there was a hint of anger in Hanifer's eyes, a slight stiffening of the muscles in her back, a shift in the angle of her jaw, there was no detectible change in her voice. "There are no other lifters in Haven at the moment, Citizen. It's part of the official policy, to keep life here as free from distractions as possible without compromising public safety and convenience. We rarely have emergencies and, if necessary, I can call for assistance from the capital."

"Well, this might not be an emergency but it's damned inconvenient." Avery lowered his voice, realizing that he was acting badly. "Come on then. If we must walk, let's get started."

They were out of his cottage and starting along the lane when something occurred to him. "What are we going to do when we get there? I mean, we're not going to carry him back, are we?"

For the first time, Hanifer seemed uneasy. "We'll deal with that situation if it arises."

"What do you mean 'if'?" The simmering anger churned, threatening to return to the surface.

"A slip of the tongue. I meant 'when,' of course." But she didn't sound sincere. "I'm carrying a beacon." She slapped one of the zippered pockets of her sleeveless uniform jacket. "If necessary, I will request that a lifter be diverted from Solitude or another nearby community to transport the body."

They trudged along quietly after that, rarely speaking. Hanifer seemed disinclined to make small talk, waited patiently at each intersection until Avery was certain they were making the right choice. There were a couple of occasions during which he hesitated longer than others; despite his asserted self-confidence, his skills had faded over the years and he had not paid as much attention as he should have. It was mid-morning now, the sun halfway up the bowl of sky. Colors and shadows were different, many of the flowering plants had unfolded their tightly wrapped leaves to catch the light, and even the sounds of insects and the movement of air through the foliage had altered. Despite these changes, he was still reasonably certain that they were following the same route, though not as absolutely confident as he had claimed earlier. Hanifer questioned him whenever he seemed to hesitate, not expressing aloud any of the skepticism written clearly on her face.

At last they reached the strip of forested land which Avery had entered just before making his startling discovery. There were at least a half dozen different paths, but he moved without hesitation toward a specific one.

"Are you quite certain this is the way you went before?" Hanifer was hanging back.

"Of course I am. Come on, it's not much further." He had regained his confidence now, and was quite certain that this was the path he'd taken earlier. When he picked up the pace, she fell back until he was forced to slow and wait for her. "You don't seem to be taking this very seriously." He made no effort to disguise his irritation.

There was a quite visible change in her expression this time, though fleeting. Anger, perhaps? He wasn't certain. "A few seconds won't matter, will it, Citizen?" She made the last word sound like an insult. "This corpse of yours isn't going to wander off. When you came this way the first time, did you see anyone else?" She came to a complete stop and turned her head to examine the high brush to their right, as though searching for Avery's co-conspirator in some elaborate joke at her expense.

"No, I told you that already. I didn't even see any animals except some insects and a winged snake nesting in a tree."

Hanifer nodded, cocked her head as though listening for something. Almost without thinking, Avery did the same, but it was very quiet now, almost oddly so, although he couldn't quite explain why he felt that way.

"Well? Are you coming or not?"

She nodded, and surprised him with a very faint, short-lived smile. "Of course. Lead on."

It didn't take long to cover the last leg of their journey. Despite the bright sunlight, the woods were still dark and gloomy, tendrils of mist rising from patches of damp soil. It had seemed romantic and mysterious before he found the body; now it simply smelled of decay. Avery realized that he was growing increasingly nervous and found himself searching the darkness for evidence of unseen watchers.

He felt considerable relief when a sharp turn revealed bright sunlight ahead and began to move faster now that they had nearly reached their goal. Hanifer lagged behind, apparently unwilling to alter her steady pace, and stepped out into the sunlight a few seconds after Avery.

She stood at his shoulder, critically silent, waiting for him to speak. But Avery had nothing to say, had completely forgotten her presence, could do little more than stare at the spot where he had examined a cooling corpse only a short time before.

The ground was bare and unmarked and they were quite alone. Although the adjacent tree looked familiar, he couldn't be entirely certain that it was the right place. But it had to be.

"Perhaps you chose the wrong path; there are several through here and they all look very much alike. We can walk along the edge of the field and check the others as we go. Almost all of them come to an end on this side of the trees." She didn't reproach him by word or look, but he could sense the change in her tone. She was humoring him; she had never expected to find anything.

Even though he knew that it was useless, he accompanied her along the edge of the field until it was certain that none of the outlets were marked by a dead body, or anything else out of the ordinary. It was an unnecessary effort. He had recognized a peculiarly twisted branch back at the original spot and knew that he'd returned to the right place. The body was gone. Either it had been taken away or, despite all appearances to the contrary, the man had not been dead after all, had recovered and removed himself.

Avery felt angry and foolish at the same time, and Hanifer's steadfast refusal to criticize him just increased his irritation, but he remained silent, responding sullenly to her occasional question. Part of him wanted to apologize for wasting her time and slink back to the cottage, but another part was determined to discover just what was going on here.

Chapter Two

❋ ❋ ❋

A thorough search failed to turn up any sign of the body, or anything else out of the ordinary. Avery walked along the edge of the tree line while Hanifer covered the opposite side, peering down the narrow rows of parasoy with silent but nevertheless eloquently expressed skepticism. It was a frustrating and entirely unpleasant experience, and he kept telling himself that someone must have taken the body away, that he couldn't possibly have been mistaken either about the location or the state of the man's health. When they were far beyond the point where he could entertain any further hope of vindication, he suggested returning to the village to organize a larger search party.

Hanifer shook her head. "I don't think you deliberately made a false report, but sometimes our eyes play tricks on us. Or perhaps someone played an elaborate and rather tasteless joke at your expense."

"I touched the man as well as saw him. He was dead, I tell you!" His voice sounded petulant, and he snapped his jaw shut.

She remained unmoved. "Hallucinations are not exclusively visual. It was hot this morning, your health has not been what it should have been, and you're in a new environment. Under the circumstances, lapses like this are understandable." Avery noted the reference to his health and realized that Hanifer must have consulted his personal profile and medical records, which would have been transferred to the main databanks on Meadow at the time of his arrival so that they would be available in the event of an emergency. She would have had sufficient authority to access privileged medical information.

"This was no hallucination." But he said it softly, realizing what this might look like to someone who had no reason to believe his unsupported word. "The man I saw was as real as you or I, Officer. Except that he had stopped breathing."

There was quite clearly nothing he could do to prove that fact here and now and, after a final look around, he agreed to end the search. They started back along a slightly shorter route suggested by Hanifer; as Avery had suspected, a direct line was impossible because of the village's secondary reservoir, but Hanifer led him along a poorly maintained but less circuitous path that saved a considerable amount of time. Avery had begun to limp slightly; he'd been less active during the last few years, and had gotten little prolonged exercise during his hospitalization. The persistent sharp ache in his ankles did nothing to improve his temper.

"There *was* a body, a man's body, and he was most certainly dead. Surely there's something you can do." But was he entirely certain? The specialists on Aragon had insisted that his implants would suppress the hallucinations and that the worst he should feel would be momentary disorientation or *deja vu,* but perhaps they had been mistaken. Most of his earlier episodes had involved dead bodies, usually of people he had known and who had died during the rebellion. But not always. Sometimes they'd been unrecognizable strangers. Perhaps he'd just experienced a relapse. That possibility worried him so much that he missed what Hanifer was saying and was forced to ask her to repeat herself.

"There are only a thousand or so permanent residents in Haven, and less than fifty tourists. If anyone is reported missing, we will certainly investigate as vigorously as possible. I do take my job seriously. But I prefer to be discreet. There's no purpose to be served by alarming the residents or other visitors unnecessarily, nor do I wish to expose you to possible embarrassment." This last seemed like a veiled threat, but he let it pass without comment.

"What if he was a transient, a visitor from another community, or even from offworld?"

Hanifer sighed, quickened her pace slightly, forcing Avery to exert himself to keep up. "I'm sure you know that all offworlders are registered upon arrival. Meadow has stricter immigration control procedures than most worlds, because of the ambiguity about our legal status. Surely you haven't forgotten the elaborate procedures involved?"

Indeed he hadn't. Meadow was an oddity, the only planet where an established human settlement on this scale continued despite the presence of an indigenous sapient species. Development was confined exclusively to this single land mass: too large to be an island, too small to be a true continent, the population strictly controlled.

"Someone from one of the other settlements then."

Hanifer shrugged. "As I said, I will take whatever steps seem advisable. You must realize that we don't monitor the entire population, only those who travel to the restricted islands. There are nearly a quarter million humans on Meadow, and we couldn't possibly keep track of them all."

"But you will try?" Avery wasn't entirely certain why it

was so important that he know the truth about the missing body. He had always been a very private, even reclusive, person, avoiding most unnecessary involvements, particularly official ones. It had been years since he had so much as voted for his representative to the Concourse Senate. He had numerous acquaintances but no real friends, and preferred the almost monastic lifestyle that had allowed him to create some of the most successful virtual dramas of all time. His social conscience was, if not missing, at least in suspended animation, and he felt no sense of obligation to the dead man.

"I am well aware of my responsibilities, Citizen," she replied coldly, not looking in his direction. "If you have a complaint to make about my performance, I would be happy to provide you the access number for my superiors in Park City."

"No, no. I didn't mean to offend you." Avery suddenly found himself on the defensive, suspected it had been a deliberate maneuver. "It's just, well, you can imagine how upsetting this must be, can't you?"

If Hanifer could, she wasn't admitting it. They completed the walk back to his cottage where she bid him a curt goodbye and kept on toward the village, not even waiting for him to respond. Avery stood at the door, watching her march off until she was hidden by a turn in the road, then sighed heavily, shook his head, and went inside. He remained in his quarters for the rest of the day, attempting to immerse himself in a new virtual from one of his competitors but was unable to concentrate and eventually opted out.

Physically and emotionally exhausted, Avery slept an unusually long time that night, and woke with a renewed though less intense headache and stiff muscles. He felt as though he had dreamed, and in fact his body was drenched with perspiration despite the cottage's very efficient climate control system. Memories of the unsettling events of the previous day recurred immediately, but he pushed them aside, washed himself in a quaintly primitive mechanical shower, ate a light breakfast, then walked to the small den where his portable virtual composer sat in a corner.

His first exposure to virtual drama had been during a visit to Camelot, using the funds he had inherited following the death of his parents. Priam City was the capital of Camelot, already famous for its exotic entertainments, some of which were illegal outside the city limits and on most of the libertarian worlds. Rebelling against his repressed upbringing, he had thrown himself into the brightly colored whirlpool of sex, drugs, fantasy, neural stimulation, and more bizarre enticements with desperate enthusiasm. The contrast between Priam City and his barren home world had convinced him to cut his last ties to Parchmont, although he hadn't expected to end up on the comparatively less sophisticated Aragon.

In the long run, most of the experiences he sampled proved themselves less than satisfying. Avery alternated between pleasures of the mind and pleasures of the body: submitted to induced synesthesia one day, sexual enhancement technology the next. He tried direct cortical stimulation, was brought to orgasm by a furry humanoid alien of indeterminate and probably irrelevant gender, and vicariously participated in dangerous physical activities by means of a rather inadequate mindlink. He was a young man from a planet with limited entertainment resources, and for a little more than a standard year, he'd immersed himself enthusiastically, stopping only when his credit balance hovered at the subsistence level and he found himself unable to indulge himself further.

It was on Camelot that his interest in virtual drama was born. It was a long established and immensely popular entertainment technology in use almost universally throughout the Concourse. Even Parchmont had a small library of material, although he'd grown up in a family that had little time for amusements and considered such things decadent at best. Avery had reluctantly sought employment and found himself entering data at the local ministry of agriculture for a wage that would not support expensive frivolities. He hadn't been to a virtual since childhood, but since the cost of admission was well within his budget, he surrendered to impulse one evening and changed his life forever. Avery was completely caught up in the experience, even though his initial selections were less than critical successes: two routine potboilers in the *Bannion Bayler, Interplanetary Adventurer* series and a historical supposedly based on Terran history, although Avery was pretty certain that Napoleon's career had predated the discovery of atomic weapons.

Within a local year, he had saved enough to buy an outdated but workable virtual recording system. Although his motivation was primarily to create fantasy worlds for his own amusement, within two years he had completed his first noteworthy drama, a subtle tragedy that achieved both critical and public acclaim when he made it available through the planetary entertainment network. He attracted patrons, some of whom were willing to invest credit in his career, resigned his position with the ministry, and began to produce commercial work. His popularity had increased steadily with each subsequent production, and he'd become a significant name in the field in a remarkably short period of time. When the Grahamites came to power and began dismantling Camelot's artistic community, he'd emigrated to Aragon for what was meant to be an extended vacation, only to be trapped there during the Lysandran invasion. By the end of the war, he'd become quite attached to his new home, and had been quite content to compose his work in his house overlooking the Jackknife River.

Then came the disorientation, the flashbacks and hallucinations, and the detection of the alien virus in his brain. He was wealthy enough to afford the best possible medical treatment, but they'd been able to accomplish little more than symptomatic treatment. The implants were designed to counteract the virus but it was in his brain to stay.

The doctors had little more to suggest. "Take a vacation. Let your body and the implants get to know one another. When you're ready, resume as much of your normal lifestyle as possible."

Haven was supposed to be his vacation. Disappearing dead bodies had not been listed among the tourist attractions.

Avery logged into the comnet for company while he set up the recording equipment and tested it, listening with only a small fraction of his mind, letting his hands assemble the components almost of their own volition. There had been renewed skirmishes along the border with the Krail Hegemony, some lives lost, rumors that the systems closest to the disputed area were agitating for a declaration of a state of conflict by the Senate, which had already formally expelled the Krail from the Concourse. The priests of Lalande were once again threatening to secede from the Concourse, citing the revelation to their High Priest that artificial intelligences were instruments of the "Other," a supposedly transdimensional entity who sought to lure humanity to its moral destruction. There had been heated debate about the Lysandran request to join the Concourse and an outbreak of Serpentine Plague on Lithia. Even more upsetting were reports of fresh rioting on Parsimony, following rumors that one or more members of the local planetary council were actually clones.

Avery shook his head in dismay. Despite centuries of expansion to what now numbered something close to a thousand worlds, the human race had been unable to grow away from its primitive superstitions. The fear that clones or artificial intelligence programs were soulless creatures undermining civilization from within had originated back on Earth and spread like a contagion, changing its outward appearance but never its true character. The Concourse Charter allowed each planetary government to set its own policy in such matters, but for many people, the desire to enforce their own personal idiosyncrasies was irresistible.

He spent most of the morning setting up the equipment, testing, calibrating, creating a few simple simulations, and playing them back to judge fidelity. The input cap was designed to fit snugly so that they matched the connections to the ports he'd had surgically implanted in his skull. Actual creation of a simulation involved a complex interaction through both keyboard and direct neural sequencing, and required much more sophisticated equipment than he had here. This was more of a sketchbook, where he recorded quick impressions or subroutines. It would be impossible to do detailed, finished work here; for that, he would need a more elaborate studio capable of the sophisticated blending and sequencing required. Customized AI routines would provide the necessary enrichment levels, using his personal reference library of backgrounds and settings, tastes and smells, sensitivity resolution and smoothing techniques, and other standard and non-standard tricks of the trade. He didn't plan to do any serious work on Haven, but he wanted to reassure himself that he could work creatively without slipping back into self-destructive habits.

Although he had been ordered to ease into the work slowly, Avery continued throughout that afternoon and late into the hours of darkness, pausing only for hastily prepared meals. He was conscious of the fact that he was overdoing things, but in that artificial world that flowed from his mind he could ignore the existence of dead bodies that walked off of their own accord, skeptical and quietly insulting security officers, and the knowledge that an alien virus would likely reside in his brain for the rest of his life. Under the input hood, he was in complete control of his environment, could even alter natural laws of the universe, although it was all illusory. A safe haven, he thought, within a suddenly threatening Haven.

When he finally stumbled to his bedroom, Avery knew he had overtaxed himself. He still hadn't adjusted to Meadow's longer day and had worn himself out physically as well as mentally. He slept fitfully that night, troubled by dreams that fled his awareness as soon as he woke, defying memory, rose while it was still dark, and returned to his equipment, throwing himself into his work with artificial enthusiasm. He napped a couple of times during the day but never left the cottage, managed to forget about the missing body, and actually produced some promising initial work on an ambitious theme he'd considered off and on for several years. Exhaustion finally overcame his enthusiasm, but despite the length of the day, the sun was down when he stumbled back to bed for another night's rest.

On the following morning, he was so lightheaded that he

fell to one knee climbing out of bed and realized that he couldn't afford to be so casual about his health. The possibility of a recurrence of the disorienting attacks sobered him and he resolved to do no further work until he was rested. He forced himself to eat an unusually large breakfast, taking his time over the food, then washed and dressed with equal deliberation. Although he had been provided with a limited range of psychotropic medications to supplement the implants, he was reluctant to rely on chemicals any more than necessary, and the food and clean clothing had already gone a long way toward improving his mood. Meadow had no weather control system, so he punched up a local forecast, which promised nothing but clear skies for the day.

His feet and ankles were no longer swollen, so he stepped outside, breathing the fresh morning air of Meadow. Oxygen content was slightly higher than that to which he was accustomed, another of the planet's selling points as a vacation world, and the sense of physical well being cheered him. There was movement behind the front window of the cottage across the way and he briefly considered walking across to introduce himself, then thought better of it. Many people came to retreats like Haven to get away from other human beings, not to make new acquaintances. If the opportunity arose, he'd be sociable, but propriety and his own natural reticence argued against imposing himself uninvited. The village proper advertised a handful of social settings, including a sidewalk café and an entertainment center, and that should satisfy his sudden craving for companionship.

It was quite warm, with a welcome breeze, perfect weather for another hike. This time Avery turned toward the village rather than away, and moved eastward along the narrow lane, moving purposefully but not so quickly that he didn't enjoy the ornate landscapes and artfully arranged gardens along the way.

Haven's center was arranged in deliberately haphazard fashion, the architecture modeled after the style made popular on Pastoral during that world's reign as the favorite haunt of the rich and bored. Most of the buildings were two stories high, none taller, though some quite obviously had additional levels buried below ground. The streets were unnecessarily wide, but acreage was not in short supply and the effect was pleasant. A mixture of native and imported trees shaded the walkways, some of them bearing the omnipresent bell vines. A handful of people moved about, some industriously, others more casually, and a small group of children of varied ages were playing some indecipherable game in a small park adjacent to the town landing grid.

Avery passed a half dozen private homes, a communal building of uncertain purpose, an arts and crafts shop, before reaching the administrative center. He hesitated in front of the security building. It was large but all on one level, with a small landing field adjacent. A serviceable but older model lifter was parked there, unattended, its windshield discolored, looking as though it could use a refitting as well as a paint job. Briefly he considered going inside to find out if there'd been any developments following his report, but ultimately he moved on without doing so. He told himself he didn't want to ruin his day having another unpleasant confrontation with Lydia Hanifer, who would undoubtedly have contacted him if anything had changed. He had enough insight to realize he also feared learning anything which might cast further doubt on the authenticity of his experience. A single hallucination was not a tragedy in itself; he'd been warned that occasional brief relapses were inevitable. But even during his worst moments on Aragon, he'd been aware that what he was seeing could not be real, just as you could tell virtual dramas from reality no matter how well they were crafted. If the dead man was in fact an hallucination, Avery was losing his ability to distinguish between reality and imagination.

He passed a commissary which carried a variety of native and imported food, household supplies, and other necessities. The building next door was the entertainment center annex, advertising holotapes and virtual dramas for loan or on-site viewing and he paused, automatically checking the display for any of his titles, then moved on. There were some professional offices, including an offworld trading company he'd never heard of, but a small tagline indicated it was a division of Intercorp. Avery wondered how viable interplanetary trade was for Haven, or Meadow in general, but obviously there was at least limited commercial activity. There was a good sized agricultural business locally, but he assumed that most of that produce went to Park City and elsewhere on the planet. Meadow was presumably self-sufficient, but its only real impact on interstellar trade was as a resort. Villages like Haven were scattered across the inhabited subcontinent. The imposed restriction on population growth prevented expansion into large scale manufacturing or other forms of trade and would continue to do so until someone made a decision about how to deal with the indigenes. Transient visitors were not counted as part of the population, and they brought with them offworld credit. Avery had never heard of Meadow until one of the medical specialists mentioned the name, and he had selected it primarily because he was worn out and discouraged and desperate to get away from the constant gentle probing by his doctors.

Just past and on the opposite side stood a smaller

building, set behind a wide patio sprinkled with chairs and tables, and an unprepossessing sign that read: *Quiet Spaces, Beverages, and Snacks.* Avery hadn't walked off his breakfast yet, but the warm sunlight had made him thirsty and a combination of curiosity and the prospect of a cool drink lured him inside. A pleasant and strikingly attractive woman told him to sit wherever he liked and after a brief tour of the interior, he moved back outdoors, selected one of the many empty tables near the perimeter of the seating area. He studied the selection displayed on the menu pad and keyed for a non-alcoholic fruit mixer. A tall young man brought the drink almost immediately, nodded politely, but said nothing when Avery thanked him.

He remained seated in one corner of the patio, watching the occasional pedestrian pass by, his drink kept cool by the cryogenic glassware. A man and woman entered, glanced briefly in his direction without acknowledging his presence, were greeted familiarly by the hostess, and moved to a table in the opposite corner. Both seemed too formally dressed to be vacationers, but Avery sensed that they were not Haveners. For one thing, they both wore their hair considerably longer than the local style. The man looked vaguely familiar to him, but he couldn't quite place the face, or perhaps it was just his imagination or a chance resemblance. He might well be a prominent public figure on vacation, a politician or military official. Avery had no interest in politics or news in general, but he occasionally watched the nets for interesting faces, images, backgrounds, and other artifacts he could incorporate into his creations, and he had a skilled eye and a retentive memory.

The woman appeared to be considerably younger than her companion, and from subtle cues of posture, he deduced she was subordinate to the other. They argued quite animatedly at times, though always amicably, but he sensed that she was reluctantly deferring to him. Avery amused himself by trying to ascertain details about their relationship through body language since he was too far away to hear their actual conversation. He watched the way they made eye contact, the posture of their bodies, and decided that while not intimately involved with one another, they were closer than casual acquaintances. Friends despite the disparity in rank. She expressed an unusual degree of familiarity, as though she were a well-trusted employee. Avery ordered a second drink, amused with his game, shifted position slightly to gain a better perspective, but was immediately thwarted when the man rose, nodded to his companion, made one additional brief inaudible comment, and walked out to the street and off into the distance.

The woman finished her drink, talked easily to the young man when he returned to retrieve the empty glass, then settled back into her chair and stared off into the distance. She seemed to be in no hurry to leave, but there was a vaguely troubled look on her face, as though she had grown uncertain of her surroundings.

Impulsively, Avery stood up with drink in hand, and walked across the patio. "Excuse me, but I'd be willing to bet you're a fellow offworlder." He felt incredibly awkward. This kind of forwardness was so utterly alien to his character that his hands were shaking.

The woman glanced up, her face neutral, and he realized she was younger than he had estimated. "Yes I am, as a matter of fact." She was not unfriendly, but wary.

"Have you been here long?"

"On Meadow? Just short of half a standard year. I'm here on a short-term employment contract." He found himself unnerved by her willingness to meet his eyes steadily. "And you?"

"Just a few days." Normally reclusive, Avery had the distinct feeling he was committing social errors with every word, but he was in the grip of a totally uncharacteristic desire for human companionship. "I apologize if I'm intruding, but there are so few of us here, and the local people aren't very forthcoming." He laughed nervously. "I think we're tolerated rather than welcomed."

"It's a little better in Park City, a bit more cosmopolitan, but I know what you mean, Citizen . . . ?"

"Avery. Wes Avery." He waited to see if she'd recognize his name, was pleased when she did not. "And you are . . . ?"

"Dona Tharmody. Would you like to sit down?" When he was settled into the seat, she touched an icon inset in the table, requesting a fresh drink. "Can I order something for you?"

"No thanks, I'm fine." He indicated his half-filled glass. "What line of business are you in, if you don't mind my asking?"

"I'm a tweaker." Avery didn't recognize the word, which must have shown in his face, because she laughed softly. "Sorry, that's jargon. The proper term is artificial personality technician."

"Ah, a programmer."

But she shook her head. "Not really, no. Actually most code is written by other programs nowadays, and that's not my area of expertise. I just make adjustments to the personality overlays. You know, if you get tired of the sarcastic sense of humor you had originally written into your home monitoring system, I adjust it on-site so you can avoid major rewrite charges. There are limits, of course, but you'd be surprised how much you can accomplish if you understand how the emulation protocols interrelate."

"I wouldn't think there'd be much call for your talents here," he gestured vaguely toward the small commercial district. "Haven doesn't seem to have much use for advanced technology."

"You might be surprised. There's a lot of automated agricultural equipment that's AI managed, and their performance parameters have to be flexible enough for them to run unsupervised. And almost all of the cottages have a low-level AI system. But most of my work is back in Park City. The last three days have been an unofficial vacation of sorts. The Senator and I get along pretty well and my employer is more than happy to have even as tenuous a political connection as I offer."

He raised an eyebrow. "The Senator?"

"Karl Damien. You must have seen him earlier; he was sitting right where you are now."

Avery shook his head. "I saw him of course, but I'm afraid I don't have much interest in politics." But the name did sound vaguely familiar, and that might explain why the man's face had struck a responsive chord.

"Senator Damien is regional representative to the Concourse. He isn't a native of Meadow, although he has a permanent office in the city and owns land all over the place. Since Meadow doesn't have an independent government, it doesn't have a delegate to the Senate, so Karl informally represents their interests. He's on his way back to Park City right now, to catch a shuttle up to the *Star of Night*."

Almost as if Dona had timed it, there was the sudden thrum of a lifter's engine and a sleek shape rose above the line of rooftops a few blocks away. The clasped hand insignia of Meadow's security service was prominently displayed on its side. It was louder than it should be, a faint irregularity in the power cycle, symptomatic of engine wear.

"That's Karl leaving now, in fact."

"Aren't you going with him?" A silly question that he regretted immediately, but she handled it gracefully.

"No, there's no room this time. Only two passengers can travel comfortably in that thing, and I was preempted by a woman who needs microsurgery. I'll be taking the commercial flight back in a few days. Frankly, I can use the time off, and the Senator is letting me stay at his private cottage while I'm waiting. It's a lot nicer than my little rental back in the city."

Avery followed the lifter with his eyes as it moved off out of his line of sight, headed roughly north. "It's a good thing they got it repaired in time."

"Got what repaired in time?"

"The lifter. It was grounded a couple of days ago, waiting for a part from the city. I wouldn't be surprised if whatever it was came in on the same flight that brought you."

Dona frowned slightly. "That would be a neat trick." She gestured toward the departing lifter with her chin. "The local security office sent their lift out at mid-morning to pick us up and bring us here. The Senator gets special treatment because there have been a few threats on his life."

It was his turn to frown. "I thought you said you'd been here three days?"

"Sure. We left Park City three mornings back. The pilot was a quiet little guy. He let us off at the Senator's cottage, early in the afternoon." She saw the confused expression on Avery's face and leaned forward. "Is something wrong?"

"No, not exactly. Or maybe there is. I don't really know." He realized how inane he must sound and forced himself to relax, even counterfeited a brief laugh. "I must be disoriented or something. Or maybe I just misunderstood. You see, I was told by one of the local security people that their lifter was inoperable."

"They must have been able to repair it then. I don't think they'd have taken any chances with the Senator aboard."

"Yes, I suppose you're right. It's really not important, I guess."

They talked long enough that a third round was necessary, and Avery found himself relaxing more completely than he had managed for some time. He admitted to having authored several virtual dramas, one of which Dona had actually experienced, although she remembered it imperfectly. "I was just curious about them, you know. I usually prefer genuine activities, even if they're less exciting. But I'm fascinated by creative people. Where do you get your ideas anyway?" The conversation drifted from subject to subject and he followed wherever she led, surprised at the breadth of her knowledge and interests, appalled at what he now perceived as the narrowness of his own.

"So you're taking a long overdue vacation away from the nerve centers of civilization."

He paused before answering, uncertain how she would react to the truth, finally decided he liked her too well to be dishonest. "An enforced vacation, more or less. I'm recuperating from a nervous disorder."

She stared at him blankly.

"I have a virus infection in my brain that was causing hallucinations until I was properly diagnosed and treated," he explained. "It's under control now." He tapped the back of his neck. "A biotechnical implant neutralizes the virus."

"I'm sorry. I didn't mean to be nosy."

"Not at all. I'm told that one measure of recovery will be

the ease with which I can discuss my condition openly. Sounds like a psychological panacea to me, but I promised the specialists I'd cooperate."

"Any lingering effects?"

He thought about his obsessive two-day session with the synthesizer, pushed the memory away. "Not to speak of. A little depression at times."

"Well, I imagine Haven is ideal for rest and recovery. Meadow bills itself as a planet of quiet leisure. The words bland, dull, and unimaginative also come to mind. I shouldn't complain really, because I've been treated well here, but I'll be very happy when my contract expires and I can go someplace where there's a little more excitement."

The conversation faltered after that and, mutually recognizing that they'd exhausted their current store of small talk, they thumbed the credit vouchers and got up to leave. Avery felt a pang of regret; he hadn't realized how starved he was for casual human companionship. But Tharmody surprised him by turning at the last minute to invite him to have lunch with her. "The Senator's place is quite well stocked. He visits here often, supposedly to confer with the people whose interests he's supposed to be representing. More likely it's a refuge where he can forget politics for awhile."

"I wouldn't want to impose. I mean, I don't even know the Senator."

"No imposition at all. The Senator's larder is more than amply stocked, and most of the perishables will just go to waste anyway. Trust me; there's enough to feed the settlement for a month."

Avery was more than happy to be persuaded.

They were both headed in the same direction, so they walked side by side in companionable silence following the winding path that led out of the village proper and into the well cultivated area that contained the various small visitors' cottages. These were widely scattered and varied in size, most of them considerably more elaborate than the one in which Avery was staying. The largest clearly offered facilities for organized entertainment, with extensive patios, gardens, even a few rummage courts for the athletically inclined. Some were situated to provide maximum privacy for their occupants, with security walls screened by heavily overgrown pathways that twisted and turned around small hillocks, clusters of manicured trees and shrubs, or patches of heavy natural creepers. Whenever the breeze came up, he could hear bell vines tinkling on every side.

"What's the Senator like?" Avery asked. "I don't follow politics very closely, but I have the impression that he's rather prominent."

"Senator Damien is an odd blend of contradictions," explained Tharmody. "Meadow isn't his real venue, although he is their informal representative. His home is on Pretoria, which is far more developed. The total population on Meadow wouldn't make more than a fair-sized city on Pretoria, but he spends a disproportionate amount of time here. Says he likes the simpler, more natural lifestyle, although his cottage is fitted with the finest AI software available for home maintenance and security, the newest model from the Socrates Company, so close to self-aware you'd swear you're talking to a real person when you interface. He was one of their first customers, had it installed while they were still debugging, and naturally they found a few glitches afterwards. This is my third trip down. It was minor stuff this time; the discrimination routines needed some work; they had a tendency to freeze in response to rhetorical questions and the automatic reset was annoying. But the first time the Senator asked me down, it was a real challenge. The damned thing developed the AI equivalent of a guilty conscience and kept apologizing for everything. It was a multi-source problem and every time I thought I had fixed it, the self-correcting master program would undo my work the next time the situation came up."

"I admit I don't know the first thing about AIs, and I even owned one back on Aragon. It was limited and very specialized and I never had a problem."

"You're lucky. Most of the consumer versions are warped one way or another. Mostly small stuff. The manufacturers usually do some fairly rigorous testing and catch most of the big problems. But when human interaction is involved, there's no way to anticipate every combination of circumstances, and sometimes things that would seem completely unrelated to you and I form a paralogical link that can lead to loops, internal logic shutdowns, all sorts of problems. I once had a lifter maintenance unit tell me it was responsible for the trade war with the Glave. Couldn't shake it at all, finally had to wipe the system and start over."

"How do you fix them normally?" He really didn't care, but he was enjoying her company and she clearly enjoyed talking about her work.

"I talk to them. Despite the fancy sophisticated interfaces, they're all very simple in their basic design. You just have to lead them through a series of logical paths until you find the one where they make the wrong choice. Sometimes you can even talk them into reprogramming themselves and correcting the problem, sometimes you have to wipe a circuit or bring in a supplementary subroutine. On very rare occasions there's a hardware failure, but mostly the trouble is in conflict resolution. It's pretty easy to find the problem once you understand how they work, although it's not always as simple to cure. The unit at the cottage is on standby right now though, so we'll have to do things ourselves." She turned her head and winked at him. "Don't worry. I can operate the kitchen manually."

"I never doubted you for a moment."

They turned away from the cluster of cottages where Avery was staying and descended a short slope beneath slender native trees covered with low hanging mosses. The cottages to either side were much larger than anything he'd seen before, hardly cottages at all. Most had security walls; he could see the telltale electronic flickering. The grounds surrounding them were much more elaborate as well. Avery hesitated and turned to his left to admire a particularly impressive display of ornamental plants, some clearly imported from offworld.

"They're really beautiful, aren't they?" Tharmody had paused a few steps ahead of him. "The ones with the pink fronds are from Pretoria. They're sensitive to motion. If you wave your hand in front of those little weblike flowers, they'll open right up. Back on Pretoria, they lure insects inside. Go on, try it."

Curious, Avery left the path and approached the plant, one hand extended in front of him. But before he reached it, his eyes flicked to one side, and he came to an abrupt, stunned halt.

Several meters away, an adult male sat on the ground with his back propped against the bole of a tree, head bowed forward motionlessly on his chest. It looked very much like the same body he had first seen lying out in the sun on the edge of a parasoy field two days before.

Chapter Three

❋ ❋ ❋

For a brief moment, Avery thought he had stepped outside of time and space. He couldn't feel the breeze on his face, all sound was muffled and distant, and he even felt detached from his own body. As the first wave of shock receded, it occurred to him that someone might be playing a bizarre joke, moving the dead man from his original location in anticipation of this moment. Was Dona Tharmody part of the conspiracy, assigned to bring him here? He regained control of his body, turned and walked slowly toward the recumbent form, but when he looked more closely he realized that this was not the same man, although he was dressed very similarly. Nor was it plausible that Tharmody was involved, since it had been he who had approached her. Or perhaps not. If he hadn't decided to introduce himself, might she not have found an excuse to approach him? He deferred consideration of that until later, and continued to walk forward. The recumbent man's face was heavy, deeply lined, and there was a stubble of hair across the upper lip and chin. With each passing second, the dissimilarities became clearer. This was not the same man he'd found lying near the parasoy field.

Tharmody appeared more curious than alarmed, but her eyes widened as she saw the expression on his face.

"What's wrong? Are you all right?"

He heard the questions as a string of individual and unrelated words, but could not immediately assemble them into a meaningful structure. There was a rushing sensation inside his skull and it felt as though his feet were no longer making solid contact with the ground. He knew he needed to subvocalize the code word to activate his secondary implant, but he had momentarily forgotten it and while he understood in some abstract fashion that this was an important bit of knowledge which he had lost, there was no sense of urgency, just a vague regret. Avery felt poised upon a precipice, about to fall into the great unknown, and wondered why he didn't feel a greater sense of alarm.

The "corpse" grunted sleepily and shifted to a more comfortable position. Avery realized that the man was lying in an anamorphic lounge chair that took on the color of its surroundings as it constantly altered shape to support its occupant. The real world snapped back suddenly, leaving him so shaken that he might have fallen if Tharmody hadn't touched him on his shoulder. "Are you all right?"

"Yes. Yes, I think so." But when he tried to turn in her direction, he nearly lost his balance. "I'm just a little bit dizzy. The medication, I guess."

"The Senator's place is just around the next curve. Do you think you can make it that far if I help? Or would you rather sit here while I go ahead and call someone?"

"No, please. I'm fine." He finally remembered the code word and whispered it to himself, felt an immediate surge of counterfeit strength as the subliminals kicked in. He'd pay for it later with fatigue and a headache, but just then he didn't care. Once his composure was restored, he felt foolish. "I'm quite all right, just a passing faintness."

Her expression remained dubious, but she released her

grip on his arm and confined herself to watching closely, as though she expected him to fall over at any moment. Avery was still shaken but he hid it as best he could, smiled, and indicated that they should go on. She hesitated only briefly before turning away, but it was obvious by the concerned look on her face and the frequent glances she sent in his direction that she was not entirely convinced.

The Senator's cottage lurked under a stand of healthy native trees just a few meters further along, the dense foliage concealing it from the walkways until they were almost at the door. She waved a passcard so that the security fence wouldn't zap them as they passed through. The grounds were well tended, with the obsessive orderliness that indicated robotic rather than human gardeners.

The lock responded to Tharmody's thumb and they went inside. Avery glanced around in curiosity, noting the richness of the furnishings. Anamorphic chairs waited patiently, prepared to adjust to the shape and posture of anyone who chose to sit on them, and the walls of the front room were decorated with elaborate, ever-changing mandelbrots. Through an archway, he saw the interface for a highly advanced home intelligence system in the corner of the small room, with what he presumed were diagnostic interfaces connected by slender connectors.

"Would you like to talk about what happened back there?" Tharmody waited until he had settled into one of the seats, which obligingly adjusted to support him as completely and comfortably as possible. "I don't mean to intrude, Wes, but you looked as though you were having a stroke. They have an excellent health clinic in Park City if you're having some kind of physical problem."

"I'm all right, honestly. Just had a brief flashback. Sometimes stress brings them on too quickly for mere meds to deal with them." He scrambled to explain himself. "That man sleeping out there reminded me of something unpleasant, that's all."

"His name's Nimby, a local," she replied. "Theoretically he does minor maintenance work at the visitors' cottages, but in practice he doesn't accomplish much. There was a lifterbus accident years ago, and he suffered severe and irreversible brain damage. He has no surviving family, so the village authority pensioned him off. He's peculiar at times, but harmless. The Senator uses him to run simple errands occasionally, but he has trouble with complicated instructions, and sometimes he just forgets what he's supposed to do and wanders off. Or takes a nap."

"It was just coincidence, I suppose, but he reminded me of someone else." Tharmody didn't reply, just sat alertly facing him, waiting for him to explain further. He hadn't intended to tell anyone about the body he'd found, but neither had he been forbidden to do so. It was only now that he realized that he needed to talk to her about his discovery and the unsatisfactory meeting with Hanifer. The first words came out haltingly, but as he lost himself in the story, it became easier, almost cathartic, and he cut short the flow of words only when he realized that he was starting to repeat himself.

"That's why I was so surprised when you mentioned coming in on the security lifter," he concluded, swinging back to the main subject. "I mean, if it was operable that morning, why didn't Hanifer fly out to pick me up? Even if I had only been able to retrace part of my original route from the air, it would have saved us considerable time. If I really did see a body, and if someone moved it after I left, we might have had a chance to catch them in the act."

Tharmody's face had grown more serious toward the end of his story, and she didn't respond immediately. Instead, she rose and began pacing the room, not looking in his direction.

"How much do you know about Meadow? Its history and government, I mean?"

Avery shrugged. "Not a whole lot. It was originally planned as a new member of the Concourse but its status is unclear because of the indigenes. Human settlement was confined to this single landmass after they were discovered elsewhere on the planet, on some chain of islands I think. There's a Concourse-appointed governor in Park City who supervises the corporate developers and, from what I've seen, its administrative functions seem fairly standard."

"That's true, as far as it goes. But what you're seeing is a relatively recent overlay. Thirty standard years ago, this was a well established company world, and Haven was a company town. Still is in many ways. The governor is tolerated, not always obeyed, although the opposition is largely passive. A lot of people who were born on Meadow were hoping for full Concourse membership and had planned to make their fortunes developing one of the most hospitable worlds we've found. There are also offworld corporate interests who haven't abandoned hope of investing here. Once it was established that the Nerudi, the indigenes, were sapient, Senator Damien and a few of his allies pushed through a ruling that gave the Concourse Senate the right to directly legislate Meadow's future on their behalf. Most of the planet is off-limits to everyone except researchers. There's considerable mineral wealth practically underfoot; the village was originally intended as a self-supporting mining community, with agriculture as a secondary industry. Then the Senate declared a moratorium on all nonessential development, and it became a tourist center instead."

"I didn't realize that." Company worlds were private enclaves, some owned by individuals, most developed by interstellar trading cartels and developers. Technically they were not subject to Concourse rules, but in practice corporations abided by certain guidelines to avoid punitive sanctions elsewhere. When a sentient race was involved, however, the Concourse acted preemptively. "So the company was kicked out and its employees stranded?"

"It wasn't quite that drastic, but a lot of people feel that way. Intercorp concealed the existence of the Nerudi for two generations, claimed they hadn't explored far enough to encounter them until just before a conscientious or perhaps disgruntled employee went public and everything blew up in the Senate. That's still their official line, but no one seriously doubts that reports were suppressed for at least several years in order to protect their interests here. I imagine that they thought once they were firmly established, the Concourse would accept the situation."

"But they didn't."

"No. Like I said, someone sent incriminating holofilms to the media. Damien was head of the investigating committee, and he's done a good job, looking out for the rights of the people who settled here as well as the Nerudi. He's invested a lot of time and effort to strike a reasonable balance. Intercorp agreed not to oppose the installation of a non-company administrative government and formally acknowledged the right of the Nerudi to retain exclusive control over any landmass they currently inhabited, but the company still has a considerable presence and dominates local commerce. The agreement was later expanded to reserve all but this subcontinent in trust for the Nerudi, with the exception of a handful of remote and uninhabitable islands set aside for researchers."

"Do you think Intercorp is still pulling strings behind the scenes?"

"They directly employ a full quarter of the people on Meadow, and indirectly many of the rest. They're too heavily involved here to remain passive."

"I thought security personnel reported directly to the civil government, in this case the governor."

"Yes, but the current governor is a supposedly retired Intercorp official named Tsien. He's probably a significant stockholder as well. Damien was also a major Intercorp investor at one time, but he divested himself completely when the Senate appointed him to head the investigation."

"I see." He didn't, not exactly; politics of this sort had always given him a headache. "Then you think Intercorp might still be influencing the local government in order to advance its own objectives."

She laughed derisively. "Might? Despite some concessions to propriety and public relations, the company still is the local government in everything except name. Trust me, a lowly security officer is unlikely to buck the top brass. Maybe Hanifer took her time so that she could send someone out to remove the body."

The same thought had occurred to him, but he still had some doubts. "That assumes that I didn't just hallucinate the entire incident. I told you, I have a problem with flashbacks, and they generally involve violent death. I was on Aragon."

She blinked. "It's possible. But if that's the case, why did she lie to you about the lifter? I think you did see a dead man. We don't know whether he was killed deliberately or accidentally or died of natural causes, but in any case, if it inconvenienced Intercorp, there might be sufficient influence exerted to hush it up."

"Then Hanifer is helping to conceal the truth."

"Probably but not necessarily. It is possible that everything she told you was true, that they jury-rigged the lifter for the trip to Park City later that morning. Or maybe they'd already received the request and were holding the lifter at the Senator's convenience and didn't want to admit that to an outsider. Hanifer might have made up the repair story to avoid letting on that public equipment was being reserved for a private party."

"I suppose I could go over her head."

Tharmody shook her head. "I'm not so sure. Hanifer is senior here in Haven. You'd have to go to Park City and take it up with the Department of Security. Even if there is no conspiracy, the bureaucracy there would set your teeth on edge. But something does occur to me." Her voice drifted off and she stared at a point beyond his shoulder without focusing.

"You were saying . . . ?"

She gave a little start. "Sorry, I was trying to remember something. Look, I've done some work for Security back in Park City, helped smooth out rough edges in their AI interface. I still have my access clearance, at least for routine level data traffic, and there's a government datalink right here." She turned and pointed at an elaborate terminal inset in one wall. "The Senator likes to be able to keep in touch with things."

"I don't understand what you're getting at."

"You reported a crime, didn't you?"

He nodded. "A possible crime, at least. But I'm still not sure whether or not Hanifer believed me."

"Doesn't matter. She was obligated to file a report and

take steps to confirm or discount your story. I think I can find out just what steps she took."

Avery felt vaguely uneasy. "I'm not comfortable with the idea of spying on the authorities. My doctors want me to rest, not have an adventure."

"No one will ever know that we've been in the system. I'll have to interface passively, but I already have an excuse to tap into the security network. I'm contracted to do periodic quality checks to make sure my tweaking was effective; that's why I still have access to the unclassified files. I can log on, browse through randomly selected transaction logs that just happen to include those I'm interested in. Even if anyone noticed, they'd have no reason to connect my name with yours."

Avery was instinctively wary of anything that even sounded like it might be illegal or dangerous, but he deferred to her expertise. She established the link so quickly and easily that he was surprised by the apparent vulnerability of the security net. Tharmody scanned the coded entries that marched up the small wall screen. "Everything I'm accessing here is a matter of public record. You could walk into any security station and request that they call it up for you. When I was working on the secure stuff, a data security specialist monitored everything I did, and I'm sure all the access codes were changed as soon as I had finished. Don't worry; I'm not doing anything that would get us into trouble even if someone does notice, which is unlikely." She touched a key and the encrypted data was replaced by coherent words.

Avery attempted to read some of the lines as they passed by, but it moved much too quickly. Tharmody was scanning irrelevant information to mask what she was really looking for. He eventually gave up, sat back silently while she worked.

Tharmody's enthusiasm made him mildly uncomfortable. He had grown up in a culture where women were expected to be as physically resilient as men, but to defer to them in most matters. The desert was unforgiving of weakness and despite growing urbanization, the majority of people on Parchmont still spent much of their time in a hostile environment. The original settlers were a comparatively liberal splinter group from a decidedly patriarchal society, and many traditional gender-determined behaviors survived. Despite having spent several years on Aragon, whose chief of state was currently a woman, he had never completely unlearned the prejudices of his youth.

He settled back into a chair and studied his companion. Dona Tharmody was of standard human stock such as was found on most worlds where genetic modification was unnecessary. She was slightly less than two meters tall, slender but well muscled, her hair a bit longer than the local fashion. Avery didn't feel actively attracted to her, but neither was he repelled. There hadn't been much room in his life for female companionship, or male for that matter, but he'd indulged in the usual experimentation as a young man and there'd been occasional, short lived liaisons ever since. Inevitably his work interfered. Either his partner would resent his marathon composing sessions, or he'd start begrudging the time spent away from his work. There were times when he regretted how completely his obsession had taken over his life, but there were also times when he felt as though his creative work was more important than anything else he might have done.

"Are you all right, Mr. Avery?"

He blinked, realized she'd been talking to him for the past several seconds. "Sorry, I was thinking about something else. And please, call me Wes. If we're going to be partners in crime, we should at least be on a first name basis."

"Wes it is then. Anyway, I've just read through Hanifer's duty logs for the past three days." Tharmody began pacing back and forth across the small room, her head tilted down onto her chest. "It was very interesting." She repeated the last two words, letting her voice trail off.

After a few seconds of silence, Avery grew impatient. "What did you find?"

"Nothing." She stopped pacing and turned to face him, smiling triumphantly, obviously pleased with herself.

"Nothing? I don't understand."

"No, and I don't understand it either. But that's what I found. Absolutely nothing. Hanifer didn't file a report about your little excursion, nor did she initiate an inquiry to the database about missing persons. In fact, there's been no official traffic between Haven and Park City at all for the past three days except confirmation of the arrangements for ferrying the Senator back and forth. I know Hanifer by reputation; she's considered a tough, committed, highly competent officer. These aren't oversights on her part; they're deliberate."

Avery was growing increasingly worried. Just what exactly had he gotten himself into? He rose from his seat and walked to the small inset window, staring out through a lattice weaver's delicate webbing at the surrounding garden.

"I found out something else as well." Tharmody waited until she was certain she had recaptured his attention. "Senator Damien was originally planning to stay until the following day. The change in his transport request wasn't received until quite late in the morning, so Hanifer couldn't have known about it while she was out traipsing through the woods with you. And there have been no requisitions for repair parts or lifter-related maintenance work orders filed for the past ten days."

"Then there was nothing wrong with the lifter! Hanifer deliberately delayed things to provide time for someone else to remove the body!"

"That's most likely the case, although there could be some other explanation. Maybe the lifter was being used to take the body away."

Avery thought about it, then shook his head. "No, I can't believe that. It was a quiet morning, Dona. I even heard the motor of a harvester from so far off I could barely make out its silhouette. If a lifter had come anywhere near, I think I would have heard it. Particularly security's lifter. It's an older model with engine problems, and that whine is unmistakable. Remember how loud it was today?"

"I suppose you're right. But she's involved one way or the other, either actively or as part of a cover-up."

"But why?"

She shrugged. "We don't even know the identity of the dead man, so it's pretty useless to speculate about motives. There could, I suppose, be a reasonable explanation, but I'd be hard pressed to invent a plausible one. We need more information."

Avery shook his head. "I'm not sure that we'd be smart taking this any further. I don't know what's going on, but it obviously involves some powerful people."

"We'll have to be careful, certainly, but the Senator is pretty powerful himself. If we can come up with something concrete, I can send a secure message to him. He has the resources to open up a full investigation without fear of reprisals."

"Dona, I really didn't mean to drag you into this. It could be dangerous."

"Yes, but it could also be very interesting. We won't take any chances, but I'd like to play detective a little longer. It sure beats teaching a domestic AI to differentiate between the family pet and vermin."

"All right," he said reluctantly. "So what's next?"

They tossed ideas back and forth for a while, but they lacked enough information to produce any useful course of action. Hanifer was implicated in the cover-up of a death, possibly a murder, for reasons unknown and in collaboration with parties unknown. Unless Hanifer herself was the killer and had arranged for the removal of the body while Avery was waiting for her to show up at his cottage. Their conversation lapsed as they realized how ill-equipped they were to pursue the matter further. Tharmody sighed and suggested that they have something to eat.

"Any requests? The Senator's kitchen is topnotch."

"Surprise me. I'm flexible."

"Living dangerously, aren't we? I could serve you Lemurian eels."

"Actually, I've had Lemurian eels. They're not nearly as unpleasant looking once they've been cooked, and the meat is quite edible, though a bit bland." He was lying outrageously, had never even heard of Lemurian eels.

"That's very interesting, since I just invented them." She wiggled her eyebrows at him and punched up an assortment of conventional fare for them both. Neither spoke again until they were sitting around a table picking at the last of their food.

"I have an idea."

Avery glanced up from his plate, cocked an eyebrow.

"How would you like to fly up to Park City on the lifterbus with me tomorrow?"

"What good will that do?"

"I know someone who might be able to help us. His name is Charles Laszlow. He used to be an Intercorp manager, but he took an interest in the Nerudi when the story broke, resigned his post, and went into politics. Charles would have been one of the leading contenders for governor if they had allowed the elections to proceed, and eventually planetary CEO. When the Concourse changed Meadow's status, they turned the governorship into a mostly honorary position, and Charles refused to enter his name for consideration. I've known him for quite a while, and he's a straightforward, honest man. But we'll have to be careful. Charles is a friend and I wouldn't want to compromise him. He's a bit of a stuffed shirt at times and is a big fan of proper procedure and playing by the rules. If we tell him too much, he'll feel duty bound to go public and agitate for a full investigation. We have to be sure that's what we want before we push him into it."

Avery sighed. "I'm an offworlder infected by an alien virus which causes occasional flashbacks and hallucinations, often involving dead bodies, and I have no evidence to support my claim other than a missing security report which could be an oversight, or an attempt by Hanifer to avoid embarrassing a tourist with an overactive imagination." He paused thoughtfully. "She might even be right, you know."

Dona nodded. "It's possible, but Hanifer is a stickler for procedure. Something funny's going on."

"This really isn't any of my business, or yours. I was irritated at the way I was treated, but not enough to risk my neck over it, or yours."

"Aren't you curious though?" There was something in her expression that told Avery she was taking great delight in their little intrigue.

He sighed again. "So how can this Laszlow help us if we

can't just tell him what we know?"

"Charles Laszlow was highly placed in the administration of Meadow when it was run by Intercorp. He survived the reorganization that followed imposition of the planetary government, but resigned a few standard years ago and chose to remain here and champion the rights of the indigenes. At the moment, he's one of the leaders of the Fraternalist Party."

Avery frowned. "Never heard of it."

"It's local. There's no reason you should have. The Fraternalists advocate immediate, full Concourse citizenship rights for the Nerudi."

"The natives? But aren't they primitives?"

She nodded. "They're technologically backward with an elaborate clan system, but they're surprisingly sophisticated in many ways. The Fraternalist position is that the Nerudi are clearly an intelligent species with a well-developed social structure, sufficiently similar to our own for fruitful intercourse, and that they deserve to be accepted into the Concourse with full rights to determine the structure of government on their home world. There's precedent for it. The Alikashi have full citizenship, and the Cthulians are represented by an observer delegation. Supposedly the Lysandrans have even petitioned for membership now that we've defeated them militarily. Naturally Intercorp is worried about what recognition would do to their property holdings, and the Senate is concerned about public opinion if the Nerudi are given the right to dictate laws to the human inhabitants."

"The human enclaves among the Alikash are subject to local law."

"Insofar as it applies to humans, yes, but the details of the relationship were worked out in advance. It would have to be retroactive here. Nerudi sovereignty would certainly impact the tourist trade, and I imagine there'd be large scale emigration. Frankly, this is too valuable a world for the authorities, even the Senate, to loosen their grip unnecessarily."

"All right, but what does all this have to do with our problem? There are no Nerudi on this landmass. I don't see a connection."

"There probably isn't one. It's not Laszlow's current activities that make him useful to us. But he has no reason to love the company, and while he was working for Intercorp, he managed several departments, including the planetwide security network."

"And . . ."

"And one of his subordinates was Lydia Hanifer. At a minimum, we ought to be able to get some background information. We'll have to be circumspect, but if we simply suggest that she's covering up some sort of minor irregularity and that we're curious, he might be able to suggest a line of investigation that hasn't occurred to us."

"All right. Let's go visit your friend."

Two days later they sat side by side on the lifterbus. Avery had suggested that they pretend not to know each other, but Tharmody dismissed his concerns offhandedly. "We've already been seen together in Haven, and it would look even more peculiar if we pretended to be strangers. No one has any reason to be interested in what we're doing. If anyone notices, they'll suspect that we're indulging in a casual affair. Don't worry about it."

He was forced to accept the logic of her argument, but it did little to help his nervous fear that he was being kept under surveillance. He kept a wary eye on the other three passengers, but if they were anything other than what they seemed, their disguise was impenetrable to him.

Park City was the largest settlement on Meadow, numbering something over one hundred thousand permanent residents and a fair number of transients. The only spaceport on the planet was just outside the city limits, small but adequate for the limited amount of traffic that touched down here. The city was compact enough that he didn't notice it until they were on their final approach into what turned out to be quite a busy midtown terminal. The lifterbus disgorged its passengers, after which they took the public tubeway first to Tharmody's apartment to drop off her luggage, then to the hostelry where Avery had reserved a room for the night. He had entertained fantasies of being invited to stay at Dona's lodgings, but relations between them had remained warm but slightly distant.

"You're certain Laszlow is willing to talk to us?" They were sitting over an adequate but rather tasteless meal in the hostelry dining room. Senator Damien's private menu had been much more diverse than that offered here.

Tharmody nodded. "I was deliberately vague over the com. That should pique his curiosity. Charles is very fond of minding other people's business." Apparently she and Laszlow had spent a considerable time together shortly after her arrival on Meadow, and Avery was experiencing brief twinges of totally irrational jealousy even though she had said nothing that even hinted that her relationship to Laszlow had been anything other than professional.

"How do you think we should approach him?"

"We provide as much of the truth as we can without being too specific. He'll know right away that we're bypassing security channels, so we might as well be up front about that. Nothing about the body, of course. We have reason to believe that Hanifer might be involved in something illegal, but we can't tell him the details. He won't like getting only a small part of the story, and he'll grumble and complain a lot before he opens up, but we don't have anything to lose, and he's best source of advice I know of here on Meadow. Don't worry; I know how to handle him."

But as it turned out, Avery was destined to visit Charles Laszlow on his own. Early the following morning, he was wakened by the insistent whispering of the com, and when he indicated he was ready to accept the call, a three-dimensional image of Tharmody's head materialized on the reception pad.

"Wes, I'm sorry to leave you in the lurch like this, but duty calls and there's no way I can get out of it. There's been a major fault in the city's credit management overseer and the governor is threatening mayhem if it doesn't get straightened out today."

He opened his mouth to answer, then noticed the icon flashing on the console. This was a recording, not live; Tharmody must have been rousted out early and would have sent the message with a timed delay.

"There's no reason why you can't visit Charles without me. He's a bit of an autocrat, but you should be able to handle him all right. And he's a man of fierce loyalties, so get him on our side and we'll have a firm ally if we need him later. Just don't tell him so much that he feels he has to take official action on his own. His sense of duty sometimes results in obstinacy, and if he feels strongly that something is wrong, he might act independently. And prematurely. Charles is not a particularly patient man. Good luck, and I'll try to reach you later today and find out how things went."

Avery was irritated, surprised himself by realizing that it was not so much that he disliked approaching a stranger alone under such unusual circumstances as it was disappointment that he wouldn't be seeing Tharmody today, or at least not until the evening. He ate breakfast alone, then waited impatiently until the autocar he'd ordered showed up in front of the hostelry. He punched the code for Laszlow's villa with unnecessary force and settled back into the cushions, oblivious to the view outside.

It was a longer trip than he'd expected. The center of Park City had been laid out in a series of grids and traffic was surprisingly light, even once they had left the commercial district serviced by the tubeway system. Like most modern human cities, it made some effort to appear decentralized, interspersing commercial, residential, and recreational areas, but there was a clear progression from larger central complexes at city center to smaller, less well maintained ones on the periphery. He assumed that Laszlow, a wealthy man, would live close to the downtown services, but the autocar moved steadily outward without showing any sign of nearing its destination. In fact, Avery was almost alarmed when he glanced out the window and saw heavy stands of trees passing on either side, and he asked the autocar to confirm its destination.

"Destination code 427804. The estate of Charles Laszlow. Do you wish to alter our destination?"

He wanted to know more. The AI unit in the autocar was sure to be linked to the metropolitan database, but he was reluctant to query it. A query would be logged and there'd be a recorded link between himself and Laszlow, a situation which he hoped to avoid.

The landscape opened up into gently rolling fields, only a few of which seemed to be under cultivation, broken by occasional upthrusts of craggy rock. Once they passed an automatic tiller, patiently turning over the topsoil not far from a narrow river, but he had seen very few buildings since leaving the periphery of the city. This area consisted largely of untouched forestland and open grasslands, with occasional farms scattered very widely from one another.

Eventually the landscape changed again; tilled fields became larger and more common, displaying crops in various stages of maturity, most of which he couldn't recognize, at least from the air. Then he spotted the telltale sparkle of a modern security fence off to the left, which proceeded at an angle that gradually closed on the course the autocar was following. They began to lose altitude just as a rather large building became visible in the distance, closely surrounded by a bewildering blend of local and imported vegetation, much of it quite colorful.

A few minutes later, the autocar landed and switched itself to standby.

Avery glanced around, but there was no indication they'd reached his destination.

"You may disembark, Citizen." The autocar's speech module had a slight flutter.

"Where are we? I mean, confirm destination."

The autocar repeated the code number. "Do you wish to input an alternate destination?"

"No, I'll get out here." Hesitantly, Avery stepped outside. There were two stone pillars nearby, framing a breach in the security fence, but evidently Laszlow's published address code was designed to deliver passengers to the gate, not the house itself. It was still a considerable distance away, and all uphill, although the slope was gentle.

Sighing, he started along the well-marked path.

He was two thirds of the way to the villa, moving parallel

to a thick, spiky hedge of some prolific plant he could not identify, when he had the sudden feeling that he was no longer alone. Coming to an abrupt halt, he turned in a slow circle, his field of vision shifting just in time to see a startling apparition rise from behind the hedge.

It was close enough to human to be disconcerting, dissimilar enough to be disturbing. The eyes were disproportionately large, the nose tubular, the mouth an odd crescent shape underlined by a massive chin. The creature was a half meter shorter than Avery but probably massed as much or more, and its skin was shiny and varicolored, with splotches of dark purple and green and even traces of amber. The skull was hairless but irregular, its surface fractured by lines that reminded Avery of crazing patterns on the baked plains of Parchmont, even though the sheen gave a false impression of moisture. The creature moved with quiet confidence, showing no obvious alarm at his presence, even though only two meters separated the two of them.

Having met both Alikashi and Lysandrans in the past, Avery was merely startled rather than frightened, until the creature slowly raised two heavily muscled arms from behind the hedge, and he caught sight of the sharp-edged, bladed thing which it was pointing in his direction.

Chapter Four

* * *

One of the early symptoms of Avery's viral infection had been an occasional inability to differentiate between the actual physical world and those he created in his virtual dramas. The technology had become extremely sophisticated, capable of mimicking sensory input of every variety, even taste, smell, and touch. There were limitations to the fidelity—nuances of texture, richness of odors, subtleties of taste—but the gaps in detail were generally filled in by the imagination of the viewer. Avery had accumulated an elaborate library of sensory memes, subroutines which he could patch into his compositions as needed, most of them generally available to artists but many that he had developed or recorded himself.

Avery had always been particularly aware of the shortcomings of virtual reality: the lack of complete detail, the myriad tiny elements that were ignored or glossed over. He could not immerse himself in the works of his rivals because he was constantly watching for those irrelevant but obvious flaws, and he was similarly aware of the shortcomings in his own creations. At least, that had been the case prior to the infection. The virus mixed memories with current sensory input and sometimes a remembered flaw had seemed to be a present perception, making it difficult for Avery to differentiate between virtual and physical reality. The implants in his body were designed to inhibit the virus and keep him in touch with the real world by suppressing the intermixing of present and past data. Even at its worst, the virus could not create new images, however, and he'd never seen anything resembling this creature before. Hence, it was real.

He stepped back hastily, almost tripping over his own feet, then felt foolish as the bladed tool descended and began rhythmically trimming fresh growth from the top surface of the hedge. The gardener must be a Nerudi, he realized, one of the natives. But what was the creature doing here? Avery had understood that the Nerudi had never settled on or even visited the subcontinent, which was physically isolated by a broad expanse of featureless ocean. They lived scattered through an extensive chain of islands on the opposite side of the globe, the upper reaches of a sunken continent where they must have originally evolved. Meadow was a warm world with minuscule polar ice caps, but at one time the climate had been colder and the oceans smaller.

The Nerudi moved steadily and efficiently, the blades trimming away every stray twig or leaf he encountered. The gardener appeared to be only remotely aware of Avery's presence and totally disinterested.

"You must be Wes Avery."

Avery had been too preoccupied with the Nerudi to notice the approach of another figure, this one entirely human, but in some ways just as outlandish in appearance. Either Charles Laszlow was too old for anti-agathic treatment to be completely effective, or he preferred to allow his bristly, close cut hair to fade to its natural white. Laszlow was a large man, well over two meters, heavily muscled, and looked unusually fit. There was just the slightest hint of a bulge at his waistline, but he moved easily and gracefully.

This is a formidable man, Avery told himself. It might be difficult to tell him less than the full story; he would not take kindly to being denied anything he wanted.

"Charles Laszlow?"

"That's right." Laszlow extended his hand and Avery took it in his, feeling the rough texture of his palm, the calluses on the thick fingers. This was a man who preferred to do things for himself rather than hire others.

"I would have met you at the gate but I had an incoming call at just the wrong moment." Laszlow glanced around pointedly. "I don't see Dona. Did I misunderstand her message?"

"No, but I'm afraid she was unavoidably detained and sends her apologies. An emergency of some sort in the city. I hope you don't mind my coming on alone."

The older man shook his head. "Of course not. Don't get enough company as it is, glad to see a new face. Dona almost always has to rush off when she visits. Meadow's infrastructure hasn't been brought up to date in over a generation. Ever since Intercorp installed that damnable AI to oversee its accounting practices, it's been difficult to get them to maintain, let alone upgrade, capital equipment in marginal profit centers. Which Meadow had become even before the Senate intervened, I'm afraid, and that's just made things worse. We're a losing proposition for Intercorp now, and since there's a Senate-mandated moratorium on development, there's no incentive for them to invest any further. We nearly had a catastrophe last year when the spaceport program developed paranoid tendencies and wouldn't allow any shuttle to land that included AI components on its bill of lading. Thought we were going to shut it down once we had its replacement in hand." He laughed shortly. "Sounds funny in retrospect, but our economy is a very fragile thing and even minor disruptions have far-reaching consequences."

Avery still found it difficult to stop glancing at the Nerudi, who was patiently trimming the hedge as though unaware of the two humans standing nearby. Laszlow must have noticed his preoccupation because he nodded toward the non-human.

"That's Tavarasan. I'd introduce you to him, but there's a rather elaborate and time-consuming greeting ritual involved which requires a little bit of preparation and a great deal of patience. Until you've been through it, he won't acknowledge your existence."

"Must make socialization a bit awkward."

"Not really. Within their own culture, there are prescribed methods of approach, all parties performing their part of the ritual until they reach the point where they can speak directly to one another. Usually there's an intercessor, a mutual acquaintance who oversees the ceremony, but things can be managed even between two complete strangers, though it becomes rather tedious. It serves rather a useful purpose, actually. Saves them the bother of interacting with strangers simply because of social pressures. We could learn a few things from them."

"It was such a surprise to see him here. I mean, I thought the Nerudi were kept strictly sequestered."

"Not exactly. There are very precise restraints on human activities in Nerudi territory, but the rules aren't as restrictive here. It's too late to conceal our presence from the natives, after all, so we're making tentative efforts to explore the ways in which our two species might be able to work cooperatively. Tavarasan is one of three Nerudi I have living with me at the moment, and there are a handful scattered in other places on the subcontinent. They don't understand the concept of ambassadors exactly, but they do trade among themselves and we think we've conveyed to them the concept of commodities with a measurable external value, although for all we know, their interpretation might be very different. They physically resemble us more than the Alikashi do, but culturally and intellectually, the gap is considerably wider. But I assume you didn't come here to talk about the Nerudi. Why don't you come up to the house? I have a bottle of wine from New Versailles that I've been waiting for an excuse to open."

Laszlow's home more than slightly resembled a small museum. The rooms were much larger than in any residence Avery had entered since arriving on Meadow, the ceilings higher, the furnishings more Spartan but all of high quality. All of the furniture had a fixed shape, no morphoforms, the carpeting was some kind of intricate and quite striking synthetic weave, and the walls were covered with natural objects rather than the standard interactive artwork. There were mounted heads of scuttlebuck and hedgeroarers and the antlers of a weirstag, as well as other trophies whose origins were less certain. There were transparent plates displaying the colorful wings of flutterbyes, slices of brain coral from the reefs of Sunset, and sections of glistening scale taken from Komoran dragons. Despite its size, the villa had much the feeling of a vacation lodge rather than a permanent dwelling place.

Laszlow hadn't completely abandoned modern technology. A state of the art master control panel was set inconspicuously to one side of what appeared to be a functioning fireplace, and there were small units scattered around the house that Avery recognized as input devices for a voice recognition system. Through a rear window, he saw a late model lifter parked on a small square of pavement that separated the main house from a handful of outbuildings. Laszlow was clearly a man of substantial personal wealth.

Avery was standing beneath a meter-long, serpentine head mounted on one wall of the front room when Laszlow returned carrying a bottle and two glasses.

"Are you a hunter or just a collector, Mr. Laszlow?"

"Primarily a collector, although I have hunted from time to time. That's one of mine." He pointed vaguely toward the scuttlebuck. "And I much prefer Charles. I tolerated the formality while I worked for Intercorp, but now that I'm retired, I prefer to dispense with such nonsense."

"All right, Charles. And I'm Wes to my friends."

They sipped their wine, Laszlow with obvious pleasure. Avery had never acquired a taste for alcoholic stimulants, but the wine had a pleasant taste and he made suitably polite comments before accepting a proffered chair. As he did so, a Nerudi entered the room, hesitating in the doorway until Laszlow noticed. Avery felt certain this was not Tavarasan, a point which was confirmed after Laszlow spoke to the newcomer in a rapid series of low sibilants.

"I apologize for the interruption but Tosilara wished to know if you'd be staying for lunch. Actually, the way she phrased it was to ask if she should prepare a larger meal than usual. Officially, she hasn't noticed you're here so don't feel snubbed if she ignores you. I took the liberty of assuming you'd be our guest."

"Must make entertaining a bit awkward at times."

"Not really. Living together, we're slowly developing compromises between our two cultures. You just saw one. Back among her own people, she'd have served as usual unless she received specific instructions to the contrary. In a sense, she really wouldn't be able to see you, at least not as a fellow being. Even the newborn must be formally introduced to the family. They're an adaptable people though, and they adjust to changes quite readily. That's actually one of the arguments against integration. There's some concern that we'll alter their cultural irreparably and imprint them with our own."

"I suppose some degree of cultural contamination is inevitable, but I don't see why that's necessarily bad. It doesn't sound as though the status quo encourages large communities, and perhaps that's why they've never developed a higher civilization."

"No, you're right about that. The concept of an organized political state seems virtually impossible for them to comprehend, at least at this stage in their development. Their culture rests entirely on a foundation of interlocking personal relationships. For example, if one Nerudi wishes to purchase an object from another, but lacks a formal introduction, he or she would have to find a mutual acquaintance to act as intermediary, either to make the actual purchase or to perform the introductory ritual. It's a bit more complicated than that, since they have no concept of currency or fixed values. I'm tempted to call it a barter economy, but even that's a misnomer. It's more like a prearranged exchange of gifts."

The trip out had taken longer than he expected and Avery really hadn't given any thought to the possibility of a protracted stay, but he accepted the offer of a meal. He was curious about the natives as well and tried to prod his host into discussing them in more detail.

"They seem to integrate into human society rather well, at least on a menial level."

Laszlow's eyes narrowed. "Despite appearances, the Nerudi are not my personal servants. They are guests here.

In a sense, they're a combination diplomatic mission and research team, sent to learn about our culture so that they can help to establish a functional bridge between our two peoples. The Nerudi have an intricate social code that emphasizes service to the clan, or in some cases the larger community, and they would be unwilling to remain here if I didn't allow them to provide some service in return for their keep. Non-producers among their people are eliminated in what might seem to us a pretty callous and uncivilized fashion. Exposure is the most common solution but sometimes more immediate steps are taken." Laszlow seemed preoccupied for a moment, then went on. "I could easily automate most of their duties, but if I did, they'd insist upon being repatriated immediately. If they remained here without contributing, they could not in good conscience eat the food I provide."

Avery hurriedly apologized for the unintended criticism. "I didn't mean to imply you were exploiting them. Dona gave me quite the opposite impression, in fact. When the Senate recognized the rights of the Nerudi, it would have been a devastating blow to the colonists as well as Intercorp. It must have taken considerable courage to champion their cause under those circumstances."

Laszlow's features softened and the sudden tension left as quickly as it had come. "Perhaps I'm a bit touchy on the subject. You have to understand, those of us who hope to integrate the Nerudi into our culture are in a decided minority. This remains functionally a company world despite the imposition of a Concourse governor, and as you imply there are powerful vested interests still unhappy with the status quo. Intercorp has petitioned for status as custodian over the planet, supposedly to watch out for native as well as human interests, but you can imagine how unlikely that is given their recent history. The Nerudi would become prisoners on their own world, supposedly for their own protection, forced either to adapt to human ways of doing things or cling to a tenuous existence as a tolerated minor species."

"Surely Intercorp couldn't have hoped to keep their existence secret forever?"

"Of course not, but don't expect a company bureaucrat to look at things that way. I know; I used to be one of them. So long as the consequences aren't likely to show up during their tenure, they can and will do whatever serves their short-term interests. And Intercorp has a lot of political muscle; they managed to ward off Concourse inspection teams for several years. By any reasonable test of intelligence, the Nerudi deserve full recognition by the Concourse, if not actual membership, but we can't get the motion out of subcommittee, and there's a very distinct danger that legislation will be passed blocking even consideration of citizenship rights. We've never encountered an intelligent species this primitive before, and there's no precedent for dealing with them. There are even forces in the Senate who would prefer to restore a modified form of the chattel arrangement that existed previously, a more or less permanent protectorate administered by Intercorp."

"What advantage would that give them? If word leaked out that the Nerudi were being exploited, surely the public outcry would hurt enough to outweigh their short-term gains."

Laszlow shook his head. "Remember, company functionaries don't take the long view. The facts are being buried under an avalanche of procedural issues. The Nerudi have no central government, just a loose arrangement among their clans. And there are all sorts of procedural issues to be resolved. The other non-human Concourse members all applied formally for admission. That's not the case here since there is no centralized government, just an informal council that meets periodically and primarily for social reasons. The petitioners are humans, acting on behalf of the natives."

"Then why not just have this council of theirs file their own petition? Surely they could do that without actually having to meet anyone?"

"More cultural problems. Nerudi form alliances through a process of mutual agreements. The concept of requesting admission to an organization, even the idea of a formal government on the scale we subscribe to, is completely alien to them. It's one of many areas in which we're not really certain that we understand enough to know where the real differences lie." He sighed, reached up, and absently scratched his chest. "I could go on about the Nerudi for the rest of the day and well into the night, but I think your visit has another purpose. You'll have to excuse my tendency to lecture. I've made the resolution of this conflict the focus of my retirement, and it does tend to preoccupy me."

"No apology necessary. As a matter of fact, it's been quite interesting. But you're right, I'm here on another matter entirely."

"Well then, how can I help you?"

Avery had constructed and discarded several elaborate and circumspect strategies, finally decided to keep things as simple and as close to the truth as possible without giving away any unnecessary details.

"I'm vacationing in one of your small resort communities, a place called Haven."

"I'm familiar with it. A quiet spot, though the scenery is much more interesting on the northern coast. Provides a good portion of the planet's grain harvest, though it's a far less profitable business than it used to be. So how is life in Haven?"

"Quiet, a pleasant change really. But recently I had a somewhat awkward experience there which I am not, unfortunately, at liberty to describe in any detail. I may have misinterpreted some perfectly legitimate activities that are none of my business and I don't want to cause trouble. On the other hand, it's possible that a serious crime has been committed, and that I may be the only witness. I realize this is a rather awkward situation, and I apologize for being vague, but until I have a better understanding of what's happening, I just can't be any more specific than that." He felt no temptation to add that he was subject to hallucinations and might have imagined the entire thing.

Laszlow let that statement percolate for a moment. "Is there a reason why you have come to me rather than security? There are ways to report to them in confidence, you realize? They can be quite discreet when required."

Avery chose to answer with a question of his own. "Do you know Lydia Hanifer?"

Laszlow blinked. "Hanifer? Know her? Of course, I do; she used to work in my department. If that's what brings you here, then certainly you're already aware of that. How is she involved with this?"

"I knew that she was at one time a subordinate of yours, yes, but I didn't know if you would even remember her."

Laszlow's forehead creased. "Lydia is hard to forget. She's the security officer for Haven now, I take it? I knew she'd gone to one of the outlying communities, but couldn't remember which. And obviously you suspect her of being involved in whatever it is you're worried about." He raised a hand when Avery started to protest. "No, don't bother. I knew you must suspect security right from the outset; there's no other reason for you to have come to me. Let me thumb through my memories for a few seconds. Lydia Hanifer was not . . . is not the sort of person you forget easily. A contradictory woman, however, and a determined one. She was bright enough to have grabbed a top administrative position in Park City if she'd been willing to unbend a little, do some minor politicking on her own behalf. A strong, analytic mind, flashes of brilliant insight, and a good sense of organization. Not much patience and a bit of a temper though . . ." His voice trailed off suggestively.

"She did seem brusque."

"Haven, eh? Well, maybe that's the best place for her. She was an obstinate woman, alienated a lot of people. I had to smooth ruffled feathers on more than one occasion. She was right most of the time, but not what you'd call tactful. In Park City, she'd have gone on butting her head against immovable objects until the laws of nature changed or her skull caved in. Most likely the powers that be would have found a way to terminate her contract or shift her to a desk job where she wouldn't have to interact with the public. And you think she's involved in something illegal?"

"I didn't say that."

"No, you didn't. But I can't think of any other reason why you'd be afraid to handle this through official channels. You're not sure or you'd have gone over her head, I imagine. No, don't bother to answer that. It's self-evident."

Avery wasn't happy to have been seen through with such apparent ease. "If I felt confident that she was involved in criminal activity, I wouldn't hesitate to report it. I assure you it's far more ambiguous than that."

"All right, then either she failed to perform to your satisfaction and you think her incompetent, which is unlikely, or she's done something unorthodox and you suspect her motives."

This was the part of his story which made Avery the most uneasy. "A little of both. There's one interpretation of events that suggests she's suppressing knowledge of a crime, and may even be implicated, and another in which she's simply not doing her job. I was hoping you might be willing to tell me your opinion of her reliability and perhaps suggest a course of action I might take."

"Without knowing more of the specifics, it's going to be very difficult to suggest anything. I don't suppose you'd be more forthcoming if I offered to keep everything you said confidential?"

Avery squirmed uncomfortably. "I've heard that you are an honorable man with a strong sense of duty. There's a chance that this involves a rather serious crime, and I'm hesitant to place you in a situation where your sense of honor about your given word would conflict with your duty as a citizen."

Laszlow thought about that for a while, then nodded. "All right, leave it for the time being. For what it's worth, here's my opinion of Lydia Hanifer. She is stubbornly loyal to an internal set of standards which, for the most part, coincides with the duties she's assumed. In that sense, she is ideally suited as a security chief, because she is also intelligent, capable, and energetic. On the other hand, I don't doubt for a moment that she could rationalize violation of those responsibilities if they conflicted with her internal value system. Hanifer was raised a Situationalist; they're a popular sect on Meadow and the keystone of their creed is that there are no absolutes, that every situation must be evaluated on its own merits. Even the oath of office would not override her personal priorities. She wouldn't hesitate once she had had time to work through the contradictions in her mind. She was also somewhat aggressive, nothing serious enough to appear on her record, but a worrisome insensitivity to the rights of others. Lydia came from an unhappy background; her father was confined for mandatory psychotherapy while she was still quite young, but not before he inflicted considerable abuse on the child. Her psychological evaluation had some warning flags, but nothing significant enough to overtly affect her career. I don't remember the details. That's pretty much all I can offer except that I categorically refuse to believe she would omit to perform her duties through laziness or inattention. If she failed to do something which should have been done, it was a conscious, reasoned choice. Our relationship was always formal, though not unpleasant. She's rather a handsome woman, as I recall, but not particularly sociable."

Actually, Avery found her about as appealing as the Nerudi woman, Tosilara. "I appreciate your frankness. Who would she report to, within the security apparatus, I mean?"

Laszlow used his tongue to push out one cheek as he thought. "Her nominal superior would be the regional division officer in Park City. I think Ogleson still covers that district, though he may have retired recently. I'm not in as close touch with things as I used to be. And my association with the Fraternalist Party has made it difficult for some of my old cronies to be seen with me publicly. We're not exactly popular in some circles. I've even had the occasional death threat."

"What would be the procedure if I reported my suspicions directly to this Ogleson?"

"You haven't told me enough to answer that. Normally, if there was a complaint about Hanifer's handling of a case, and if Ogleson believed it might be a valid charge of dereliction, she would be immediately summoned to Park City to give her own account. If more direct involvement was suspected, she'd be suspended pending the results of a formal investigation." Laszlow twisted his face uncomfortably. "Ogleson's not exactly a ball of fire. He'd do what was absolutely necessary and no more. Doesn't like paperwork, and hates scandals. He'd probably cover up a minor transgression if he thought he could get away with it. I can't imagine him risking anything more than that; he doesn't have much steel in him. I suppose it's not entirely unwise that you remain cautious, although I'm uneasy about this."

"No more than I. And what would he do if the charges were simply a personal observation, with no substantiation?"

"Most likely he'd just com Hanifer and ask for her side, then file a report with no comment. His presumption would be to favor his people in the absence of corroborative evidence. Any good officer would do the same."

That was pretty much what he had expected, but it was still depressing to hear it spoken aloud. "Is there any other course of action you could recommend?"

Laszlow sighed dramatically. "I'd recommend that you be a bit more forthcoming first, but I accept that there might be valid reasons for remaining silent. This isn't exactly a frontier world, but it's not far removed from it. As far as official channels go, you're out of luck. We're not officially a member of the Concourse, and it hasn't been very long since we were an exclusively privately-administered society. There's not much of any supportive infrastructure even for our citizens, and you're just a transient. The local legislature is just a debating society, setting regulatory standards but with no real teeth. The governor has absolute veto power under the interim charter, but he's a retired company bureaucrat, and his decisions in turn are subject to reversal by the Senate committee overseeing Meadow. Haven is represented by Councilor Deng, a nice woman lacking in either imagination or common sense, I'm afraid. She'd either throw you out of her office and forget the entire matter, or deliver some ill-advised speech at Government House. And she lives in Solitude, which is also in her district, and is frankly less than interested in what happens outside her home town unless she's up for re-election. It's not likely you could advance matters there, and you might do irreparable harm if there really is a plot afoot. I don't think the woman has a discreet bone in her body."

"Then if anything is going to be done, I'll have to see it through myself?"

"I'd be the last to suggest such a thing, frankly. Neither you nor Dona have either the training or sufficient reason to risk yourselves. You might be wasting your time needlessly or, even worse, involving yourself in something dangerous."

"Dona's only connection was to introduce me to you." Laszlow's face betrayed his skepticism but Avery was determined not to involve her any more than he had already. "I hadn't even met her at the time of the incident, and I haven't told her much more than I've told you." Avery didn't like lying, but thought he could do so convincingly. "I suppose for the time being I'll just have to wait and see what develops."

"Sometimes that's the wisest course of action. But I won't allow you to leave today without promising me that at some point, assuming things are resolved satisfactorily, you'll at least tell me what this conversation was really about. I have an absolute intolerance for bad endings, you know, and you've made me very curious indeed."

"If there is ever anything to tell, you may rest assured that I'll be more than happy to return." He raised his empty glass. "If for no other reason than to provide you an excuse to open another bottle of this excellent wine."

They ate lunch on a small patio at the rear of the house. One of the Nerudi brought in the food, an elaborate platter of fresh native fruits and raw vegetables, some of which Avery recognized, and small meat pies with crisp, tasty crusts. Without acknowledging Avery's presence in the slightest, the native set the plate conveniently close at hand.

"They don't eat with you?"

Laszlow shook his head. "Nerudi only eat in the presence of family. One of their worst punishments is to force a criminal, if that's the right word, to consume food publicly. Apparently it's deeply shameful."

"Do they judge us by the same standards, or do they just think we're all related?"

"No, they're actually quite sophisticated about humans. Their word for us is roughly 'more than animals but not the same as people.' We're more like a force of nature to them. Not an insult, exactly, but not a compliment either."

"Sounds fascinating." Imaginary aliens were a staple plot device in virtual dramas, one Avery had used on two occasions himself. They were almost always recognizable variations of humans, whether covered with scales or fur, with varying numbers of limbs, sometimes with unlikely, impractical shapes.

"If you're staying in the city for long, I'd be happy to have you visit again. I could even introduce you to my guests if you were willing to sit through some rather dull ceremonies."

"It's tempting, but I need to get this other matter straightened out first, and I'm headed back to Haven on tomorrow's lifterbus. Perhaps some other time before I leave."

"By all means."

They spoke of other subjects for a while, but Avery's attention wandered and his host seemed to be repeating familiar anecdotes rather than actually engaging in a conversation. Laszlow reminisced about his early career on Meadow and his eventual break with Intercorp management following a growing disenchantment with the purely mercantile interests of the trading group.

"They have to maintain their profitability, of course; I never quarreled with that. But too often their horizons were unwisely close at hand. What mattered was maximizing income for the very next reporting period, even if that meant an overall decline in profitability in the long run. In practical terms, that involved ruthless exploitation of each resource rather than planning for a prolonged investment. They were prepared to strip Meadow of all of its accessible resources and once there was nothing left worth taking, move on to someplace else and start the cycle all over again. After all, the universe is full of empty planets."

There was more wine, enough that Avery felt a bit unsteady when he said goodbye and he dozed off on the trip back to the city, wakening only when the lifter placidly announced that they had reached the requested destination. He returned to his room, tried unsuccessfully to raise Dona on the com, then stripped off his clothing and used the shower. When he emerged, there was another recorded call waiting for him.

It was Dona. "Hi, missed you again, I guess. I hope you hit it off all right with Charles. He's pleasant enough, but sometimes a bit stiff and self-important. Anyway, I have to apologize for leaving you yet again without warning, but duty calls and all that. The master controller in Westfield has apparently had a psychotic episode and refuses to talk to anyone. Since all calls to that lovely little town are routed through the controller, that effectively leaves them out of touch with the rest of the planet until someone goes out and talks the little darling into resuming its duties. So I may be gone for a day or two, and you'll be back in Haven by then. I don't want to discuss our little project on an open line, but I'm owed some more vacation time and the Senator did tell me I was welcome to use his cottage for as long as I wanted, so maybe I'll drop by for a visit once I get this mess straightened out. Best of luck, however you've decided to proceed."

She sounded and appeared perfectly natural, and there was really no reason to suspect that anything was amiss, but Avery was troubled by the call. It was just a bit too convenient that she had been called away twice now, depriving him of his only ally. He was well aware of the ease with which an individual's image, voice, and mannerisms could be counterfeited with modern recording equipment. Perhaps it was just paranoia, for there had been, after all, no overt action taken by either himself or Dona that might have alerted Hanifer or anyone else. But Avery was too sensitive to coincidences, which made for simple but very bad dramatic scripts, to ignore them when they arose in real life.

That evening he dined in the hostelry, went to bed early, still uncertain how he should proceed. There were no further messages from Dona, and the fact that he hadn't really expected one did nothing to make him feel better about the situation.

Chapter Five

❋ ❋ ❋

Avery returned to Haven the following afternoon, uncertain whether he felt better or worse. The conversation with Laszlow had brought home to him how limited his options were. His only consolation was that it was unlikely that he knew enough to be a threat and was probably not in any immediate personal danger. Dona's continued absence was disquieting, but there was no reason to believe that it had any connection to his experience. He wanted very much to talk to her again, if only to reassure himself that he wasn't acting foolishly. He felt confident that the incident was not just another manifestation of his illness, even though the doctors admitted that they didn't fully understand how the virus functioned.

That didn't eliminate the possibility that he was misinterpreting things. Could the man have been alive after all? He was no physician and he supposed it was possible that the man had recovered from some mysterious ailment that mimicked death and had simply walked off on his own. Or perhaps he really had been dead, but the facts were being suppressed for perfectly legitimate reasons. What those might be, he couldn't even begin to imagine, but Avery couldn't summarily rule out that explanation.

When he disembarked from the lifterbus, he looked

around as though seeing Haven for the first time, no longer seeing it as just a rustic stopover for rich tourists. Suddenly it had become a place of potential mystery, subtle intrigues, missing bodies, and sinister conspiracies. He felt a thrill of excitement that made his pulse race, and the feeling wasn't entirely unpleasant. He couldn't remember ever being as sharply aware of his environment as he was now. Sounds seemed crisper, colors brighter, the perfumed scents drifting from the gardens more evocative. Still carrying his overnight bag in one hand, he set out not toward the shaded lane that wound westward to his cottage but randomly southward, moving methodically from one street to another, noticing for the first time how small Haven's commercial district actually was: a few dozen buildings spread over a disproportionately large plot of land, the streets curving back on themselves in a complex pattern.

Despite his new perspective, Avery found little of interest in the village and nothing noticeably amiss. Pedestrian traffic was light and casual; several passersby nodded polite but disinterested greetings. It was even warmer than usual today, almost uncomfortably so, and he took refuge in a small canteen called Soothers, sliding the bag under his chair while he studied the table menu.

Unlike the place in which he had first met Dona Tharmody, Soothers apparently drew most of its patrons from among the permanent residents rather than transient guests. The interior was very crowded, small tables set close together, animated conversations on every side. Avery had selected a table near the rear wall, a good vantage point from which to watch the other patrons. It felt as though he had stepped back through several centuries of time, or into the world of an alternate species that looked very much like human beings, but ordered their lives in a subtly different fashion. It was so loud that he had trouble focusing on any one voice and heard instead fragments of sentences in different voices, sometimes laughing, sometimes argumentative. At one table, an attractive woman harangued a sullen, older man, waving her arms to emphasize her points. At another, three young men seemed to be swapping ribald stories, and two elderly women sitting nearby were alternately amused or pretending to be offended.

He read through the menu quickly, noticed that the prices were considerably lower than at the tourist concessions, and eventually ordered a mildly alcoholic fruit drink by touching the appropriate icon. A harried young man arrived at his side a few seconds later, giving Avery a surreptitious once-over while setting down a tall, colorful drink in a frosted glass.

"Quite a crowd. Are you always this busy?"

"Most times, after mid-day. This isn't Park City, so there's not much else to do." He nodded and was off before Avery could entice him to say more.

The noise level continued unabated: numerous conversations punctuated with raucous laughter, occasional shouts, mock insults, and once a prolonged burst of good-natured applause when someone tilted a chair too far back and fell over with a crash. Not for the first time, Avery felt regret that his compulsive dedication to his art had taken up such a large portion of his adult life. There had been no clear-cut transition, but he had realized one day that he had somehow become disconnected from everyone else, had no close friends, and might have lost any chance to enjoy what most people thought of as a normal personal life. The success of his virtual dramas had been financially if not socially rewarding, particularly once he had switched from meticulously researched documentaries to wholly imaginary stories in which good always triumphed over evil, and evil itself was usually just mediocrity. Critics still complained because the originality that brought so much attention to his early work was largely absent from his later productions, but they also never mentioned that he had hovered on the brink of insolvency for several years, breaking through only when he produced the still-popular adventure classic, *Into the Pit of Bohara*.

His drink hadn't been very strong but Avery still wasn't used to alcohol and he found himself growing lightheaded, even sleepy. In one of his dramas, this might have indicated that the protagonist had been secretly drugged. He wasn't paranoid enough to believe that was happening now, but he decided against a second drink and was preparing to reach down for his bag and leave when one of the mock arguments suddenly became much louder.

Although he hadn't been paying particular attention, he'd been vaguely aware that a party of young men to his left were teasing one of their number about his recent involvement with a girl. Their victim had protested his innocence with considerable heat, but in that ambivalent fashion that balances boasting against tactful reticence. The party had ordered three rounds of drinks in the short time that Avery had been present, their fingers pressing icons on the table so frequently that the harried server was visibly annoyed.

Just as Avery finished entering his credit code into the table to pay for his drink, the star of the show pushed back his chair, stood up abruptly, his red face twisted into a rather unflattering grin, and raised his arms for attention.

"All right, all of you. I can see it's impossible to keep any secrets here. If I confess the truth, can we talk about something else for a change?"

"Details! We want details!" That and similar cries were his answer, and he kept his arms raised until the noise dropped back to its previous level.

"All right then." He swayed, put the palm of one hand on the back of his chair to steady himself. "The truth is that Dini Torgeson finally surrendered her honor to me on the banks of Wobbly Brook just two nights past. Her obvious enthusiasm more than made up for her lack of experience in that area, and it was clear to me that I was sowing my seed in an untilled field."

There was a loud outburst of laughter just as Avery turned toward the door, already tuning the conversation out, but the volume of sound dropped so abruptly at that moment, in a cascading effect that swept across the room, that he blinked and turned to look back. The young server was standing frozen nearby, clearly alarmed.

An older man had stepped out from a recessed corner concealed from the main seating area and was walking slowly toward the once-raucous party. Several of the young men rose quietly to their feet, discovering a sudden need to get a breath of fresh air or to relieve the pressure of their bladders. Even without knowing the particulars, Avery was quite sure he knew what was coming. He'd written a scene very like it in one of his most melodramatic compositions.

"You've got quite an active tongue in your mouth, Nils Karnov. Too bad it seems to have come separated from your brain." The older man's voice was level, unexcited, but filled with menace.

The young boaster, Karnov presumably, turned slowly and raised his arms in an unconsciously defensive position. "Mr. Torgeson, I didn't know you were there." His voice trembled nervously, a blend of defiance and uncertainty.

"That's more than evident." They were within arm's length of each other before the older man slowed his advance.

"I was just kidding around, sir. You know how it is. Nothing really happened, nothing you wouldn't approve of, I mean. I really admire your daughter."

"You might be surprised at the range of behavior I disapprove of, boy." There was strong emphasis on the last word; it was clearly meant to be provocatively insulting. Torgeson remained outwardly calm, but it didn't require a practiced eye to see the anger that seethed beneath the surface.

Karnov glanced at his friends, obviously seeking support. There was a nervous rustling and at least one head turned deliberately away. Evidently he was on his own. Avery wasn't sure he blamed the others. Torgeson looked to be past his prime, but his arms were still thick with ropes of muscle and he massed considerably more than Karnov, as well as standing at least a full head taller. There was some quality in his voice and posture that expressed silent self-confidence and convinced Avery that this was not a man to be trifled with lightly.

"There was no harm done," Karnov answered sullenly, his eyes dropping to study the table in front of him. "We were just fooling around. It was a private conversation anyway."

"No conversation roared at the top of your lungs in a public place can be considered private, and I'm not so sure my daughter would feel that there was no harm done if she'd been present to hear it. She might have a different version of the story to tell."

"What happens between Dini and me is our business, and we'll deal with one another as we see fit." Anger deepened Karnov's voice. He raised his head and made an effort to square his shoulders. "She's old enough to make her own decisions. We both are."

Torgeson nodded. "I agree with you there, boy, and you're also old enough to take the consequences of your bad judgment."

At this point, Avery realized that by standing he might be drawing attention to himself, so he eased quietly back down into an empty seat. He didn't want to leave in the middle of this scene. I couldn't have written it better myself, he thought wryly.

"I don't have to listen to your threats, old man!" Karnov's flush deepened. "You've no right to cause trouble over this!"

Torgeson's expression changed, becoming just slightly more aggressive. His voice dripped with sarcasm. "Ah, I'm an old man now, am I? And I suppose you don't think I should find your brainless, bragging fantasies irritating?"

Karnov dropped his hands to his sides and they suddenly clenched into fists. "I told you, I didn't know you were there."

"And that excuses your slandering my daughter, does it? You know full well that Dini wouldn't give you a second look, Nils Karnov, that she'd rather lie with a scuttlebuck than share the sheets with a lazy wastrel like yourself."

Karnov moved then, without any visible warning, although Torgeson was clearly anticipating him, had intended from the outset to provoke exactly that response. He avoided the first thrown punch with a quick twist of his torso, swinging one arm up to strike his opponent high on the right side, just below the armpit. Karnov stumbled away, his hip banging into the table, and upset drinks splashed those of his friends who still remained seated. The expression on his face was almost comical, surprise and anger all running together. He hadn't begun to feel the pain yet.

Recovering his balance, he started to swing again, but this time Torgeson stepped inside the blow, raised one knee sharply into the younger man's groin. As Karnov gasped and bent forward, Torgeson's fists moved in near unison, two blows against the chin which lifted his opponent into the air. He crashed down onto the table, which promptly overturned, depositing the now unconscious combatant on the floor.

Torgeson glanced around the silent room as though waiting for someone else to impugn his family's honor, then turned and walked through the crowd to the door without speaking another word.

As Karnov's friends moved to evaluate the damage, the server breathed an audible sigh of relief and walked over to ask Avery if everything had been satisfactory.

"Does this sort of thing happen in here often?"

"Sometimes emotions run high, particularly when there's been drinking. We've had worse than this before, and we'll have it again." The man's voice was sullen, suspicious.

"The gentleman seems to have quite a temper."

"Kier Torgeson is a man of strong opinion and decisive action." The server dropped his eyes, turned, and walked off with a brusque nod.

The young man was still unconscious when Avery made his way out of the canteen.

Emerging onto the narrow street, Avery was briefly disoriented and headed north rather than south, although he soon realized his error and reversed course. He passed the canteen a second time, continued to the end of the block, then took an unfamiliar alleyway that led southwest, suggesting a shorter route back to his own lane.

He had barely rounded the first corner, however, when he noticed a small group of people standing to one side a dozen or more meters ahead. They were deep in conversation, although they kept their voices low enough that he caught not a word. There were four in all, two men and two women, but to his surprise, he recognized half their number. The man doing most of the talking was Kier Torgeson, and judging by his posture, he remained or was once again angry about something. Facing him directly was Lydia Hanifer, her understated security sash not immediately visible from this distance. She appeared to be listening calmly, interjected a brief comment from time to time, but did not seem unduly upset.

Avery was only mildly curious. Evidently someone had notified security of the incident at Soothers and she was investigating. In a community like this, word would spread quickly and, he suspected, security would use considerable discretion in dealing with the situation. The young boaster had clearly been out of line, seemed the type who would have been in previous but minor trouble, and he would not be at all surprised if Torgeson escaped with nothing more than a stern warning.

He was walking along the opposite side of the street and decided not to cross until he was well past the small knot of people, not wanting to intrude into their private affairs. But before he had covered half the intervening distance, one of them glanced in his direction, and what followed was, if not exactly menacing, at least very disquieting.

The cluster opened suddenly like a flower greeting the rising sun, the two unfamiliar figures stepping back to flank Hanifer and Torgeson, so that all four had a clear view of his approach. The unknown woman was short and barrel-chested, the man of medium build, memorable only because Avery noticed that his left arm was a prosthesis. None of the group acknowledged his presence in any way and their expressions remained neutral, but it was obvious that they were watching him with some interest. Avery nodded in their general direction as he passed, hoping that he appeared unconcerned and inattentive, but he was acutely aware of the quick exchange of guarded looks, a brief, inaudible comment from Hanifer, and the silence that continued until he was well out of range.

His nerves were on edge for the rest of the walk, his mind examining and discarding explanations that included the possibility that the entire village, or at least a substantial subset, was involved in an elaborate, possibly murderous, conspiracy, that his discovery in the fields had caused them no more than a minor inconvenience, and that they were acutely and actively aware of his presence.

His dreams that night included a nightmarish sequence in which he was running through an infinite expanse of parasoy, pursued by Hanifer, Torgeson, and the others he'd seen, as well as Charles Laszlow, Senator Damien, and a handful of specialists he'd known back on New Vienna. Occasionally he would elude them long enough to rest, but whenever he did so, he invariably stumbled across more dead bodies, sometimes duplicates of the one he'd actually seen, sometimes the bodies of people who'd died during the uprising on Aragon, and on more than one occasion it had been Dona Tharmody's blood-soaked corpse lying before him.

He woke well before daylight, soaked with perspiration, his head throbbing relentlessly.

Avery spent the remaining hours of darkness practicing

the various techniques of mental and chemical self-control he'd learned. Once his equilibrium had been somewhat restored, he sat in the darkness, replaying the events of the past few days in his mind. For some reason, he had the nagging impression that he was overlooking something, that he had more information than he realized but hadn't made the right connection. The more he thought about it, the stronger the conviction grew, until he finally used the data console to make an itemized list of everything he had learned or suspected: the body, Hanifer's response, the interview with Laszlow, the encounter in the village, even the fight in the canteen. He broke the information down into small units, ran it through the limited AI interpreter, then examined the resulting list of cross-references. All of them were observations he'd made on his own; the AI hadn't found any new correlation. He saved the file and blanked the screen in frustration.

After breakfast, he left a message for Dona, who had apparently still not returned to her apartment in Park City. A direct call had resulted in an error message indicating that Citizen Tharmody's com was not currently in a functional network area. That worried him, but there was nothing he could presently do about it, and the odds favored a perfectly innocent explanation. Still dissatisfied by his inability to scratch the subconscious itch that had bothered him in the hours before dawn, he set out on a brisk walk back to the village, this time going directly to a single-story building which bore a sign that read: *Village of Haven, Administrative Services.* He hesitated only a brief moment before determinedly climbing the steps, slipping through the doorway as it sensed his approach and slid obediently to one side.

The outer office appeared to be completely deserted. Most of the floor space was occupied by a number of small partitioned cubicles, each fitted with a com screen. An exceptionally neat desk and work area was separated by a waist-high partition that appeared to be natural wood. One wall displayed a small comnet interface, text only, and he scanned the scrolling headlines for a few seconds, noting that the rioting on Parsimony had subsided, at least temporarily, and that the mining colonies in the Belial system were being evacuated as a precautionary measure, pending analysis of the data collected by solar probes. The last flare, over a standard century earlier, had caught the population unprepared, resulting in tens of thousands of deaths. The solar monitors hadn't been serviced on a timely basis and had failed to broadcast a warning, an oversight which had ended several prominent careers.

There was a doorway in the rear wall, leading to another room whose details he couldn't see.

"Hello! Is anyone here?"

Something moved in the back room, and a woman's voice called out cheerfully. "Be with you in a moment. Make yourself comfortable."

Avery amused himself by rehearsing the story he'd prepared as a cover for his real interest, wondering if he could lie convincingly. He was mildly surprised to realize that he was actively enjoying acting out the kind of fantasy he'd created in his dramatic work.

"May I help you?"

He turned to face a tall, slender woman wearing what he thought of as the informal Haven uniform: plain, loose-fitting, pastel-colored clothing obviously designed more for usefulness than decoration. Her hair was cut unusually close to her skull and there was a flatness to her cheekbones that made her mouth seem too wide. The only visible embellishment was a locket that rested against the center of her chest, a small but exquisitely crafted serpent's head fashioned of metal, inset with jewels, with two sharp looking curved fangs protruding from beneath a slender snout. It was so striking that Avery realized that he was staring and hastily raised his eyes.

"Beautiful, isn't it?" She was watching him with friendly amusement.

"I'm sorry, I didn't mean to stare."

"That's perfectly all right. Happens to most people the first time they see it. It's from Earth, you know, dates from the solar period."

Avery was impressed, although he wondered if that was true. An authentic piece of that vintage would be quite valuable. "Family heirloom?"

"No, a gift from someone I know who indulges my whims from time to time. Now how can I help you?"

Avery returned to the matter at hand, replaying the first line of his prepared script. "I was wondering if I could access some of Haven's public records."

"We have a fairly complete database on-line here and everything except confidential data is available, of course." She spread her arms to indicate the array of cubicles. "I might be able to save you some time if you could be more specific about what information you'd find of interest. Oh, and my name's Tanya, by the way. Tanya Churienko. I'm the local data manager." She laughed and tossed her head. "As well as village registrar, licensing officer, tourist guide, and a few other duties no one else is willing to take on."

"Sounds like they keep you busy."

"Not as much as you might think, Mr. Avery. We have a very small population, our economy isn't particularly complex, and there hasn't been a new business started here in almost a generation. Haven is so stable it's almost ossified.

So are you interested in crop yield ratios for the past twenty seasons or credit disbursement patterns for male citizens over the age of twenty-five standard?"

This was the point where he needed to be clever. By Concourse law, any inquiry made against public records also became a matter of public record. He was specifically interested in Hanifer, and to a lesser extent Torgeson, but he would have to be circumspect in order to avoid revealing his real intentions. He figured he was safe so long as no one believed he was a threat, but if there was even the slightest suspicion that he was sticking his nose into local matters, his status might well change quickly and unpleasantly.

"Nothing like that. I'm staying at one of the rental cottages just west of here, but since you already knew my name, I imagine that's not news."

She laughed lightly. "This is a small community and most of our guests are regulars: Intercorp executives, government officials, and a few wealthy citizens from Park City. Other than yourself, there's only one stranger currently in residence, and I was pretty sure that you weren't the Dowager Duchess of Gloon."

He relaxed slightly, unable to see anything threatening in the woman's manner. "I've lived in urban centers for the past several years, and it's easy to forget how hard it is to keep secrets in smaller communities." Avery watched to see if she'd react, but her expression never changed. "I hadn't realized how much I missed the sense of community and the more relaxed pace you enjoy here."

"I'm afraid at times it's more comatose than relaxed. Most of our young people can't wait to leave for the city because that's where the excitement is."

"I assume you're a native Havener, then?"

"You assume correctly. The Churienkos have been here

since Haven was first settled, although as a family we're dying out. I'm not quite the last of my line, but neither of my sisters have chosen to bear children. My parents emigrated to Downunder when they retired, but personally I have no real desire to travel offworld. Everything that I need and want is here."

"I'm not surprised," he lied. "I've been very favorably impressed with Haven, so much in fact that I hope to make this more than just a brief, one-time visit." Churienko's face expressed only friendly interest. Avery hurried on, hoping the explanation he had prepared beforehand would sound as plausible in practice as it had when he'd rehearsed it.

"I was rather hoping to purchase a small parcel of land in the area, preferably one of the existing cottages, although I suppose I could build if there are none presently for sale."

She frowned slightly but her voice remained amiable as she shook her head determinedly from side to side. "I'm afraid I don't even need to check to assure you that's impossible. It has been at least twenty standard years since any local real estate changed hands other than through inheritance. I don't think ownership has passed outside the existing circle of landowner families in living memory. This is a stable community; we're comfortable with ourselves and with each other. A few of our young people leave, of course, but most of them stay, or return after they've satisfied their wanderlust. The guest cottages help support our economy, and most of our visitors are regulars, but even if one of our residents decided to sell out and move away, the rest of the community would pool its resources and buy the owner out to prevent an influx of . . . outsiders. I suppose that sounds unfriendly, but we're very conscious of the need to maintain our way of life. Tourists are only here for short periods and have very little impact on the core of the community; a new permanent neighbor would be far too unsettling."

"Surely it isn't that serious. The population here can't be large enough to be self-sustaining."

"Not entirely. It is possible to marry into one of the local lines from outside, but you'd be surprised at how rarely that happens, and usually part of the marriage contract is a right of reversion in the event of the death of the original resident. I suppose it all seems a bit paranoid to those who don't live here, but it has helped to maintain Haven as a . . . well, as a haven from some of the less desirable aspects of civilization. We're old-fashioned in many ways, and don't have a lot of the luxuries you can find elsewhere, but as a tradeoff we have a peaceful community where everyone knows everyone else. It has its drawbacks, of course, and a few of the younger people rebel against it from time to time, but it works for most of us well enough that there's not likely to be any significant change in our lifetimes."

"Including yourself?"

"Most assuredly including myself. I come from several generations of Haveners, Mr. Avery. My great-grandfather was the project manager when the first settlement was originally built."

She sounded a bit defensive and Avery decided to mend fences quickly. "I meant no offense."

"I never thought you did." If she had, it was quickly forgotten and she talked some more about the colony's early history. None of it was of immediate concern to Avery, but he nodded and made an effort to appear interested. She spoke straightforwardly and with some pride, her manner open enough that he decided to take a risk when she reiterated that Haven's population was stable and content.

"Perhaps I misunderstood then, but I overheard a conversation yesterday that led me to believe one of your residents was in fact contemplating moving out. I forget the name, something like Taliesin, Forlesin, Torgestar . . ." He let his voice trail off, hoping she'd fill in the blank.

"Torgeson?" Churienko made no attempt to disguise her disbelief. "Kier Torgeson?"

"That sounds right. I really wasn't paying that much attention."

She was shaking her head energetically back and forth. "You certainly did misunderstand something. Kier Torgeson is fourth-generation just like me, and he's as firmly rooted in this village as anyone. More than most. He even pays an export agent in Park City so that he doesn't have to travel there to arrange shipments of his produce. If you were to tell him our sun was about to go nova, he'd shrug and keep planning next season's crop rotation. The soil of Haven will be a part of his body until his body is a part of the soil."

"As you say then, I must have misunderstood. But I would still like to learn more about the village, perhaps browse through your historical files, and the current physical survey."

"I think you'd find our historical data pretty dry." It was a flat statement, with no indication she was concealing anything. "Most of it consists of births and deaths, tables of statistics, production figures, and the like. There's no real narrative. I could probably tell you everything of general interest faster than you could call up the index files."

"All I'm really looking for is an overview. I'd certainly prefer your company to that of an AI."

She thought about it a moment. "All right, make yourself comfortable. I'd offer you something to drink, but I'm waiting for Soo Yen or Noric Klanth to come over and repair my autochef. I don't often get to do anything here but input data and file reports. Our charter says there has to be a village administrative technician, but it doesn't make any provision for ensuring there's enough work to do to fill the hours I'm expected to stay on duty. Our equipment isn't state of the art, but it still doesn't leave much opportunity for frail and error-prone humanity to compromise data integrity."

Although Avery paid close attention, Churienko revealed nothing that seemed relevant to his real interest. At times she fell into a rhythm which he suspected meant she was repeating memorized summaries. She described Meadow's discovery by an exploration team and Intercorp's prompt action to pick up the option for development and exploitation. The planet as a whole had been mapped by automated satellites, but plans to expand rapidly to the other land masses, mostly located in one enormous chain of variegated islands, had faltered when Intercorp was briefly plagued with business reversals and teetered on the brink of insolvency during the years leading up to the Lysandran war. Meadow had been relegated to standby status, and development operations had not gone forward. Its income came primarily from food exports to Drago and an extensive mining operation in the eastern hills.

Haven had originally been planned primarily as an agricultural center, but several Intercorp executives had managed to divert funding to build several private vacation retreats in Haven and elsewhere, and steps were taken to shelter the area from the large-scale plans being formulated for the rest of the world. The war with Lysandra had changed the pattern of development in this entire sector, however, and the projected markets had never materialized.

Then the existence of the Nerudi caused a scandal and there was a planetwide moratorium on development that had helped ensure that the comparatively simple lifestyle of the village and its environs was not materially altered.

Intercorp had hoped to introduce a larger and more diverse farming operation than the current one, with major support from technicians, geneticists, and other specialists. The Concourse had blocked those plans and Haven had actively promoted itself as a restful getaway, attracting a few small entrepreneurs who helped shape the tourist village to supplement the farming income. Haven's permanent population had grown slowly to slightly over a thousand and stabilized there. Food exports were expected to decline even further because of the more aggressive development of nearby Camphorus and the demand for everything other than basic grain crops had already begun to dwindle. Although Park City and a few of the other communities on Meadow were too valuable to be summarily abandoned, Haven had become a borderline investment, its slide toward extinction arrested only by the popularity of its limited but expensive tourist business.

"The local farms support their owners, but they're only marginally profitable. Some of us are rather bitter about it, I'm afraid. The Nerudi have never even visited this land mass in the past, so there are many who say it's unfair to penalize the farmers just because Intercorp tried to conceal their existence."

"It must have been quite a surprise here, learning that there was already an intelligent species living on the planet."

She shrugged. "No surprise. The local people knew at least a generation ago. There was no contact, of course. I don't think the Neroos . . . the Nerudi . . . even knew there was land in this part of the world until the government told them. We're pretty far from the inhabited regions, and the Nerudi never developed any real system of navigation. Their fishing boats never go beyond sight of land."

"Then I'm surprised no one reported their existence earlier, before things were so firmly established here, I mean. They certainly must have known that the Concourse would never have sanctioned development of a world with native sentients."

"You'll find that people in Haven, on Meadow in general, mind their own business to a degree you might consider obsessive. I know that's not a popular trait abroad in the universe, but it's considered a virtue here."

Properly chastened, or at least feigning so, Avery indicated she should continue her recital.

There had been a considerable debate both on Meadow and in the Concourse Senate, and undoubtedly in the offices of Intercorp, following the revelations about the Nerudi. There was a serious proposal to remove every evidence of human presence on Meadow except for a small, concealed research mission. Intercorp argued that the substantial investment involved should not be abandoned so cavalierly, although few were inclined to worry about the corporation's financial losses given the fact that they'd acted knowing full well that the colony on Meadow was of questionable legitimacy. The Senate canceled Intercorp's development credits and the company promptly stopped subsidizing the colony and began charging for every service rendered.

Avery couldn't conceal his surprise; colony worlds were almost invariably credit sinks for the first several generations, and only survived because of long-term investments and loans from one of the giant interstellar corporations.

"Then how have you survived? I mean, is there enough income coming in from the tourist trade to support a community of this size?"

"Actually we are fairly self-supporting, although we do without a lot of services that you can find elsewhere, and we sell grain and a few other crops in Park City. Fortunately, we had a friend in the Senate who took up our cause, a friend who called in a lot of political favors to ensure that we weren't all relocated to Park City or one of the outlying villages."

"Who was that?" But he already had a suspicion, which she confirmed with the very next breath.

"Why Senator Damien, of course. His family has owned property in Haven since the second generation and he comes out to visit us two or three times every standard year. Our most illustrious citizen, I suppose you could say, although he's offworld more often than not."

Chapter Six

❋ ❋ ❋

It was not a particularly startling revelation, but it was interesting and coincidental, and Avery was always suspicious of coincidences. They were cheap shortcuts in drama and he didn't trust them in real life.

"It sounds as though Haven has tried to insulate itself from outside contact."

"That's not an entirely unfair characterization, although we're not fanatical about keeping our distance, not the majority of us in any case. About half of us have even been offworld once or twice, all of the bigger farmers except Kier Torgeson, and almost everyone goes to Park City now and then. A vacation from vacationland, I suppose. We enjoy living in a stable environment that doesn't bend and sway with every change in public opinion, but that doesn't mean we don't stay in touch with what's going on. We're just selective about how much of that influence we allow into our daily routines. We're more cosmopolitan than it appears."

"I gather Torgeson is an exception to the rule."

"Yes, but Kier is a force unto himself. He's a complex and intelligent man despite his attempt to appear dull and single minded." She paused, as though uncomfortable talking about her neighbor, but she continued without prompting. "He's had a great deal of trouble in his life and as a consequence he's very wary of change. Most of it was just bad luck, though he has a tendency to put the worst possible interpretation on even mild setbacks. I think he considers the drop off in grain exports a personal affront." She laughed, as though to indicate this was a joke, but Avery thought he detected a hint of exasperation.

He waited for her to elaborate further, but she determinedly reverted to the general history of Haven and he could think of no way bring up Torgeson's name again without making his specific interest obvious.

There wasn't much more to tell, and little of it new to him. A negotiated compromise had resulted in the establishment of Meadow as a Concourse protectorate with special status for the Nerudi. A group consisting primarily of those with vested interests, farmers and investors, remained bitterly opposed and had formed a vocal but largely ineffectual political party on Meadow. There continued to be considerable local debate about the wisdom of accepting the Nerudi as Concourse citizens, but to the Senate it was just an embarrassing problem that wouldn't go away. Most of the human population of Meadow were understandably concerned that their interests would be overwhelmed by a "misguided" sense of obligation to the natives.

"There has even been talk of enfranchising them within the next few years," Churienko confided, making no effort to conceal her uneasiness. "It sounds good in theory, but we know so little about them . . ." She didn't complete the thought. "I suppose everything will work out eventually. These things always do."

"When I was in Park City recently, I was introduced to Charles Laszlow, who seems quite interested in the welfare of the Nerudi."

Her animosity was evident by the change in her expression, and her voice also crackled with tension. "Charles Laszlow. Yes, indeed. Quite a change of heart for the man. He was assistant to the planetary administrator of Meadow prior to the change of status. They hadn't even installed the provisional government before he began questioning corporate policies, criticized his superiors and their motives quite publicly even before his resignation. Forced resignation, more than likely, although no one talks about it much."

"I imagine it took a great deal of courage to stand up to a corporation as big as Intercorp."

Churienko's mouth curled skeptically. "Or a great deal of naiveté. Don't misunderstand me, Mr. Avery. Despite my obvious personal interest in the future of Meadow, I want to see the Neroos treated decently. I suppose we should have realized sooner that by putting off the crisis we just made it worse, but when you grow up in the middle of a situation like this, it's hard to be objective or to feel any sense of urgency. Charles Laszlow may be an honest man, acting out of conscience and a sense of obligation, but he supports a quick, narrowly-focused solution that addresses only the most obvious problem and ignores a large number of very complex questions. I can't help feeling that he'll cause endless, unpredictable problems if he succeeds." She drew a deep breath before proceeding. "I apologize. I didn't mean to make a speech."

"That's perfectly all right. It makes a far more vivid impression than columns of statistics."

She returned to her prepared recital, adding few details that interested him. She described changes in the way the village had been administered over the years, including some mildly petulant comments about the lack of funding for a state-of-the-art infrastructure. Haven drew less support from Park City than it contributed in taxes and fees and was clinging precariously to existence by undercutting the prices asked by other agricultural communities, sometimes below cost just to protect their markets. They survived by continuing to use outdated equipment, suspending unnecessary public services, and milking the tourist trade for everything they could get.

"And that's essentially where we are today. Our only two real sources of revenue are tourism and farming. We have room to expand in both areas, obviously, but only if we can attract outside investment and convince the authorities to allow us to continue the development process. There's fertile land that we could plant, but we can't afford the equipment that would be necessary to work the increased acreage, and there's a virtual prohibition against land conversion. Even if we manage those hurdles, no one will loan us the credit necessary."

"What about tourism then? It's quite beautiful here and there are no extremes of weather or dangerous wildlife, and I understand there are some spectacular canyons and rivers to the south. I find it quite refreshing to be able to walk about for hours at a time without encountering another human being." At least, not a live one, he thought to himself.

She shook her head. "If everyone in Haven pooled their available credit reserves, we might be able to raise enough to build another handful of cottages. But it would take years just to earn back our investment, and we might not have those years. Haven could be irreversibly altered by forces beyond our control, the government in Park City or even the Concourse Senate. They're still debating the future of Meadow and the outcome is far from obvious. One extreme wants us to confine the Nerudi to reservations, and the other advocates packing up and leaving them to their own devices. It's not presently worth the risk."

Churienko seemed to recollect herself and waved her hands dismissively. "That's probably already more than you wanted to know. Is there anything else I can do for you?"

He nodded, trying to maintain as casual and friendly a demeanor as possible. "I'd still like to take a look at the survey, if you don't mind. Hopefully, it'll help me to get the whole place into perspective. I have a map, but it's hard to visualize the scale."

She nodded unsuspiciously and rose, led him into one of the cubicles. He sat at the console of a retrieval system so old he wasn't certain of the controls until she explained them. Once she was satisfied that he understood the icon system, she left him alone and he bent to his task with more energy.

On the pad in front of him, a section of downtown Haven centered on his present location was holographically projected from the overhead hood, part of a digitized recording of the entire area. Avery glanced through the enhancement icons, tapped the one that superimposed a three-dimensional grid which identified the individual buildings, with floating icons that yielded owners of record, year of construction, and other information. There was a string search function as well, but he thought it might be dangerous to enter Torgeson's name. He would have to scan until he found it, although he knew enough that it would not be necessary to search completely at random. He changed the focus to the outlying regions, moved around the perimeter of the village until he found a complex of storage sheds, equipment huts, and silos, obviously one of the major farms, located slightly northwest of the village center. The owner was listed as Ulrica Chan, so he passed it by.

It only took a few minutes to pan around the perimeter of Haven, activating each icon until he found the one he wanted. A rambling one-story house was listed as the residence of Kier Torgeson, wife deceased. Avery took careful note of the location, felt confident that he could find it in the real world, then systematically widened the search area.

He found four more homes nearby, two of whose owners were also named Torgeson, relatives presumably. One of the others was registered to Eli Karnov, and Avery wondered if this was where Nils lived. Avery hadn't particularly cared for the young man, but he seemed the kind who might become talkative under the right circumstances, and it was certain that he was no friend of Torgeson. Avery couldn't think of a plausible way to approach him, but if the opportunity arose, he'd try to take advantage of it.

Once he'd finished the perimeter of Haven, Avery turned to the village itself. The holographic display enabled him to examine in minutes what would have taken hours on foot. Few of the annotated names meant anything to him, although he was surprised to discover that Tanya Churienko's home was one of the largest in the village, several blocks east of the administration building. Senator Damien owned almost one third of the resort cottages in town, mostly on the west side, so it was probable that he was not among those who wished to abandon Meadow completely. Avery himself was one of the Senator's tenants, he discovered; he'd booked the cottage through a major travel agency and had wrongly assumed that it was a corporate holding.

When he was finished, he tapped the unit's power icon and sat back in his seat, trying to decide how to proceed. A nagging internal voice insisted that he was in over his head, at best wasting his time running full tilt toward a dead end, at worst risking his life. Even if the dead man had died of natural causes, the simple fact of his subsequent concealment proved that someone had something to hide.

Avery rose and stepped outside the cubicle. Churienko was sitting at her desk, studying the face of a data console. "I'm all through here. Thanks again for your help."

For just a split second, her eyes betrayed more than casual interest. He felt a sudden, strong impression that there were deep currents invisibly rushing around him, that he had dipped his toe into a fast-running stream, sending ripples of disturbance toward either shore. Then the moment passed.

"You're quite welcome. Come back any time if I can be of assistance, Mr. Avery." She seemed to genuinely mean it, and Avery wondered once again if his subconscious was suggesting a melodrama that didn't exist.

It was still morning, though rapidly approaching midday. Avery realized he was ravenously hungry, his body still unaccustomed to the longer day of Meadow. On impulse, he returned to Soothers, where a limited selection of hand-prepared foods was available and, as he would later discover, at much more reasonable prices than in either of Haven's two tourist-oriented restaurants.

Fortified by a hearty meal, Avery felt more optimistic and energetic. He admitted to himself that he was getting a perhaps childish pleasure out of playing detective. There was still the possibility that he was deluding himself, that the body had been just another variety of hallucination and that the contradictory story about the lifter had some rational and trivial explanation. His feeling that he had brushed up against some wider conspiracy could be equally illusory. His past episodes had always had a dreamlike quality; he had known them to be false even as his infected brain insisted that they were real. This felt different, more convincing, and if it was indeed just another facet of his ailment, then the disease was taking a much more serious course.

His cottage lay to the west, but Avery turned north toward the farm complexes and the homes that lay around them. He didn't have a clear plan of action, wasn't even sure what he should be looking for, but he was too restless to just sit and wait for something to happen. There was no hurry; the largest part of the day still lay stretched before him. A casual stroll would be in character; a determined march would not. The lanes and byways were not laid out in utilitarian grids, but he had a pretty clear picture of the general geography in his mind and was reasonably sure that he could find Torgeson's farm without much difficulty.

While examining the survey, Avery had noticed a fairly largish home owned by Haven's security chief. There was enough attached land to indicate that it was probably a small farm. He wondered if Hanifer had family; it didn't seem likely that she ran a farm herself in addition to her official duties. For some reason it had never occurred to him before that Hanifer could be a native Havener, perhaps because he was aware that she had previously worked with Laszlow in Park City. It seemed likely that she'd been born and raised in Haven, and had returned there after leaving Intercorp's employ. He would very much like to know more about her past, particularly the circumstances of her resignation, but could see no way to inquire along those lines except through Laszlow, and that he would not do on an unsecured line.

There were fewer signs of habitation as he left the village center behind him. The patches of undeveloped woodlands were thick and luxurious with growth, although neatly trimmed back from the lanes and the edges of the cultivated fields. There were times during which Avery could neither see nor hear any sign of a human presence other than the roadway itself. Even the synthetic pavement was engineered to blend in with the surrounding foliage.

There were a few powered vehicles in Haven; he had seen at least two autocars and a handful of wheeled vehicles, mostly powercarts propelled by storage packs, but Hanifer seemed to have the only lifter. For the most part, people here were obviously disinclined to rely on technology to move themselves from one place to another. Mostly they walked and he had seen at least one wagon drawn by a pair of yoked animals whose origin he didn't know. He had no doubt Haveners were as industrious and hard-working as he had been told, but there was undeniably a slower, more relaxed pace here than in most communities.

A short while later, he passed a pleasant little house owned by one of the Torgesons. The foliage was less luxurious here, giving way to long stretches of open ground, most of it under cultivation, with crops like parasoy, barley, singana, suprawheat, and others he couldn't identify. The only non-grain crops he'd seen so far were small vegetable plots that appeared to be personal rather than commercial, hand-tended, most of them close by private homes. Once he spotted a distant figure standing in a field, motionless, too far away to identify, possibly inspecting the crops rather than working. Despite the almost primitive atmosphere, Haveners used automated equipment for most agricultural chores. It just wasn't cost-effective to till or fertilize or plant or reap by hand, and the population wasn't large enough to tend the extensive fields manually even if they'd chosen that option.

At the next intersection, he paused until he was certain that he knew where he was, then took the left fork, moving slowly past the Karnov house. It was the only home he'd found registered in that name, apparently another family line in danger of extinction. He assumed that this was the home of Nils Karnov, self-proclaimed lover of Dini Torgeson. It was a smallish holding, in not particularly good repair. A windowless outbuilding had a pronounced lean to one side, the roof of the main house was missing a dozen shingles, and the yard itself displayed evidence of long-term neglect. For the benefit of any theoretical observer, Avery pretended to be fatigued, stepped off the road into a small, untended clearing opposite, sat, and removed his boots. In fact, he wasn't at all tired and found the physical exertion pleasantly stimulating. Part of his therapy had been supervised outings, some of them involving long hikes through forest preserves. Improved circulation and endurance helped keep the virus dormant, and he was more physically fit at present than he had been in years. One of the specialists had been fond of saying that there was no point in putting strong wine in a weak vessel.

It had occurred to him that even if there really was some bizarre conspiracy taking place beneath the placid surface of Haven, he was not likely to stumble across the solution without assistance. He was too much the outsider here. His best chance was to cajole someone like the Karnov boy into revealing some clue about his neighbor that Avery could use to build a theory, although given the animosity between the two men, it was also unlikely that the young man was in Torgeson's confidence. He watched the Karnov house surreptitiously for several minutes. At one point a shadow passed across the front window, indicating there was in fact someone inside, but there had been no other sign of life and, bored, Avery retrieved his boots and pressed onward. He hadn't really expected to have Nils emerge just as he was sitting there.

The lane he was following merged into another, larger one, an extension of the main road he had initially followed while leaving the village center. Off toward the horizon, a cluster of buildings were visible behind a row of trees set as a windbreak, including two large silos and what was probably a barn or equipment storage shed, but he lost sight of them almost immediately because this lane wasn't as well maintained, and thick ropes of vines and branches adorned with spatulate leaves pressed disconcertingly close. Most of the foliage here was native to Meadow, although a few familiar offworld imports had already secured a foothold in the local ecosystem.

Kier Torgeson's house looked larger than it had in the holograph. In addition to the main structure, which could have accommodated two good-sized families in itself, there were several outbuildings, one of which appeared to be a guest cottage. The land rose just beyond, a gentle slope that had been cleared for cultivation but was presently lying fallow, crested by two small clusters of wide-branching trees. Between them, the unfinished frame of another building was a misshapen silhouette against the sky. Although he wasn't close enough to judge, Avery assumed it was new construction, since there'd been no indication of its existence on the survey he'd examined. Apparently not everyone in Haven was constrained from expansion.

Now that he'd come this far on impulse, Avery wasn't certain how to proceed. He couldn't very well stop and ask for directions, since there was but a single route back to the village. A more plausible excuse would be to inquire about a tour of the farm complex, but he couldn't think of any reasonable way to explain why he hadn't made an appointment before trudging all the way out here. Although it reduced his chances of learning anything useful, he decided that it would be best just to continue past, as if this particular house held no more meaning for him than any of the others along the way. Avery remembered the mocking smile Torgeson had displayed in the village, and could not dismiss the feeling that the Havener had been deliberately if subtly taunting him.

He slowed his pace as much as he dared until he was well past. There were no signs of life: no children playing in the yard, no sounds from the interior, no movement except the slight sway of branches in a gentle breeze and the buzz of a swarm of tiny mites that hovered around his head for a few seconds before deciding that he was too alien to be bitable. Everything that he could see appeared to be in good repair, the yard was neat and orderly, a sharp contrast to the Karnov holding. Avery was disappointed, but not greatly; he had not really expected to learn much from this expedition, but had felt the need to reconnoiter personally. The survey hadn't told him how well the property was maintained. What he had seen indicated a rigid, orderly personality, someone who took pride in his possessions without feeling the need to boast about them. He felt that he might be able to admire Torgeson, but would never be able to like him.

The lane terminated at the farm entrance, which was surrounded by a quiltwork of fields. A harvester was silhouetted against a patch of sky in the distance, barely visible, the sound of its working so low he had to concentrate to hear it. There was other activity near a low building adjacent to the closest of two very large silos; oversized mechanical devices moved slowly through the inner yard. There was also a fairly large fenced area containing several dozen grazing animals of a species Avery didn't recognize. They were quadrupeds, massing about double his own weight, their thick bodies slung low on stubby little legs, draped with a pelt of fine hair so long that it brushed the ground. Just beyond, several smaller feathered animals milled silently about in an oblong pen.

The larger of the two fenced areas was roughly rectangular and one of the short sides extended all the way to a footpath on his right. Avery walked slowly across to the fence, which was constructed of native wood rather than the plastisteel he'd expected, weatherworn to an undistinguished gray. Several of the animals eyed him warily as he approached but showed no particular alarm and made no effort to move away. Avery was fascinated. He had seen animals from close at hand before, but always in zoos. Parchmont's rare fauna resembled small lizards and insects and a few varieties of a rare, cold blooded creature that was analogous to Earthly snakes. Aragon was another farm world, but he'd rarely ventured outside of the city of Aladdin in the few weeks he'd been resident before the Lysandrans invaded, and the largest native animal could have rested comfortably in the palm of his hand. He wasn't surprised to find domesticated animals here; the survey had indicated that there were extensive grazing lands northeast of the village.

The animals were even stranger looking from close at hand. They had a fairly conventional head, though the muzzle seemed disproportionately long as were the cup-shaped ears mounted high on the sides of their skulls. They chewed the tough grass with an unusual set of jaws which appeared to be articulated vertically instead of horizontally. He was watching the odd movements so closely that he didn't realize he was no longer alone until a hand clasped him firmly on the shoulder.

"May I help you, Mr. Avery?"

It was Torgeson, of course; he recognized the voice even before he saw the face, which bore the same derisive smile he'd seen earlier. Avery was distressed by his sudden conviction that Torgeson was not going to believe that his presence here was coincidence, might even have been aware of his approach for some time. Could Churienko have seen past his false disinterest and alerted her neighbor? Or was he being kept under surveillance routinely? The conspirators could be toying with him, laughing behind his back, anticipating his every move. It had been purest chance and bad timing that he had stumbled across that body, a mistake they were not going to repeat. Avery was both alarmed and angry, suddenly more determined than ever to play the part of detective. And Torgeson would undoubtedly continue his role, even though neither of them were particularly good actors.

"I beg your pardon. I didn't mean to trespass."

"There's nothing to apologize for. This is a public roadway and you've done neither me nor mine any harm staring at the sloggards, though I'd have thought a visitor like yourself would have found better things to do with his time." He nodded toward the herd, which hadn't reacted to his arrival any more than they had to Avery. "They're brighter than they look. Sometimes I think they know when it's slaughtering time even before I do, although they've never voiced any objection. They just mind their own business and don't cause problems when I set out to do mine. Dumb beasts they may be, but there's people who might learn a thing or two from them, wouldn't you say?"

Avery was careful not to let his expression change in response to the veiled threat. "Your business involves their eventual death and dismemberment. I'm not sure that's a lesson that I'm interested in learning. I don't think I could be quite as docile if I were in their place."

"You have a point there," Torgeson admitted. "The sloggards could be dangerous if they weren't so narrow in their minds. I can walk in right now and winnow out one for slaughter and the others wouldn't raise a squawk, even though they're smart enough to know what's coming. Don't be fooled by their dainty appearance. A grown man wouldn't last long under those hooves if they acted together. I'm careful and treat them with respect. I helped my father and his father thin the herds almost as soon as I was old enough to walk, and I've learned to accept the way things are. We all have our roles to play, and most times trouble comes only when people try to step out of their own and into that of others. Appearances to the contrary, this is still an alien world, and there's always danger lying in wait for unwary strangers."

Avery remembered the cruelly unforgiving nature of Parchmont, still treacherous despite nearly five hundred standard years of human habitation, with its sandstorms and earthquakes and poisonous thistles and spectacular lightning storms. He'd emigrated to Aragon seeking a calm and quiet environment in which to pursue his career, and was caught up in the Lysandran invasion and then infected with an alien virus. And now he'd fled from Aragon to Meadow seeking rest and recuperation, and had stumbled into some kind of conspiracy, possibly including murder. Torgeson might think that he was no more than a soft outworlder who'd lived a pampered life, but Avery had survived a good deal of adversity and thought he might have a surprise or two left in him. If Torgeson underestimated him, that was all to the good.

"I've never actually seen an operating farm before. It looks quite interesting."

Was there a hint of uncertainty in those dark eyes, or was it amusement? "It's actually rather boring, Mr. Avery. The machines do most of the work, after all, so long as nothing happens that's outside their programming. We have eight grains we raise here, staggering the planting season so we can keep a level workload. There are automated programs to plan the crop rotation and schedule fertilization and such. I spend more of my time working on a console or repairing equipment than I do with the crops. It's honest work, but has nothing to interest those not called to it. Most farmers are born to it nowadays."

Torgeson suddenly came closer, looming above Avery for a brief time before moving to the side of the pen, ostensibly interested in a curious sloggard that had come close to the fence. Avery glanced around appraisingly, realizing that they were sufficiently isolated that anything that happened here would be easy to conceal. Had he placed himself at risk foolishly? Would Torgeson chance killing him if he felt sufficiently threatened? It would be simplicity itself to bury a body out in one of the nearby fields. He could disappear as easily as the dead man he'd stumbled upon, might perhaps share his grave. Avery began watching Torgeson closely, alert to the possibility of a physical assault.

"Do you do all the work here alone? It seems like quite an extensive operation for a single man, even with the robot equipment." His voice sounded odd to him and he wondered if Torgeson could sense his nervousness.

"I have a couple others work for me, and there's more help when I need it, but one day is pretty much like another around here, which suits me. I'm a man of simple interests;

I don't push myself into other people's lives and I prefer that they show me the same courtesy."

The mocking smile was still there, but Avery thought he detected an undertone of irritation. He was beginning to think it might be best to retreat while it was still possible. "I see. Well, I don't suppose there's anything else to be seen out here. Nice to have met you, Mr. . . . ?" He waited for Torgeson to supply his name, but it wasn't forthcoming.

"I don't suppose there is either. This is a simple place, Mr. Avery. But we're content with what we have." That was the third time Torgeson had called him by name, which was certainly intentional. Torgeson was saying plainly that Avery had no secrets here, that his identity and, by implication, his purposes were known. "People from outside come here to rest, listen to the quiet, walk our lanes, enjoy the clean air, and tend to themselves. They don't care what happens in Haven that doesn't affect them, and we don't care who they are or why they're here so long as they mind their own business and leave us to mind ours." He paused, waiting for some reaction, and Avery struggled for something to say.

"I understand why you feel that way," he answered finally.

"Good day to you, Mr. Avery." Torgeson said the words with such obvious dismissiveness, turning away as he did so, that Avery experienced a flash of anger that overwhelmed his caution.

"And good day to you, Mr. Torgeson." The other man gave no reaction to the use of his name, but it was unlikely he'd failed to take notice of it.

The adrenaline wore off long before Avery had completed the long walk back to his cottage, and he had by then progressed beyond second thoughts into third and fourth. Enough of his anger remained to anesthetize some of the fear, but by the time he reached home, he was still wondering if he had behaved foolishly.

There was a blinking icon on the comnet console, indicating there was a message waiting to be played, and he rushed across the room, hoping it was from Dona Tharmody.

But it wasn't; she still seemed to be incommunicado. Instead, it was a routine notification that someone had queried his personal database.

Chapter Seven

❋ ❋ ❋

Avery was not particularly surprised to discover that someone had looked into his personal history. What did surprise him was the name of the person initiating the inquiry—Lydia Hanifer. As chief of security, she clearly had a valid interest in knowing as much as possible about people visiting her community—particularly those who reported disappearing dead bodies—but as a security officer, she would have been able to make the query without triggering the automatic notification feature. She hadn't bothered. The fact that she could have accessed his file without alerting him but had chosen not to do so was significant. Clearly she wanted him to know that he was under scrutiny, which led him to believe either that he knew more than he realized, or that the conspirators felt vulnerable to his inquiries, however inept. He checked to see when the query had been made and was only mildly surprised to see that Hanifer had acted only minutes after his brief conversation with Torgeson. That was such an improbable coincidence that he concluded Torgeson had spoken to her immediately following his trip to the farm.

Avery was perversely pleased to think that he'd at least made them uncomfortable, but he also felt the symptoms of nervous tension that he'd been warned to guard against. He decided not to wait for the implants to respond and administered his medication proactively, then lay down and waited for it to take effect.

Although he didn't think of himself as a coward, Avery entertained no illusions about his capacity for heroism. His adventures had almost all been experienced at secondhand, derived vicariously through virtual dramas, or dredged up from his rich store of imagination. Although he'd taken part in the uprising against the Lysandrans on Aragon, his role had been largely supportive, and it was only during those last violent days that he'd actually risked his life and carried a weapon, a weapon he had never even discharged. The action sequences in his own productions had all been products of his imagination or shamelessly adapted from the work of others. He had never felt any compulsion to improve their authenticity by experiencing that sort of thing at first hand.

Virtual melodramas provided an illusion, however short lived, that allowed people to participate in great events, assured them that they had the courage, strength of character, intelligence, and tenacity to triumph over evil, survive against overpowering odds, endure in the face of adversity. In reality, violence was loud, painful, and repulsive; it was the only aspect of his work where he made no effort toward verisimilitude.

Avery knew that in real life most people would panic and run if faced by an onslaught of silicon-based lifeforms from the rim of the galaxy, hysterically demand that security deal with a serial killer rather than investigate on their own, or watch holos of the initial landing on an unknown world rather than risk disease or disaster for themselves. As a child, he'd been told repeatedly that caution and circumspection were the keys to survival in the desert, that heroism was an unnecessary and generally stupid approach to life. The lesson had been reinforced whenever a neighbor took a foolish chance and paid the price. One of his childhood playmates had wandered too far from home and had perished in the desert, and there'd been other, lesser tragedies.

"The reason there are so few heroes in the universe is that most of them die while they're still young." It had been one of his father's favorite observations.

All that notwithstanding, Avery believed, as did most people, that he possessed a core of inner strength that could be called upon if the situation demanded it. He had always imagined that such a confrontation would be forthright and clear-cut. This net of implied threats, subtle menaces, and quiet mysteries was disorienting as well as alarming. But once the drug had soothed his nerves and slowed the racing impulses of his mind, Wes Avery still felt anger, pure and cool, and knew that he wasn't ready to back down. At least not yet.

He stood up and walked over to the com. With steady hands, he brought up the query screen and requested access to Kier Torgeson's public datafile. It was an act of pure defiance, and he scanned the information provided without paying close attention. When he reached the end of file marker, Avery cleared the screen, then decided it was too late to be cautious. He pressed a few more keys, and within seconds was examining the shorter but somewhat more interesting profile of Lydia Hanifer.

There was nothing there to contradict what he'd already learned, but there were some interesting embellishments. Hanifer had risen rapidly in Intercorp's private security agency, distinguishing herself through hard work, intelligent analysis, and a willingness to assume responsibility.

She had singlehandedly subdued a pentha addict who had slipped into violent psychosis in a crowded market, uncovered a rather clever misdirection of company funds by a moderately highly-placed executive, and after she was appointed as section supervisor, her department was invariably rated close to the top in its efficiency and performance ratings.

The change in Meadow's status had forced Hanifer to make an important decision. Intercorp had offered her a position on Durham, a frontier world where they were heavily involved and which was experiencing a high incidence of violent crime. Theoretically she would have taken a slight reduction in rank but in fact she'd have assumed much wider responsibilities and would have had a large staff supporting her. She would also have been perfectly situated for a much better posting or a significant promotion. It was clearly intended as a temporary holding place designed to broaden her experience and groom her for better things. The new private government of Meadow had made a counter-offer, with a better title but lower pay and less chance for advancement, as division chief in Park City. Hanifer had turned down both opportunities, instead applied for and eventually received her present assignment, an almost certain dead end. Haven was too quiet and out of the way; there was nothing Hanifer could do here, no matter how well she performed, that would single her out for advancement. And if the records were complete, she had never applied for a transfer or made any other effort to find a better position. Was she just another parochial Havener or was there something else holding her here?

When he blanked the screen, Avery felt that he understood Hanifer even less than before. Was the Haven cliquishness so strong that a promising security officer would abandon her bright prospects just to remain as village constable? Would a bright woman standing on the brink of a successful future shrink back rather than leave the familiar?

He left another short, cryptic message for Dona Tharmody, and once again received the automatic reply that her personal com was not currently accessible. Disturbed, he requested enhancement and was referred to an official news release indicating that the comnet was unavailable for several communities southeast of Park City due to technical difficulties. Emergency calls only could be relayed through alternate facilities in Park City, probably a radio transmitter.

Restless but hungry, he made himself a light supper, carried it back to the small sitting room, wondering if he could concentrate enough to work this evening. There was no pressure to do so; the specialists had told him to ease into it as quickly or slowly as felt comfortable. "Just don't strain yourself. The virus is most active when you're fatigued." There was no financial pressure compelling him to resume his old career; his investments outside Aragon had done quite well during the years of the occupation, and he could live in moderate luxury on the income from his savings even if he never worked again. It had been many years since Avery had thought of himself as anything other than a virtual composer, however, and he felt a mild sense of guilt if he went too long without working.

He was still trying to decide whether to activate his equipment when he glanced out through the side window and discovered that he was not alone.

At first he didn't notice anything out of the usual, although later he realized that the intruder had made no serious effort to conceal his or her presence. It was early dusk, the sun invisible behind the thick foliage, the sky streaked with fingers of fading color. The figure standing in the trees was partially silhouetted against a patch of lighter sky but remained motionless, not quite blending into the background.

Curiosity rather than alarm drew him to the window, but the lurker must have spotted him because the intruder withdrew into the shadows so quickly that there was no sense of movement. It was more like a shutter suddenly closing: there one second, gone the next. Under ordinary circumstances, Avery might have blinked and turned away, believing he'd misinterpreted a chance arrangement of light and shadow, or that he'd witnessed nothing more than a curious neighbor. These were not ordinary circumstances, however, and he felt a totally uncharacteristic surge of anger. Whoever had been watching had acted with deliberate furtiveness, waiting until Avery knew that he was being watched. There could be no doubt that this was the latest in a string of warnings designed to intimidate him, or to convince him that he was experiencing a fresh attack of the paranoia that had accompanied his illness.

He felt his face flush with anger, anger suddenly so intense that it overwhelmed good judgment. Foolishly, without waiting to consider the risk he was taking, Avery strode over to the door and flung it open.

Nights in Haven were much cooler than the days, and the temperature had already dropped noticeably. A brisk breeze stirred nearby branches, the rising sound of its passing punctuated by sporadic insect noises and the incessant sound of the bell vines. In the distance, muted lights showed where two other cottages stood, but there were no signs of human activity, nothing to indicate that he was not completely alone.

Avery oriented himself and moved directly to the place

where the mysterious figure had stood a moment before, just a few meters from the edge of the lane. The sky was partially clear at the moment, both moons close to full, the stars quite distinct, and he could see his way clearly. In the distance, heavier clouds rolled in from the horizon, warning of an imminent change of weather. Their leading streamers were drifting across the nearer sky, sending phantom shadows slithering across the landscape.

Despite the quiet, Avery felt as though he was still being watched, but he was rational enough to realize that his imagination might be running away with him. It was possible, after all, that his mysterious visitor had been a casual passerby. He might well be making a fool of himself prowling around in the darkness. Undecided, he was seriously considering going back inside when he heard a sound that didn't fit.

It was a single, sharp crack, as though someone had stepped on a dead branch, originating somewhere around the side of the cottage out of his line of sight. Avery felt a small thrill of fear and resisted the impulse to rush forward and investigate. His anger still simmered, threatening to boil over at the least provocation, but it was no longer in danger of overwhelming his natural caution. So instead of advancing straightforwardly, he moved slowly to his left, placing his feet tentatively until he was sure he wouldn't betray himself by making unnecessary noise. He wanted to reach a better vantage point, one from which he would have a clear view of the suspect part of the property without betraying his presence.

The side yard consisted of open lawn broken by a handful of small trees that didn't offer enough cover to conceal a small child, let alone an adult. A brief movement startled him briefly, but it was only the shadow of a passing cloud. There was no one in sight. Avery bit his lip, uncertain, wondering if he was reacting disproportionately to the innocent presence of another tourist. He had almost convinced himself to go back inside when he heard a second sharp crack, this time from the opposite side of the house, the side now hidden from him. Avery felt more strongly than ever that he was being taunted, possibly threatened.

Suddenly aware of how vulnerable he was, unarmed and alone in the darkness, Avery walked slowly back to his door, slipped inside, quickly touched the maximum security icon. Reinforced bars slid soundlessly into the door as the shutters closed and locked in place, and he turned immediately to the com, reaching out to summon security.

With his fingers poised to press the emergency icon, Avery hesitated. Security meant Hanifer, and he still believed she was involved in whatever it was that was happening in Haven. In all probability, she was already aware of his situation. She might even be the intruder. Did he really want to call her? Would it do any harm? Would it do any good? A show of panic might reassure the conspirators that he was properly cowed; on the other hand, it might also encourage them to step up their campaign and drive him off the planet entirely. He hovered indecisively, the arguments for and against struggling against each another with such intensity that he developed an instantaneous splitting headache. His hand dropped to his side and he turned away from the com, frustrated, raging inside.

Ultimately he put the incident out of his mind and went to bed. His dreams were not restful, filled with dark images.

Once he wakened from a particularly vivid sequence in which he pursued a prowler into the shadows and found a Nerudi lying in wait. This wasn't the reserved, apparently docile Nerudi he'd seen at Laszlow's villa but rather a larger, more menacing figure with clawed fingers and eyes that glowered malevolently.

Later he dreamed that he was down on elbows and knees in a muddy pen, one of a dozen or so human prisoners that included Dona Tharmody, all waiting docilely for their turn in the slaughterhouse. In the distance, he could hear Kier Torgeson and Lydia Hanifer talking to one another.

"Sometimes I think they know it when it's time to cull the herd." Torgeson spoke flatly, his voice a monotone.

"Doesn't that make them dangerous?" answered Hanifer. "They might decide to attack."

"Not if you keep your wits about you. They're bright in some ways, but as long as they don't think their turn has come, they don't cause any trouble. I doubt they care much what happens to others of their kind so long as they're spared."

In one of those dreamlike transitions that ignore logic, Tharmody was suddenly outside the pen, being led off toward the barn. Avery scrambled forward, stuck his head out between two rails of the fence, and shouted desperately for them to stop.

Hanifer glanced in his direction. "One of them seems to be upset about something."

Torgeson shrugged. "Don't pay it no mind. Once this one's out of sight, he'll forget all about her."

Avery woke so distraught that he felt the implants sedating him before he had a chance to medicate himself voluntarily.

When he released the cottage security system the next morning, the shutters opened to reveal a fairly heavy rain falling from a tumultuous, dark gray sky. The ground was already so heavily saturated that there were small pools of standing water scattered across the lawn. Meadow was not wealthy enough to have its own weather control system, a standard feature on most resort worlds, and advertised the unpredictable patterns of storms and fair weather as one of its rustic charms. Even after his time on Aragon, rain fascinated Avery, who had been fully mature on Parchmont before he'd seen anything other than a brief squall, and he stood in front of the window for almost an hour, abandoning his post only when his legs began to cramp. The rhythm of water spattering against the window was hypnotic and somehow reassuring, and even the melancholy effect of gray skies and drooping leaves was perversely pleasant.

He spent the morning working with his equipment, a lengthy session that was not specifically linked to a coherent plot, but consisted of experimentations with emotional states, drawn in part from what he had experienced during the past several days. He recorded a few brief character sketches that were modifications of people he'd met in Haven, fragments of imaginary conversations, bits and pieces of actual experience that he wanted to recall and preserve before they faded. Most of this would probably never be used, but he had spent much of his life recording and cataloguing such fragments, many of which would be recalled and merged into his more serious work. His best compositions had been assembled like mosaics from myriad unconnected fragments. Eventually his unconscious mind would begin to connect these disparate visions into a plot sequence.

It was particularly difficult for Avery to create the human characters that peopled his creations, possibly because the culture of Parchmont had emphasized the virtue of self-reliance so strongly that close friendships were rare and he'd always been at a disadvantage figuring out the nuances of how others acted. Fortunately, he'd specialized in thrillers, usually set on invented planets, rarely featuring characters who were not essentially interchangeable. Once the basic plot was set, he began the slow process of assembling the elements into a coherent whole, smoothing over inconsistencies, then incorporating the supporting details, texture, color recognition enhancement, aromas, temperature. It was in this aspect that he'd surpassed the majority of his peers. Most dramatists concentrated on the foreground, ignoring the tiny details that made a virtual setting seem real. Avery attributed his success to a willingness to spend the extra time to flesh in the supposedly inconsequential details so that the environment seemed authentic and consistent, as well as interesting. It was essential that the viewer feel the story rather than just observe it, and his gift for crafting an authentic environment, despite some outrageously incredible story lines, was unrivaled.

By mid-day he was satisfied that he'd done enough for one session. He ate an unusually large meal in the front room, watching the sun finally break through the cloud cover, feeling his spirits lift as bright sunlight spilled down through the overhanging branches. The rain had stopped some time earlier, but the ground and foliage were still visibly wet and a sheen of moisture glistened on the outside of his window.

The work had been an effective diversion, but now he was forced once more to consider his situation here on Meadow. Was he in any actual danger? If so, would he remain safe if he forgot about the body and the Haveners and minded his own business for the rest of his stay? Would his personal pride and stubbornness allow that course of action? If not, what could he do to pursue the issue, alone among strangers?

He realized guiltily that he had forgotten about Dona Tharmody, who still hadn't answered his messages. There seemed no point in sending another. Either she'd get in touch with him or she wouldn't. Logic insisted she had not become the latest victim of the conspirators; if they were sufficiently alarmed to strike again, he would certainly be their chosen target. Either the communications problem had proven more difficult to solve than the official announcements suggested, or for reasons of her own she was ignoring his efforts to reach her. He entertained the possibility of calling Charles Laszlow and asking if he could use his resources to check on her status, but couldn't think of a plausible reason to make such a request that wouldn't be either alarming or intrusive. He did call up her personal datafile, found nothing in it to contradict or particularly supplement what he already knew, and felt vaguely guilty for intruding on her privacy, even though it was a matter of public record. Laszlow was still an option, but he reluctantly decided against taking steps in that direction, at least for the moment.

He walked into the village early that afternoon, bored and tired of staring at the walls of his cottage. Restless, alternating between concern for his own safety and frustrated anger that he was unable to think of anything that might enlighten him further, he had planned only a casual stroll and hadn't realized where his subconscious was taking him until the commercial district was in sight.

He avoided the tourist area, although there didn't seem to be much pedestrian traffic about today. There wasn't much of a crowd at Soothers either, and they were a subdued lot, so intent upon their own business that not one head turned in his direction when he entered. Avery had started toward an empty table when he noticed a familiar face sitting alone in another corner and altered course.

"Hi. Remember me?"

Tanya Churienko glanced up, nodded, her face only slightly animated. She appeared drawn, tired, looking years older than on the first occasion they'd met. "Of course, Mr. Avery. And how have you been enjoying your stay with us?"

"It's not exactly what I expected," he answered candidly, "but the contrast to what I'm familiar with has been very refreshing. May I join you for a moment?"

"Of course. Can I order you some refreshment?"

"Why, thank you. Yes, as a matter of fact, a cool fruit drink of some sort would be delightful. Nothing alcoholic." He slid into the chair, scanned the room for other familiar faces, then turned back to his host. "Is it always this somber after a rainstorm?"

She shook her head. "We've had a small crisis during the night, I'm afraid. A young woman missing."

Avery made a polite sound of sympathetic concern. "How did it happen? I mean, I've walked around quite a bit lately and there don't seem to be any real dangers here."

"None that are obvious."

She seemed to be speaking more to herself than to him, and he waited, hoping she'd say more, finally prompted her. "Is there any suspicion of foul play?"

Churienko laughed with bitter amusement. "Depends on your point of view, Mr. Avery, but given your vocation, I can see why that would be your first thought. I'm afraid in this case it's a good deal less exciting. Everyone but her father believes she's run off with her lover and will be found when she wants to be, but he wouldn't accept anything less than an all-night search, and Kier Torgeson is not a man you deny lightly."

Avery struggled not to overreact to the name. "Would

that be the same Torgeson we spoke of briefly when I visited your office the other day?"

"One and the same. Dini's a headstrong child, much like her father in that regard. Kier complains constantly about the girl, but he loves her dearly, more so now that her mother is dead. Dini's an adult and anxious to make her own decisions, but Kier feels he knows better than she the shape her life should take. I don't think he's forgotten the titanic battles he and his own father used to have when he was her age, but he's managed to convince himself that it's different between him and Dini. His father was always in the wrong, of course, but Kier's judgment is beyond reproach. Or at least so he believes."

"So you think his daughter's all right?"

She nodded. "Most certainly, physically at least. The Karnov boy is missing as well, you see, and they've been keeping each other's company a great deal of late. Can't say that I don't agree with her father about the boy; he's empty-headed, boastful, and lazy. Dini's a strong-willed, intelligent young woman and should be able to do better for herself, once she realizes she doesn't have to arrange her life solely as an act of rebellion against her father. Nils Karnov is about as unlike Kier Torgeson as two members of the same species can be, and I suspect she's been seeing him just to irritate her father."

"Surely if they're both adults and they've broken no laws, her father has no recourse. Why didn't they just leave openly and avoid the uproar?"

Churienko regarded him levelly and he realized he was being evaluated, judged, that his companion wasn't sure just how much she should say and how she should say it. The silence was becoming uncomfortably long when she finally reached some sort of decision.

"We're a small, isolated community here in Haven, as I'm sure you've realized by now. We respect the system of law that Park City imposes and we abide by it. But there's another set of imperatives that operate here as well: uncodified, flexible, even subjective. We have a saying here, that the law is a servant of justice, but not the only servant. I suppose you could say that we impose a different standard of behavior on Haveners than we do on visitors like yourself, or people in Park City and elsewhere. Haven is a self-contained ecosystem; a small change in population in either direction could upset the equilibrium that holds us together as a community. A breach in the agreement to sell land only among ourselves would open the floodgates to an inflow of outsiders, people with different value systems, aspirations, and cultural behavior. There are dozens of ways in which an individual could seriously damage the structure of our community. So we have developed means of defending our way of life that don't rely on the planetary code of conduct. Sometimes they don't even follow the letter of the law."

Avery wondered if, once again, he was being subtly warned to back off. But he saw no hint of subterfuge in Churienko's eyes, although there was a fierce warmth in her voice. Pride, perhaps? He knew there were entire planetary societies outside the Concourse who had refused to join because they didn't wish to surrender certain rights that helped them define themselves as a culture, even though that cut them off from many of the advantages of membership in the larger culture. Even Aragon had briefly declared itself independent when the Concourse had tried to install a temporary military government following the liberation. But it had never occurred to him that a single village might lay claim to limited sovereignty.

"But Karnov is a Havener, isn't he? I don't see where an

elopement poses even an insignificant threat to the village. You told me that some of your younger people have moved away before, to Park City or even offworld. If your population is to remain stable, I would think you'd even welcome it when the discontented pull up stakes and move elsewhere."

Churienko nodded. "That's absolutely true. Our younger generation is just as contrary as you'd expect. I myself married against the wishes of my family, although I did so openly. I was shunned by my own parents for almost three years before we were reconciled. But Nils has always been a problem child. He has no real friends; the other young men his age include him in their activities because one of those unwritten rules I mentioned requires that no one of us be excluded socially without good reason. But toleration doesn't mean friendship. Most of the time Nils is ignored, but he has frequently been the target of cruel jokes, and he's made no secret of the fact that he doesn't care for Haven, considers us provincial and uninteresting. The boy lusts after life in Park City. He's fascinated by size and complexity and the rapid pace of life."

"There's nothing wrong with that. I mean, if he doesn't fit in here, perhaps the village would be better off without him."

She nodded. "If that was all of it, I'd contribute to the price of relocating him myself. But there's more. When Dini's mother died, she left her daughter a considerable parcel of property, about one-third of Kier's arable land, and another small, detached parcel that has been left fallow for years. Tara Tshombi was the last of her family. After they were married, Kier worked her holding along with his own, but there was never a proper transfer of title. Kier has been building Dini a cottage on a piece of her inheritance.

Though he's been taking his time about it. It'll break his heart when she moves out, though he'll never let on."

Avery remembered the new construction he had seen the previous day and found himself nodding. "I took a walk up that way yesterday. I think I saw it, up on a hill between two stands of trees. A fairly small place with an oversized stone fireplace."

"Kier started work on it almost two years ago, but he tore down the original frame once and he's redone the stonework twice, always finding some flaw that needs to be corrected. The shell is done now but the interior still needs a lot of work, although I suppose you could live in it now if you didn't mind a few rough spots. I'm sure he's afraid that once Dini has a place of her own to go to, she'll make herself scarce in his house. Probably true, given the atmosphere there. But she does own the land free and clear, while Nils is still living with his parents and has no plot of his own."

Avery suddenly suspected where the conversation was headed. "And you think Nils might convince Dini to sell the land to an outsider, is that it?"

"That's what Kier fears, or claims to. I discount it myself. Dini might be loud and contrary, but she's a Havener through and through, and there's no doubt in my mind which of the couple is the dominant one. My guess is they've run off to assert their independence from their families, and they'll be back to take up housekeeping at Dini's place after they're certain that everyone knows they're making their own decisions. Kier won't like it, but once he's had a chance to come around to the situation, he'll adapt. The Karnov boy might even steady down once he has some responsibilities, though I confess I'd be happier if Dini dumped him in the city and came home alone."

"If they'd been found last night, what would have happened? I mean, they are within their rights if they're both legally adults."

Churienko didn't answer at first, then made a decision in his favor and visibly relaxed. "It would depend on who found them, I suppose. There's a few sympathetic to the girl, and Kier isn't the most popular man in Haven. Wouldn't surprise me to find out someone turned a blind eye to them. They're on foot, so there's only two possible places they could have gone, to take a lifterbus from Manor Village or over to Southport Depot. Solitude's too far to reach without transport. If they really don't want to be seen, there's not much chance of finding them. Too much cover for an air search, too many potential routes for the limited number of search parties we could organize here. Hanifer took up the lifter last night but even with infrared sensors, she had no luck. They'd hear that faulty engine coming well enough in advance to get out of sight. Dini's smart enough to have taken an insulated blanket with her. They could just throw it over their heads and keep right on walking."

"Would you turn them in, if you knew where they were, I mean?" The words were out before he realized he had no right to ask that question.

But she answered without hesitation. "Yes, I would. Haven is my family. Wouldn't you protect your own if the situation were reversed?"

Avery responded noncommittally, explaining that he had no living family, then allowed Churienko to change the subject to something neutral. They chatted about the weather and she recommended a tour of the Diva Valley, but Avery could tell she was reciting from memory again rather than conversing. She excused herself a few minutes later, explaining that she was due to return to the administrative office for another shift. Avery finished his drink thoughtfully, and left a short time later.

Soothers was located directly across from an unmarked building whose entrance was recessed from the street, with a natural stone wall and an electronic gate warding off casual intruders. When Avery stepped out into the now quite intense sunlight, there were two men on the opposite side of the roadway, just entering through the open gate, which closed and locked behind them. Neither of the men noticed him, but just before they disappeared, the taller of the pair turned to say something inaudible to his companion, and Avery had an excellent glimpse of his profile.

It was Senator Karl Damien, who had supposedly left Meadow for a political conference several days earlier.

Chapter Eight

❋ ❋ ❋

When Avery returned to his cottage, there was a message waiting for him. It was from Dona Tharmody, indicating she had finally completed her assignment and was on her way back to Haven. She looked and sounded tired but there was no indication that anything else was wrong and he felt a lifting of tension that he hadn't realized was weighing so heavily with him.

"I'll try comming you again later, but first I'm going to spend a good long time unconscious. I don't know who programmed the interpreter subroutine into the Socrates line of intelligent managers, but there are some logical contradictions built into the system that are fatal if the wrong set of conditions arises. Which is exactly what happened here. After I convinced the overseer routine that I wasn't a virus, it decided I must be a schizophrenic loop in its flexible interface code. It kept invoking a data integrity logarithm to reject signals when they tried to clear the transmission node and would only accept incoming or outgoing signals that fit a narrowly defined set of conditions." She paused. "Sorry, I'm blathering. Anyway, I've already filed a report recommending a preventive patch to the entire line, and now I need to catch up on my personal down time. Catch you later."

Relieved, Avery's thoughts turned to an even more interesting though perhaps unrelated puzzle, the apparent secret presence of one of the Concourse's most influential political figures in Haven when he was supposed to be attending a planning meeting in anticipation of the upcoming session of the Senate. It was always possible that he'd been mistaken, fooled by a chance resemblance, but that seemed unlikely. Damien was at least an honorary Havener; almost certainly had close friends in the area, perhaps even family, some of whom might resemble him physically. But there had been just too many coincidences and unexplained incidents happening in his vicinity lately. If this were a neatly scripted melodrama, all these loose ends would tie together neatly at the end. Even though this was real life, with no omniscient author controlling events, he could not shake the conviction that everything was related, advancing toward a specific conclusion. It did occur to him that, even in virtual drama, not all endings were happy ones.

Senator Damien's presence in Haven was probably unrelated to the missing body, Avery realized, but at least it offered him a new line of inquiry. A query of Damien's data file should not raise any eyebrows. The Senator was a public figure and probably received so many query notices that he no longer paid any attention to them. Indeed, when he retrieved it, Avery discovered that the file itself was the most extensive he had ever examined, much more information than he actually wanted or could absorb, and he browsed through the Senator's voting record without understanding half the issues involved. There was extensive financial information, and links to position papers and scholarly articles he'd written.

Avery was more interested in the biographical profile. Damien was the only child of two powerful and influential parents. His father had been on the board of several interstellar corporations, a man whose substantial personal investments had been spread throughout hundreds of planets. His mother served two terms as governor of Cascade and had held a seat in the Concourse Senate at the time of her death. Damien's upbringing had been orchestrated to prepare him for a leadership role. He had chosen politics rather than commerce, but had not divested himself of the family fortune. A large portion of his holdings were held in a blind trust administered by an anonymous AI management company on Midway, but there was a quite lengthy list of properties over which he maintained personal control.

Damien had first run for office shortly after his mother's death, representing twelve settled worlds, not including Meadow. Although that first victory had been by a narrow margin, he'd become increasingly popular during his second and third campaigns, carrying ten of the twelve on both occasions. Avery didn't feel qualified to judge the Senator's performance, but it appeared that he was energetic and not afraid to support a position opposed by the majority of his constituents if he felt they were wrong. During his first term in the Senate, Damien had proven himself capable and hard-working, much to the surprise of those who had considered him a dilettante more interested in a showy title than actually representing the people who elected him. He quickly won the respect of his colleagues and enough of his constituents to easily weather a concerted effort to unseat him during the next election.

There were three data tags relating to Haven, all of which Avery read in detail. The first was a summary of his privately-owned property on Meadow, which included two small tracts of undeveloped land, a somewhat more extensive investment in Park City, and several vacation cottages in Haven and two other resort communities. He was also listed as co-director of a small agricultural export company. Avery's eyebrows rose when he noticed the name of his business partner. It was Kier Torgeson.

Avery found a summary of Damien's recent activities and the text of his speeches during the last Senate session, and discovered that the Senator was a vocal opponent of Laszlow's enfranchisement plan for the Nerudi. The Senator advocated protectorate status for the natives and a continued moratorium on expansion of the human presence on Meadow. It was likely that Damien had more to gain financially if the planet was opened to development, so Avery tentatively assumed that he was acting out of conviction rather than self-interest. He followed a link to a series of commentaries, most of which seemed critical of Damien's stance, two of which were authored by Charles Laszlow. Judging by the tenor of most of the remarks, if the Senator was depending on support from Haven for re-election, he might be in serious trouble, at least in the rural areas. There was no indication of anything unsavory or suspicious and Avery's hope of finding something that might cast light on his personal mystery had almost completely evaporated.

Frustrated, he tapped the icon to close the file. It seemed less likely than ever that Damien's apparently clandestine return to Haven would suggest any new line of inquiry. He checked the time, realized there was more than enough for a brief reconnoiter of the Senator's private cottage before darkness fell. Avery had only carried a laser once or twice even during the Lysandran occupation, and had never used it, but for the first time he wished that he had one concealed among his belongings. Meadow had very strict rules about the possession of lethal weapons, however, and it would probably have been confiscated when he came through customs. Even Hanifer had carried nothing more serious than a nerve stunner.

Damien was almost certainly staying in his private cottage, which was only a few minutes away. The weather had turned warm again and he blinked as he stepped outside the climate-controlled cottage. There was no one in sight, but he could hear casual conversation from the patio of the adjacent cottage. The fact that there were no visible indications that he was under surveillance meant little, so Avery tried to appear casual for the benefit of any theoretical observer. He took a somewhat circuitous route, stopping occasionally to admire a particularly vivid patch of flowers or to watch the elaborate aerial dances of flutterbyes and other insects. On two occasions he encountered other people, an elderly couple who nodded to him in passing, and an intense-looking young woman who strode past so quickly that he never had a chance to identify her.

When he finally reached the Senator's cottage, he surreptitiously looked around, decided that if he was being watched there was nothing he could do about it, and slipped off the path and into a patch of intricately intertwined vines and shoots. They proved more resistant than he had expected, catching in his clothing and tangling around his ankles, but he pushed on quickly until he was confident that he couldn't be seen from the road.

Picking his way carefully, he progressed to the rear of the cottage, acquiring a painful scratch across the back of his left hand in the process. The Senator seemed to prefer more robust plants, ones which armed themselves with thorns, stickers, and minute barbs. Once past the worst of it, he advanced more carefully, hoping to determine whether or not the cottage was currently tenanted. The windows were unshuttered, but that proved nothing, and he couldn't find anything to indicate the Senator was in residence. He crouched beneath a spongetree for a while, then summoned the courage to move closer, almost to the perimeter of the cleared yard and the outer rim of the security fence.

There was unmistakably someone in the cottage. There was music playing softly in the background, and he saw an unidentifiable shape moving just inside one of the windows. It was there for only a few seconds, and didn't reappear. He waited impatiently, trying to will whoever was inside to return.

After several minutes passed uneventfully, Avery started to feel foolish. He was on the verge of admitting defeat and leaving when the cottage door slid open. Panicking, he dropped hastily to the ground, banging his right knee painfully. He clamped his jaw shut to keep from crying out, and it was only then that he saw who had emerged.

"Dona! What in the world are you doing here?"

He rose awkwardly and stepped out into the open, hoping he didn't look as foolish as he felt. Dona stood with her hands on her hips, watching him thoughtfully. "I might ask you the same thing. What are you doing lurking in the bushes?"

Avery sighed and shook his head. "It's a long story, but there's a good explanation. At least I think it's a good one. But aren't you supposed to be asleep in Park City?"

"That's what I planned originally, but then I found out there was a commercial lifter heading this way and I still had the invitation from Senator Damien to use the cottage, so I decided to cash in some of my accumulated vacation time. I just arrived about an hour ago."

Avery bit his lip. "This might be complicated. Your host is apparently in Haven."

She frowned. "Senator Damien? In Haven? That's impossible. I told you, he left for Ozymandias to attend a party caucus. He couldn't possibly come back here for at least several more days, and it's more likely that he'll go directly to the Senate."

"I'm not convinced that he ever left in the first place. I saw the Senator in town this morning. Dona, it's possible that Damien is linked to whatever else is going on in Haven. The place is just too small to have more than one group of conspirators."

"You might be surprised about that," she answered quietly. "But that's another question entirely. Are you absolutely certain that it was the Senator you saw?"

He hesitated, decided to be honest. "Well, no, I suppose not. I've only seen him in person that one time with you and only from a distance, although he looked vaguely familiar even then. But things are starting to come together. I've found definite connections between Hanifer and Torgeson and I think they're both involved in the cover-up." He briefly told her of his cryptic conversation at the farm, the background he'd picked up from Tanya Churienko, and his discovery that Damien was Torgeson's partner.

"That's still all pretty tenuous, you realize. Aren't you drawing conclusions from what might be just coincidence? As you said, Haven is a small place. It's inevitable that connections exist among its residents, including the Senator. Come on inside. I have an idea."

They sat separately in the front room while Dona used the com to contact Damien's office in Park City. Avery remained outside the scanning field, but in a position from which he could watch the holographic image of the woman who answered the call.

"Senator Damien's office. How may I be of service?"

The woman's smile was professional and polite and totally insincere, so Avery assumed she was real and not an AI interface.

"Yes, I hope so. My name is Dona Tharmody and I'm a friend of the Senator's. A few days ago he offered me the use of his cottage in Haven, and I wanted to confirm that it was still all right if I did so for the next three days. Could I speak with the Senator for a moment?"

The woman shook her head but answered politely. "I'm afraid that's impossible. The Senator is not presently on Meadow and we don't expect him back until after the next session of the Senate. I would be happy to forward a message for you, but I'm afraid that I'm not authorized to give out the access code to the Senator's property." She didn't appear to be particularly sorry.

"That's all right; he gave it to me before he left. In fact, I'm calling from his cottage right now."

There might have been a faint hint of disapproval in the set of the other woman's features, but if so, it vanished quickly. "In that case, I assume there is no problem. As I said, the Senator is offworld and won't require local lodging."

"Well, thank you for your patience. I won't take up any more of your time."

Once the connection had been broken, Dona slowly shook her head. "I suppose that doesn't really prove anything, but at least it establishes my right to be here. I'm not sure what I'll do if Karl shows up looking for a place to sleep this evening. If it really was him that you saw, I mean. Play dumb, I guess. He made a point of telling me he was leaving Meadow for a while. But if you saw him . . ." She let her voice trail off.

Avery hesitated before answering. "It's possible," he said

slowly, "that I superimposed a known face over that of a stranger. That's how the virus works. It retrieves old memories and mixes them with my current sensory input. I have implants that are supposed to keep the virus dormant, but sometimes it takes a moment or two for them to react."

She was quiet for a few seconds. "Do you think the body you saw might also have been some kind of relapse?"

"No, as a matter of fact, I don't. My symptoms are almost always stress-related; the overt symptoms are accompanied by anxiety and physical pain, headaches, fatigue, things like that. I felt wonderful when this all started; it was a bright cheerful day, my implants hadn't been keyed since I'd arrived, and I'd had a stimulating walk. Even when I realized that the man was dead, there was no sense of dread, none of the irrational emotional responses which normally accompany my attacks. And I examined the body for quite some time before going for help. Even if the implants had been slow to respond, they would have adjusted given that much time. Some of what followed is more questionable, I admit, and could be explained away quite innocently. But something is wrong here, something sinister and dangerous. I'm convinced of it, and I'm determined to see it through. But I can't let you involve yourself without your knowing that I might not be the most reliable witness."

Dona said nothing at first, dialed herself a mildly alcoholic drink, and finished it before answering. "All right, we have to accept the possibility that you've been hallucinating. But regardless of whether or not your mind has been playing some tricks on you, there's still something going on here. Even if we assume that you did imagine the disappearing body, why didn't Hanifer file a report as a matter of routine? We know she didn't and we know that would be standard procedure for anyone with as good a reputation as hers. Why didn't she even take the simple steps of requesting data on missing persons? She wouldn't overlook such an elementary step."

Avery nodded. "And why did she tell me the lifter was inoperable when that was not in fact the case?"

"That too, although it's still possible there's a reasonable explanation for that. You said Charles described her as fiercely loyal. I don't suppose he made any suggestions about where those loyalties might currently lie? She's not working for Intercorp any more, after all."

"No, but if she's a typical Havener, she identifies with this village a lot more strongly than she does with the government in Park City. Maybe she and Torgeson are lovers. I know his wife is dead. He strikes me as being capable of almost anything. If he's involved in something illegal, like smuggling, he might have coerced or cajoled Hanifer into helping him keep things under control."

"She doesn't strike me as the type who can be manipulated easily. I can't see her as Torgeson's pawn."

"All right, then maybe they're equal partners. Or she might even be the boss and Torgeson her hireling."

Dona's expression remained doubtful. "With Senator Damien as the third partner? I can't see him accepting a subordinate role either." She shook her head in frustration. "I'm sorry but none of those scenarios seem likely to me. Did Damien's name come up when you talked to Laszlow? I know Charles doesn't care for him very much; they're diametrically opposed on more issues than just the status of the Nerudi. Charles is a thorough and methodical man. I'd be very surprised if there is much about Damien that he doesn't know."

Avery shrugged. "I don't think either of us mentioned the Senator, though it's possible. I didn't have any reason to connect him with this situation at that point, remember? Maybe we should talk to Laszlow again."

She shrugged indecisively. "Do you have anything concrete to link Torgeson to the dead man? How certain are you that he's even involved?"

"Logically, not very; emotionally, I'm absolutely convinced. When I was out at the farm, he chose his words very carefully, but it was pretty obvious that he was making threats. He's not the most pleasant of people, but there's no reason for him just to have taken a general dislike to me."

Dona nodded. "I've only met him once. He doesn't mix with the tourists, considers them a necessary evil, I suppose. And he's not universally liked even by his neighbors, although they all seemed to respect him."

"And it's not surprising that Hanifer should speak to him after he assaulted someone in a public place. But someone moved that body, probably while Hanifer and I were en route, and Haven is a small community. There are a limited number of people who could have been involved. I can see Torgeson handling the dirty work, or arranging to have it done, and if so, he wouldn't think twice about paying me a little visit later, to warn me off." He told her about the incident at his cottage, and Hanifer's query to his personal database. "The prowler might also have been my overactive imagination, and Hanifer's could be explained in light of the report I made. The fact that it came just after I had spoken to Torgeson could be dismissed as coincidence, but I don't believe it for a second."

"You think they're telling you to mind your own business?"

"Emphatically. Not in so many words, but the message has been loud and clear."

"Then if you don't mind my asking, why are you pursuing this? This isn't your planet and you never met the dead man."

Avery fell silent, and when he spoke again it was to himself as much as to Dona Tharmody. "I guess I'm trying to pay an old debt. I grew up in a culture that elevates self-reliance above all other virtues. It makes sense on Parchmont, because if you can't trust yourself in an emergency, you're probably going to die. It's not a very forgiving world and it hasn't been tamed even after a dozen generations of human habitation. As children, we were taught that putting ourselves at risk, even to help another, was foolish at best. If a playmate fell into a crevasse and was trapped, we went for help rather than attempt a rescue. That was usually the smart thing to do regardless of the circumstances, but from time to time there were unnecessary deaths, victims who could have been rescued if they'd been reached promptly."

"And you were involved in one of those incidents?"

"Actually, no. My parents spent most of their time monitoring remote survey stations. I had almost no childhood friends. I emigrated from Parchmont eventually, but I never entirely left the planet behind me. Aragon was very different. The major land masses have an ideal climate, there are no dangerous predators, and the colonists are much more inclined to support one another. My background made me hold aloof from my neighbors, but they tolerated my idiosyncrasies and there were a few that I even came to think of as friends. Then came the Lysandran invasion.

"The Lysandrans held the planet for more than two years and they were reasonably benevolent conquerors who seemed quite honestly surprised when we continued to resist them. I joined the underground rather late in the day, I'm afraid, and only after being urged to do so by a young woman with whom I was involved." His mouth felt dry and he had to pause for a while before continuing. "We went on our first mission together. It was supposed to be routine reconnaissance; we weren't even armed. Unfortunately, someone panicked when a Lysandran patrol came too close, and they tried to arrest us. Things got out of control, weapons were fired. Kim was hit while we were running away. It wasn't serious, but she couldn't walk. The Lysandrans were chasing us and if I'd stopped to help her, we might both have been caught. But possibly not. I'll never know. I hesitated and almost started back for her, but that damnable conditioned selfish response screamed at me to run and I listened and ran."

"And you feel responsible for her death?"

"No. She didn't die. The Lysandrans treated all their prisoners quite well. I saw her again a few days after the uprising. She didn't appear to be angry at all. She just looked right through me and walked past. I never saw her again after that, but I kept track of her. She's married now." There was an awkward silence. "I don't think I could live with myself if I abandoned someone like that again, even someone I've never met. I know it's irrational, but sometimes I think this virus in my brain is a punishment for abandoning Kim the way I did. I was taught that the only person I could rely on was myself, and now I find that I can't trust myself either, that my own mind is playing tricks on me. It's rather ironic."

Dona waited patiently while he recovered his composure, and when she spoke again her voice was softer. "If the man you found was murdered, what is preventing the conspirators from eliminating you as well? You're a stranger, you have no family. If you had a fatal accident out here, it's unlikely anyone would question Hanifer's report."

"I don't know the answer to that question. Maybe they

don't think I know enough to pose any threat and the warnings are designed just to keep me off balance, discourage me from carrying things any further."

"That could change if they think we know more than we do."

"The same thought had occurred to me. I'm not sure if they're aware that I've confided in you. We've only been seen together once or twice. I don't want to put you at risk."

"Don't worry about me; I walked into this with my eyes open. And there's still a chance that there is a perfectly innocuous explanation for everything that's happened."

Avery shook his head. "If that's the case, why are people going to such great efforts to keep me from finding out about it? Even if it wasn't murder, it's something that people want to cover up."

Dona refilled her glass and offered to punch one up for Avery, but he shook his head. "We need to talk about Senator Damien."

"Yes, the mysterious Senator who manages to be in two places at once. A valuable ability for a politician."

Avery sat back and massaged his chin. "As I said, it's possible that I was mistaken, that the man I saw simply resembled Damien very strongly and triggered an old memory. I don't believe it, but I have to accept the possibility. If it was some kind of misperception, it would help to know for certain. I don't suppose you could access spaceport records and find out if Damien actually did take a shuttle offworld?"

"I could check the liftoff schedule. It wouldn't necessarily tell us anything, though. Senator Damien has his own ship and shuttle. Even if it did leave Meadow, there'd be no way to prove whether or not he was aboard. If I were in his place and wanted to give the impression that I was elsewhere, I think it would be rather easy to convince the port authority to accept my version of events. His crew could even have transmitted a pre-recorded or AI-manipulated message from orbit to convince the port controller that he had actually left."

"I had no idea the Senator had his own ship." Private shuttles were rare but not unheard of; private starships were a different matter entirely. Then he remembered the list of investments and holdings that had scrolled down his data screen earlier and realized Damien might well control enough wealth to buy his own planet if he so desired. Perhaps that was the secret motivation behind whatever was happening here; perhaps Damien was attempting to build some kind of personal empire on Meadow. That might also explain his opposition to elevating the Nerudi to full Concourse membership.

"What significance is there even if he is on Meadow secretly?"

"Damien's grandmother was one of the major stockholders of Intercorp, but he sold his shares shortly after his first election to the Senate. Most of his personal wealth is in a blind trust, but there was enough left over for him to invest heavily here on Meadow and elsewhere. Laszlow sent a position paper to the Senate that hinted Damien personally arranged the leak about the existence of the Nerudi so that the company's stranglehold would be broken, and he's taken a very personal interest in local affairs ever since."

She nodded. "I've been on Meadow less than a year, but it's obvious to me that he's a very controversial figure here. Some people loathe him and question his motives, but there are others who welcome his involvement. Charles Laszlow and I were close for a few months, and the only time I ever saw him drop that polite, mildly pedantic style of his was when I said something or another sympathetic to Damien. I thought he was going to explode."

Deep within his mind, subtle connections were being made. "So it wouldn't matter to Damien, financially at least, if Meadow's status changed?"

"Not at all. As a matter of fact, he authored the bill that eventually passed, and he's the chief sponsor of the initiative to put them in some kind of protective status. If it hadn't been for Senator Damien, Meadow would most likely still be an Intercorp fiefdom."

"But he opposes citizenship for the natives."

"That's right. Charles could explain all this a lot better since he's involved in it directly, but Damien wants to maintain the status quo, at least for the time being. The Nerudi keep their lands, the humans keep theirs, and contact between the two cultures is limited to research teams and a single permanent outpost. He doesn't rule out citizenship at some point in the future, but opposes granting them full rights now. I don't really remember the details of the arguments for and against, but essentially it boils down to Damien's contention that the Nerudi will be exploited if they're subject to unrestricted contact, and Laszlow's counter that the native culture will never be allowed to progress in its own way if it's subordinated to a government committee based in another star system."

"Laszlow favors full, immediate citizenship for the Nerudi?"

"That's right."

"And Damien wants them more or less sequestered?"

"Apparently. He was quite upset when Governor Tsien approved Charles' request to bring some of the Neroos to live in his home, but there wasn't much he could do about it. I don't see any connection to our current problems, though. There aren't any Nerudi in Haven, and as far as I know, Torgeson isn't political. Or am I missing something?"

"Everyone and everything is political. But I can't see how any of this is connected to our problem." He sighed. "And I have no idea what to do next."

Chapter Nine

That night, Avery slept much more soundly than he had in a long time, and although he dreamed as actively as ever, he wasn't troubled by the usual nightmares. When he looked outside the following morning, the scattered clouds of the previous day had disappeared from the sky and the sun was back in full force, the cheery light spilling through the unshuttered cottage windows. His mood had improved considerably and he alternated between enthusiasm for renewing his investigation and the urge to just abandon what was clearly not his business in favor of pursuing his original purpose in coming to Meadow, a prolonged vacation.

Before taking his leave the previous evening, he had arranged to meet Dona at a secluded spot on one of the paved lanes not far from Damien's cottage. He had expressed continuing reservations about involving her any further than she was already, but if anything she had stiffened her resolve to see the matter through to its conclusion. She insisted that she was perfectly willing to accept the risks, and it was only when he countered that it might prove useful to conceal their friendship that she grudgingly acquiesced.

"It's probably a wasted effort. Haven is too close-knit and gossipy. I'm sure that there have already been stories that we've been intimate. When everyone knows everyone else, it's hard to keep secrets."

Avery left the cottage, wondering if his efforts to seem casual and unconcerned were as transparent as they felt. He hesitated at the crossroads before choosing the path to the right, hoping that his choice would appear to be random if anyone was currently spying on him. Although he'd surreptitiously watched for observers since leaving the cottage, there was enough cover along the route to conceal a small army.

Dona was waiting for him, sitting on a rotting tree stump with her legs crossed, staring off into the distance.

"Good morning," he called cheerfully.

She greeted him with artificial casualness, then lowered her voice. "I feel pretty silly, you know. I haven't seen a living soul this morning. Do you really think this play acting is necessary?"

"I don't know, but it can't do any harm. With any luck, no one took any notice of our leaving the canteen together that first day, and there were no Haveners with us on the ride to Park City. I can't think of any way they could know about Laszlow, and there's no real reason for them to suspect that I've told you anything. For the time being at least, I'd like to keep it that way."

Although she had seemed prepared to argue the point, Dona subsided, apparently bowing to his wishes. She was as fascinated by this mystery as Avery, but for different reasons. His motivation was primarily guilt and a need to redeem his honor. Dona's was less noble. Her intuitive talent for diagnosing and dealing with artificial intelligences meant that she'd always be able to support herself in reasonable comfort, but the work was often tedious, particularly on a comparatively low tech world like Meadow. She was bored and curious and desperate for some sort of diversion. She also found herself drawn to this quiet, self-effacing visitor. He was completely unlike the men to whom she was usually attracted and sadly charming in his own way.

"Meadow has been almost a vacation for me," she had admitted to Avery the night before. "My contract means I have to be on call, but this communications breakdown I just fixed was the first serious problem since I arrived. Four out of five days I have nothing to do except monitor self-diagnostic routines and erase the residue of old conflicts the systems have already sequestered as bad data. Park City is more cosmopolitan than Haven, obviously, but it's still very provincial, and a lot of the attitudes are similar. The multi-generation residents are very hesitant to open up to outsiders, and the transient community exists almost as a separate caste like they have on New Hindustan. It's very rare for the two to interact other than in business matters. After you've hiked through the native floral preserve and what passes for a wildlife refuge and visited all of the scenic spots, the only things left to do are the same you can find in almost every city in the Concourse. Virtual drama has its place, of course, but it's no substitute for real life." Her face suddenly twisted in concern. "I'm sorry, I didn't mean to criticize your profession."

"Don't worry about it. I've long since come to much the same conclusion," he answered easily and truthfully. "People turn to entertainment to escape from boredom, and in the short term, virtual dramas, holobooks, and all the other media are perfectly acceptable ways to break the monotony. But none of them measure up to the pleasure and satisfaction which comes from doing things ourselves."

She stretched both arms above her head and Avery realized for the first time that while Dona Tharmody was by no means conventionally beautiful, he was very strongly drawn to her. She had a casual grace and easy self-confidence that was very appealing. He hadn't been involved with anyone since Kim and had believed that romance would no longer be part of his life, but now he found himself wondering if Dona might be attracted to him as well. Could that be why she was so willing to believe his unlikely story?

"What kept you anyway? I thought you said first thing in the morning. It's a glorious day." She glanced around as though suggesting he look to see the truth of her words.

"The local day is longer than I'm used to and my body hasn't adjusted yet. I wake up in the middle of the night expecting it to be morning, and I feel like taking a nap in the middle of the afternoon."

"Well, the day was even longer on Southmark, which is where I served out my last contract, so I had the opposite problem for a while. So where exactly are we going? Do you still think there's any chance of finding something after all this time?"

The path split into three distinct routes a few meters away. Avery pointed to the path that curved gently to the right through a thickly overgrown stretch of land. The trees dripped with some grayish green moss. The last vestiges of morning dew sparkled in the sunlight.

"You're certain you can find your way back to the same spot? Everything around here looks the same to me outside of the village, you know. I'm a city girl at heart."

"Absolutely. Back home—on Parchmont I mean—we learned to retrace our paths as soon as we started to toddle. Getting lost in a desert is extremely easy, and generally fatal, and there are far fewer landmarks there than here."

She stood suddenly, brushing dried leaves from her trouser legs. "Let's get started then."

Avery set an easy pace which Tharmody had no difficulty matching. City dweller though she might be, Dona maintained an active, physical life and was at least as fit as Avery, perhaps more so. Avery realized that he was feeling surprisingly good at the moment, and it wasn't just because of what he was doing but also because of whom he was doing it with. If he had been able to forget that their destination was a possible murder scene, he would have been positively buoyant.

Although there were signs of life at most of the cottages they passed, they encountered no other travelers as they walked. They spoke infrequently after their first exchange, falling into an easy comradeship that didn't require words. The ground rose and fell slightly beneath their feet, but never enough to cause a strain. Haven was built in a very shallow hollow which had probably been a lakebed in the distant past. They passed beyond the area set aside for tourists and the path narrowed, in some places becoming a virtual tunnel through the native foliage. At each intersection, he chose the proper path after only the slightest hesitation. The trail was less well maintained here, and the native growth encroached from both sides. He slowed their pace, partly to avoid being snagged or slapped by stray branches or tendrils, partly because of a growing reluctance to reach their goal. Eventually he saw the cultivated fields in the distance and knew that they were only minutes away.

"It's not far now." His voice trembled slightly and his mouth was dry.

They emerged from the trees and turned to their left. A solid mass of two-meter-high grain swayed slowly back and forth as a brisk wind swept in from the west. Avery felt his pulse quicken and he half expected to find a new body, or the original back in its place. He was greatly relieved to see instead a smooth expanse of yellow grass skirting an unremarkable tree. Everything was perfectly ordinary, but as he approached he had a vague feeling that something was missing, something other than the problematic body.

"Are we looking for anything in particular?" Dona walked back and forth, examining the tree and its environs briefly and emotionlessly. She turned and scanned as much of the horizon as was visible, with one hand raised to shield her eyes from the sun. The parasoy continued to move back and forth; the sound of the fronds rubbing against one another was almost like that of rushing water. Two swarms of newly hatched pinflies hovered just over their heads, arranging themselves in ever-changing, brightly colored patterns that shimmered like holographic images and producing a faint hum that was almost subliminal. It was otherwise so quiet that they could have been the only humans within a thousand miles, and if the parasoy hadn't been planted in such artificially regular rows, he could have imagined that they were alone on a virgin planet.

Avery crouched, running his fingers over the native grass, then up the bole of the tree, searching for he knew not what. He studied the path in both directions, then walked in a slow circle around the tree, pushing aside the undergrowth and examining the ground. Dona mimicked him, but with less patience; there was nothing special about the spot, nothing out of the ordinary, no indication that a murder or any other noteworthy event had ever taken place here. She didn't appear to be bored, exactly, but she didn't look particularly interested either.

When Avery stepped back out into the clearing, his face was troubled.

"Find anything?"

He shook his head, sighed, ran his fingers through his thinning hair. "No, I'm afraid not. But there's something wrong."

She waited for a few seconds before prompting him. "Everything seems pretty ordinary to me."

"Something's different," he said at last. "I'm not sure what exactly."

"Well, there's no body here to start with. That's a pretty big difference in itself."

"Not that." He glanced around nervously. "I don't know. It's like the scene has been re-edited. You see, virtual dramas are put together in layers, foreground and background tracks, main visuals, and backdrops and subsidiaries. Composers keep libraries of the background elements so that we don't have to recreate them every time. The larger the number of background elements, the easier it is for the viewer to identify with the viewpoint character, at least up to a point. Anyway, it feels like one of the elements is missing. I can tell that things are different, but I can't identify the change."

Dona turned her head back and forth. "There doesn't seem to be room here for a lot of options—just trees, the pathway, the sky, and the fields. You can't see the village from here, no buildings at all for that matter."

And that's when he made the connection. She saw it in his face instantly, as quickly as the thought entered his mind.

"The harvester. I forgot about the harvester."

She waited this time, knowing he would speak when ready. Avery walked to the very edge of the field, so close that the first row of grain brushed against the front of his shirt.

"There was a harvester out there last time. I remember hearing it even before I saw it, just as I was coming out of the woods. It was a good distance off, barely visible, and it was moving in this direction. It was red, I think."

Dona's expression made it clear that she failed to recognize any significance. "This is farmland. I imagine there are machines going back and forth all the time. I don't know much about parasoy but I'd guess these plants are about ready to be harvested."

Avery shook his head but didn't explain. "Help me look." He dropped to his hands and knees, began moving slowly along the perimeter of the field.

"Sure thing." She dropped down beside him. "What are we looking for?"

"Anything that might indicate something was dragged off into the field. Broken leaves, marks on the ground, scraps of cloth, anything out of the ordinary."

They found them so quickly that Dona was immediately suspicious. "This is too easy." There were several broken and bent leaves just inside the field, as though someone had pushed the first rank of plants carefully aside, but had continued beyond with much less concern about leaving evidence. The trail of bruised and broken plants led directly away from the path. Less than two meters away, they found two shallow gouges in the soil, as though something had been dragged across it. "Someone did a pretty poor job of hiding his trail," Dona said caustically.

"Remember, whoever was responsible may not have known that anyone had found the body until later. There was no reason to suspect anyone would be looking for the dead man. More significant is the fact that Hanifer was here with me. In fact, she walked along the edge of the field in both directions. Given her reputation as a thorough investigator, I can't believe she wouldn't have noticed this. Which confirms my suspicion that she's mixed up in this conspiracy, whatever it is."

"Whose farm is this, do you know?"

Avery tried to remember the layout he'd examined holographically. "If I'm not mistaken, this field is part of a plot adjacent to Kier Torgeson's farm. His land is crescent-shaped and reaches nearly this far. We could walk to his farm in less than an hour. I think this field belongs to a small holding company that Torgeson and Damien jointly administer."

Dona still considered Damien a friend and was reluctant to admit that he might be a criminal. "That still doesn't necessarily mean the Senator is involved."

"No, but if it really was Damien I saw in Haven when he was supposed to be elsewhere, then he's up to something he doesn't want people to know about. Something devious, if not unlawful. Frankly, I find it a little hard to believe that we have two separate mysteries here. They're much more likely to be connected in some way."

"It does seem unlikely. But I've known Karl Damien for a long time; I met him on Ozymandias and he has helped me get some good assignments since then. I installed equipment for him in his Park City office as well as in Haven. He's strong-willed and opinionated and sometimes I don't agree with him, but he's always struck me as having more integrity than most politicians. I can't imagine him working clandestinely unless it was unavoidable; he'd much rather confront situations openly, even if that meant he was at a disadvantage."

"Maybe there are aspects of the man you haven't seen, or maybe he's been forced into a situation that he can't handle in his normal way. I don't know. I can't even speculate at this point. All I know is that a man is dead, and a couple of prominent citizens of Haven, maybe more, don't want anyone to know about it, and they're willing to resort to some pretty nasty intimidation to get their way."

Her expression was troubled, but she didn't argue. "So what next?"

"We follow the drag marks. If my guess is right, they'll end when we reach a cleared field, probably not far away. That's where Torgeson, or someone working for him, will have loaded it onto the harvester."

"I thought those things were all automatic, that they ran from a program and didn't need a human operator."

"They don't. But they're all fitted with a small utility cabin. The discrimination functions on the older units need to be adjusted every so often, and operators periodically go along to monitor their work or to see the fields at first hand. Aragon's a farming world. I've even ridden on one myself a couple of times."

The trail was easy to follow and ended more quickly than they had expected. Perhaps twenty meters from where they had left the path, the fields were freshly harvested ahead and to both sides; all that remained was the stubble of the parasoy crop, which was already extruding new shoots, and the finely shredded leaves and stalks which had automatically been mulched and sprayed behind as the harvester passed.

"Now what? There's nothing to indicate which way the harvester went from here. Where would they have taken the body?"

"I suppose he could be buried in one of the fields, but that doesn't seem likely. There'd always be the chance that someone would decide to turn over the soil for a new crop and snag the body."

"Not if Torgeson's involved. Didn't you say he practically runs the farm himself?"

"Yeah, you're right. He wouldn't have any trouble making sure the grave wasn't disturbed."

"So where does that leave us?"

Avery wasn't willing to give up easily. Discovering physical evidence had been an enormous boost to his self-confidence, the first confirmation that he hadn't hallucinated the body, that it had been removed between his first and second visits. "I figure the harvester stopped here while whoever was riding it slipped over to the path, grabbed the body, and dragged it back. The dead man was pretty good-sized; it would have taken a strong man to drag him this far." Torgeson could have managed it quite easily, he thought.

"And either he buried the body somewhere out here . . ." She let the thought hang in the air.

"Or he took it back to the farm to be disposed of some other way." He turned to face northwest, but the crops in the adjacent field had grown tall enough to limit his view. "It's in roughly that direction."

"He couldn't have gone that way," she answered dubiously. "Not unless he got off the harvester and carried the body."

"No, he must have taken a roundabout course, if that is in fact where he went. And there was no reason for him to go to that much effort. If he didn't know at that point that I'd stumbled across the body, he could have taken it back on the harvester without much risk. If Hanifer tipped him off after I called, then he could rely on her to distract me or misdirect me, which in fact is what she did. There was no reason for him to make the job any more difficult than it already was."

"The cleared land must extend back as far as the farm

then. But in which direction?"

"It doesn't matter. If we're out in the open, someone might see us coming. I think we'd be wiser to stay under cover for as long as possible."

"How good is your sense of direction?" She gestured toward the distant field. "We won't be able to see any landmarks once we're in that mess."

Avery considered that. "We'll stay in the open for the time being, but close to the edge of the unharvested area. If we have time to hide, we'll duck into the field. If not, we're just out for a casual stroll, remember. There's no reason why anyone other than Torgeson or Hanifer should be concerned about us."

"Sounds all right to me."

They started to walk. Neither of them spoke for a long time, locked in an unspoken agreement to see this through, more binding than ever now that there was no longer any doubt in either of their minds that Avery's memory was not at fault.

The fields seemed to stretch endlessly ahead of them, although the walls of grain began to merge together as they progressed. Unharvested parasoy formed a border immediately to their right and, six fields later, fairly close at hand to their left as well, leaving them in a narrow corridor the width of a harvester's single swath. They had gradually turned further to the northwest, and eventually a cluster of buildings became visible ahead, an irregular break in the horizon line. Even from this considerable distance, Avery was able to identify Torgeson's farm. Beyond it was a small rise and beyond that, invisible from their current location, the farmhouse.

"Are we going to walk in openly or sneak up on them?" The land immediately ahead of them had been scythed to ankle height, but taller plants spread away from them in both directions, one arm of which reached almost to the rear of the largest of the buildings.

Avery hesitated, realizing that a direct approach was not necessarily the wisest course of action. He paused, swept the horizon with his eyes, trying to decide how best to proceed.

"If we walk through the parasoy," he pointed to their right, "we can get around to the opposite side. I don't know what that will gain us; I never saw anything but the roof of this building when I walked out the other day. There might be enough cover for us to get in closer, but I can't tell from this angle."

"I'm ready when you are. We're not going to accomplish anything by standing here and it's starting to get hot."

It was harder to move through the close-packed grain, even though it bent aside obediently when they pressed forward, arms raised to keep it away from their faces. The individual plants were quite tall here, half a meter over their heads, providing more than ample cover. This field was almost certainly ready to be harvested. From time to time they disturbed clouds of winged insects, pinflies and others, but fortunately none of them seemed interested in sampling human blood, although a few buzzed inquisitively and persistently around their faces. The sun was rising higher in the sky and, even shaded as they were, they began to feel the heat in earnest, moist air rising from the soil underfoot. The breeze appeared to have died, or perhaps they were just too well sheltered to feel its effects, and the stickiness was increasingly oppressive.

They spoke rarely and only in whispers, partly to avoid being detected, partly because of their growing fatigue. Avery felt his earlier enthusiasm fading, but he was still determined to finish what they'd begun. Dona was obviously distressed by the heat but gave no indication she was ready to turn back.

When they were finally close enough that the main building loomed over them, Avery came to a halt. "There it is," he whispered warningly. "We're right across from the equipment bays. The animal pens are way at the opposite end and extend down to the road. I think Torgeson has a small office on the far side of the hill."

Dona had been lost in her own thoughts. She blinked and was obviously replaying his words in her mind. "It's very quiet, isn't it? Doesn't sound like much is going on. What do we do now?"

They had both moved toward the edge of the field, but there was little to be seen from their vantage point. Dona's observation was correct; other than a slight hum from the small power plant, the complex was remarkably quiet. He could hear what sounded like an autotiller in the distance, but it seemed to be quite far off, almost directly to the west. "Let's keep on for a bit. Maybe there's enough cover to get closer once we're around the corner."

As it happened, the grain crowded fairly close to the building on the far side, but not enough to allow them to reach the building unobserved if anyone happened to be looking in their direction. Fortunately, all of the windows on this side were dark, either boarded over from within or blocked by equipment or supplies piled up against the interior walls. A partially disassembled harvester stood to one side, obviously cannibalized for spare parts, and the grounds themselves were poorly tended, weeds growing knee high in some places, bunched around discarded parts, containers, and a handful of rotting wooden crates. The contrast between this and Torgeson's house and yard were dramatic.

They hesitated at the edge of the cleared space. "Torgeson must really need to hire some help. I've seen his place, and this kind of sloppiness isn't like him."

"Doesn't look very promising." Dona sounded tired.

"Nothing worth the having is ever easy," he answered lightly.

"There's a marvelous platitude for you. Does the converse hold true? Is everything difficult worthwhile?" She sounded mildly irritated, and mopped sweat from her forehead.

Avery grinned, but turned so she couldn't see him doing so. "We're about to put that to an empirical test. If you're game, that is."

"I've come this far. I'm tired and sweaty and itchy and not really sure where I am, but at least I'm not bored, right? What's the plan?"

There was nothing to indicate their presence had been detected, or that there was even another human being in the area, but Avery led Dona on a brisk run across the clear ground to the wall of the building, then more cautiously toward the next corner. There were no windows close by, but there was a small door, which Avery expected to find locked. To his surprise, it opened when he pressed the catch, although the hinges were stiff and protested noisily for a second before grudgingly giving way.

The interior was dark and silent.

"Not many thieves around these parts, I imagine." There was still no sign of life, but Dona's voice betrayed her tension. "And not that much worth stealing."

It was certainly quiet enough. Avery heard a faint whirring that was probably a ventilation fan. They slipped inside, eased the door shut, and found themselves in a small, cluttered storage room that didn't appear to have seen much use in recent days. An elderly data terminal sat under a coat of dust in one corner, bracketed by piles of abandoned furniture and boxes filled with old style written materials and a wooden crate packed with rusting tools. Three steps away was another door, this one powered, which also opened obediently when Avery touched the access pad.

Beyond was a much larger area, open to the rafters far overhead. There was a small loft, accessible by ladder and a small powered lift at the far end. Light entered through large panes set in the slanted ceiling, and through smaller slit windows in the outside wall to the right. There was a set of overhead doors in the opposite wall, currently closed, each wide enough to accommodate a harvester. The floor had been freshly swept.

"Must be one of the equipment sheds," whispered Avery. "There's room for five or six of the big harvesters in here."

"Isn't this a pretty extensive operation for just one farm?"

"I'll bet Torgeson leases the equipment to some of his neighbors. Only one of the other farmers has a building nearly this size."

There was another door to their left, which they approached cautiously. There was no way to tell what lay beyond, but it was unlocked and opened quietly, sliding into the retaining shell. The dim light was no brighter here, and a strong, acrid odor caused them both to hesitate.

"What is that?" Avery had to concentrate to avoid gagging.

"Blood, I think. This must be the slaughterhouse, and freshly used too, I suspect."

Dona had guessed correctly, as they discovered seconds later. Automation here seemed limited to a conveyor and an automated flenser, both currently powered down. A heavy door led to a large refrigerated storage room which they made no effort to enter, but through a small window they could see several animal carcasses hanging motionless, already covered with frost.

"Do you suppose the body's in there?"

Dona shook her head. "You have a cheerful imagination. I don't think it's likely. Over there's a better bet." She led the way to a recessed pit in the floor. It was completely surrounded by a safety rail except where a sluice slanted down from the conveyor toward the interior. Even in the shadowy light, Avery could see that the bottom of the pit consisted of heavy metal teeth interlaced in a series of rows.

"What's this?"

"My uncle called it a masher, but the official name is much longer and less evocative. All the inedible parts are thrown in here, ground up into paste. Makes great fertilizer."

"Your uncle?"

She nodded. "He owns one of the largest herds of beefaloes on Frontier. I spent a couple of seasons living with him, learning the unpleasant facts of life. I still think about it sometimes when I'm eating meat. He had half a dozen units like this, industrial grade, about three times as large, and they worked almost every day. The smell was so bad we wore masks."

Avery glanced down at the metal teeth. "I don't suppose enough would survive to identify."

She laughed quietly. "By now, your missing body is probably spread across a pretty wide acreage. We might even have stepped on parts of him on the way here. These things grind so fine you usually spray the end product where you want it to go. You might be able to come up with a DNA match if you had an original sample for comparison but otherwise . . ."

Avery straightened up, turned slowly, examining his surroundings. "This doesn't look very hopeful. I don't think Torgeson is the type to leave any incriminating evidence lying around, even if we knew what to look for in the first place. I suppose we might as well start back." Avery was beginning to worry that things had gone too well, and a prickly tickling on the back of his neck was demanding his attention.

"Don't be in such a hurry. We came this far, we should at least do a thorough job of checking." She smiled at him. "Besides, I'm not looking forward to another trek through the fields. My life tends to be a bit more sedentary than yours. I like the outdoors just fine, and I have lots of holos of it in my apartment, but I think the actual experience is rather overrated."

The next interconnecting door led to what was obviously a repair shop. A robot tilling machine was mounted on a raised platform, its access panel missing, several components lying neatly on a shelf to one side, a thick bundle of cables hanging loosely from its interior. Photo-etched circuitry was exposed where someone had apparently been searching for a malfunction. To one side, a short set of stairs led down to a storage room which contained nothing more incriminating than spare parts for the heavy equipment, bins of thresher teeth, command relay units, cotter pins, bolts, chain links, power couplings, and other subcomponents neither of them could identify. There was no exit on the far side this time; it was apparently the end of the line of interlinked rooms, if not of the building itself. The only other door led outside, one large enough to provide access for whatever equipment was in need of repair.

"Should we risk it?" Dona seemed to be enjoying their escapade, but Avery had been growing increasingly nervous and jumped at every unexpected sound. Torgeson clearly had ample means of disposing of incriminating evidence and Avery was convinced that they would never find the missing body, that it had already been rendered unidentifiable. In all probability, it had been destroyed within hours of his finding it propped against the tree. He could not help thinking about how easily two overly inquisitive individuals could be made to disappear in the same fashion if they were discovered here.

"I don't think so. We're not going to accomplish anything else." He stopped suddenly and grabbed Tharmody's arm. There were two narrow windows set in the outside wall, one completely obscured by a stack of cartons. The other was clear and through it he could see two figures approaching, both heavyset men, their heads hidden by the upper rim of the window frame.

"Quick! Down here!"

Although Dona hadn't seen the newcomers, she responded immediately to the urgency in his voice, following him down into the parts room, where they concealed themselves as best they could behind a wooden rack. Above, they heard the outside door rumble open and two voices, indistinct at first, then more audible. One was unmistakably that of Kier Torgeson.

"We can take the scanning unit out of this one. The damn thing isn't going to be any good until I get a new control circuit from the city and they slapped me with a surcharge because it has to be special ordered. Too old a model to keep in stock, they say."

A deeper voice answered. "Will it work with the scooter? It doesn't have much of a power pack on it."

"Should do. Doesn't draw a lot of juice, just needs to be steady. Won't give you much range though."

There was a prolonged series of thuds and thumps from above as the two men set to work, apparently removing part of the tiller's instrumentation. Avery and Dona exchanged looks but remained silent.

"You decided yet what you're going to do about him?"

Torgeson's reply was immediate and chilling. "I'd like to arrange an accident, a very serious accident. I should have done it a while ago but got talked out of it. He came out here all by himself and I could have done it then, dropped him down the sluice like the other. No one would ever find him, and as far as I can see, no one would even come looking for him."

"Can't say as I blame you. Sure would make things simpler. But you know the Senator wouldn't like it much and Hanifer, she'd have a fit. They're both still upset by what's already happened."

Despite his nervousness, Avery felt a tiny thrill of satisfaction. At last, confirmation that Senator Damien and Torgeson were in this together, not to mention Hanifer and whoever the nameless man above might be. The look on Dona's face indicated she had realized the same thing.

"The Senator doesn't always understand the risks we're taking here. If there's an accident and an inconvenient person dies, no one's going to look at it twice. There's some as are better off dead."

"What about *her?* They went to Park City together and it wasn't just a shopping trip."

Both eavesdroppers stiffened. They had hoped that no one suspected Dona's involvement.

"We could lock her up somewhere maybe, where she can think things over for a while, come to see it our way. If she doesn't, well, it would be a shame, but we've known from the beginning that this was going to be risky. Here, give me a hand with this."

Something heavy shifted above them, and for the next few minutes all they heard were short, uninteresting comments as Torgeson and his unknown companion wrestled a major component out of the tiller's control module.

"There, that should do it. Not much room for maneuvering in there." Torgeson sounded as though he was out of breath. "You take it along with you now and I'll be down to help you later."

"Whatever you say. Look, Kier, I'm really uneasy about this. I mean, I know we have to keep a close eye on them, but there's no proof that they can cause any real trouble. Things might still work out all right. Why don't we just give them their head and wait to see what happens? There's not much harm they can do, is there? How much can they possibly know?"

There was an awkward silence, but when Torgeson finally answered, he sounded infinitely weary. "I don't know about that, Noric." Avery made a quick mental note of the name. "I'd like to be able to see it your way, but I don't think he's going to leave me much choice. We've warned him off, quietly but obviously, and it hasn't done any good."

"There's got to be a better way. Everyone knows how you feel about the situation, and there's a lot of sympathy for your point of view, but no one wants another killing."

Torgeson let the silence stretch before answering, and when he did, Avery thought he sounded sullen. "I'll leave it up to the Senator, but I'll not be shy about making my feelings known."

They waited until the two men had left the building, the

sliding door slamming into place resoundingly, then for several minutes longer, before creeping upstairs and reconnoitering through the window. Neither man was in sight.

"Do you still want to stick around?" Avery tried to make it sound light, but failed utterly. His pulse was elevated and his legs felt as though they would fold at the knee at any moment.

Dona's voice was thin and shaken. "No, I think I've had my fill of lurking in dark corners for the day. Let's get out of here before they come back."

They retraced their route through the interconnecting doors, making as little noise as possible, until they reached the one through which they had entered. After pausing and listening intently for any indication of activity outside, they opened it and stepped out into the daylight.

Just a few meters away stood the edge of the heavily grown field which had concealed their approach. But to their left, Kier Torgeson was standing alone in the sunlight, slowly turning in their direction.

Chapter Ten

❋ ❋ ❋

They almost made it to cover before Torgeson completed his turn, but not quite. Dona had just reached the first of the tall grain with Avery a step or two behind when they heard an inarticulate shout and knew they'd been discovered.

"Keep going! Run!" shouted Avery, but Dona had already anticipated him.

Thick stalks and broad leaves whipped past on both sides, and even though they raised their arms to protect their faces, occasional strands landed stinging blows on exposed flesh. Avery risked a glance back over one shoulder to see if Torgeson was following, but the intervening grain was so thick that an entire squad of pursuers could have been within a few meters without being visible.

They had trouble keeping their footing in the next field, where the ground was packed around the stems of the plants in small, linear mounds set close together. The soil was dry but crumbled underfoot, and they began to lurch and stagger on the treacherous surface. A few meters further, Avery fell to one knee, recovered quickly, but a short time later Dona lost her balance completely and landed jarringly on her hip. Avery was close on her heels, leaped to avoid tripping over flailing legs, landed awkwardly and fell onto his back.

There was sudden silence, no sound of pursuit at all, just the faint hum of a distant harvesting machine audible over their labored breathing.

"Do you think we're safe?" Her voice was a thin rasp. "I don't hear anything."

Avery had a painful stitch in his side and his first attempt to answer was an inarticulate gasp. He tried again, more slowly. "I think we're okay for the moment, but we can't stay here. I'm not even sure where we are. This isn't parasoy; it's some kind of wheat. We didn't come this way before. I don't know how many of the Haveners are in on this but we have to get back to the village before he finds us. We'll be safe there, safer anyway. They can't all be involved, and I doubt Torgeson and his friends will want witnesses." He didn't feel as confident as he was trying to sound; for all he knew, the entire village of Haven was part of a sinister cabal, kidnapping innocents and sacrificing them to some pre-spaceflight god. He'd used that very plot, with variations, in two of his virtual dramas.

"All right." She stood up awkwardly, brushing debris from her clothing. "I'm ready when you are."

This time they walked rather than ran, but as briskly as they could manage without risking another fall. Having strayed from their original path into very tall grain, there was no real vantage point from which to orient themselves, although the sun gave them a rough heading. Avery assumed the village was almost due south, depending upon how far they had run in their initial panic, but one of the small reservoirs was somewhere in between and he hoped they were heading far enough southwestward that they could bypass it and reach a lane that led back to the settlement. After several minutes they reached a cleared field, but there was another crop beyond, and the harvested area ended just to their right. They could hear at least two machines working in that direction, closer than before but still out of sight.

"Any idea where we are, Wes? I'm all turned around." Dona began to jump up and down on her toes, turning, trying to pick out a landmark, but the grain was too tall for anything to be visible.

"I think we've been heading roughly west and southwest, and if so we've gone far enough that we should be beyond the reservoir and have nothing but forested land directly south of us once we're out of the fields, although I have no idea where along the way we'll end up. There's a rough pattern to the way things were laid out, concentric circles, but it's hard to recognize where you are from inside."

"Do you think they'll be coming after us? Or waiting for us to show up?"

"I don't know. You heard what Torgeson said back there. Sounds like he wants me dead and you held some place where you can't say anything."

"Why not just kill both of us?"

"I've no idea; I couldn't even begin to guess. Maybe it's because I'm a direct witness and all you know is what I've told you. It wouldn't make any sense for them to keep you locked away indefinitely, and from that I infer that there's some kind of time limit for all of this. If they can keep the lid on long enough, it won't matter what we know or say."

"Then why not just lock both of us up?"

"I don't know. I guess Torgeson wants my blood even if it's not necessary. I don't know what I could have done to antagonize him so much, but I don't think he's going to accept an apology, do you?"

"So what do we do?"

"I don't think they can move against us openly. If we can

get to someplace where we can call for help, the authorities in Park City should be willing to intercede."

"You think so? The Senator swings a lot of weight in the capital as well as Haven. And where's our proof?"

He thought about that for a second. "You're right. Even if we keep the Senator's name out of it, there's a good chance he has people watching to counter any move we might make. It's still just our word against theirs, and theirs includes Hanifer and apparently Damien as well. The only way the authorities will move on our behalf is if we hand them something so damning they can't ignore it."

"Maybe I could call some people I know. I'm owed a few favors."

"It couldn't hurt, but what can we tell them that we can back up with real evidence? All it would take is for Hanifer and the others to say we'd both been acting strangely lately and then point out that I'm here recovering from a bout of hallucinations. Once my story has been impugned, it's not much of a leap to suggest that my hysteria affected your interpretation of what was actually happening."

Her face drooped. "I suppose you're right. What if we both just pulled up stakes and went back to Park City, forgot all about missing bodies and sinister plots and devious public figures with mysterious secrets? If we pose no threat to them, they'll have nothing to gain coming after us."

"I'm not so sure that will do any good. As you said, Damien has a long reach, and if this is important enough to justify one murder in his mind, a couple more won't make him lose any sleep. If he decides we're better off silenced, I don't think there's anywhere on Meadow that's safe. Or off it, for that matter."

That had clearly given her pause. "I don't suppose you

have any powerful friends somewhere. I'm beginning to feel outclassed."

He shook his head. "Which means we may as well see things through here. Torgeson's friend back there said the Senator was unhappy about the killing, so maybe we're safe so long as Torgeson doesn't have a chance to act on his own initiative."

"That doesn't exactly fill me with confidence."

"Well we can't do anything until we find our way out of these fields and back to the village." Avery stood up and brushed off his knees.

"Wes, if there really is a time limit after which nothing we know will matter, I think I know what Torgeson may have been talking about."

He had been about to start off but he paused, waiting for her to continue.

"The Senate will be considering the Nerudi question just a few days from now. The reason Damien left Meadow was to prepare for the debate, or I suppose I should say that's the excuse Damien used for letting everyone think he was gone. I'm guessing that's the time constraint. Without Damien's support, the motion will most likely fail. The majority of the Senate just wants the problem to go away; they're not as concerned about how it gets solved."

"I'd say there's a good chance you're right, but we just don't know enough to be sure. And if that's the case, I still don't understand why that man had to be killed. What did he know that could have affected the outcome? As for us, all we can do is find someplace with lots of people around and try to stay alive."

They walked without speaking for several minutes, eventually reaching another cleared field. The stubble of a recently harvested crop reached barely to their knees.

Although Avery was reluctant to emerge from cover prematurely, he realized that they would have to do so now if they had any hope of reaching safety. It was mid-day and they were hot and thirsty. One of the harvesters was so close that they could see the top of its superstructure and hear the threshers gobbling up mature grain, stripping away the unwanted stalk and leaves, mulching the latter and spraying the residue in its wake. There was no sign of Torgeson or any other human.

"Let's cross as quickly as possible. If we're spotted, then we run. If for some reason we get separated, try to make it back to the village. We'll meet at Soothers."

The harvester was closer now, just a few dozen meters to their right, cutting through the field toward which they were moving. The oversized hood was a dark red, blood red. Another of the automated units was visible as well, this one painted a cheerful bright blue, working a parallel course just beyond and a short distance behind the first one. The crop in this field didn't look mature to Avery, although he was hardly an authority on the matter. The stalks were only shoulder high and the grain itself looked unformed.

They were halfway across the open field when the third harvester appeared, this one forest green. Avery felt a tremor of alarm, his suspicions confirmed seconds later when the first of the oversized machines turned toward them, not stopping when it reached the cleared ground. It continued straight forward, even though there was nothing here to feed its insatiable appetite. Or at least nothing it was meant to ingest.

"Come on, run!"

"What . . . ?" Dona was clearly puzzled but did as she was told, following Avery as he turned away from the harvesters, angling away from the approaching machines.

When the fourth harvester came into sight, its upperworks bright yellow, she no longer needed an explanation.

"They're trying to cut us off!" She stumbled but recovered without falling.

Avery glanced back over his shoulder. "Torgeson must have overridden their programming. He can't know exactly where we are, so he has them working a preset search pattern. If we're quick and lucky, we can get past them. They're not very maneuverable." The blue harvester had emerged and turned to parallel its mate; Avery could no longer see the remaining two, and their threshing blades were inaudible over those of the closer machines.

"I thought they had safeguard programs built into farm equipment so they couldn't accidentally injure anyone."

"The newer models certainly do. I don't know about these, and I'm not interested in testing the possibility empirically. Are you?"

Two smaller but still formidable autotillers appeared ahead of them and to their left. Their blades were raised and motionless but they moved in concert, clearly aiming to intersect the course of the harvesters. The gaps between the individual machines were large enough that Avery felt that they could slip through with room to spare, but the blend of immense size, loud noise, and implied threat was frightening. The harvesters moved relatively slowly, turned in wide, gradual arcs, and should be easy to evade, but a bad misstep could be fatal. With each passing second, the gaps narrowed. Avery realized that slow and cumbersome as the harvesters were, the enormous breadth of their maws made them a tangible danger. Each harvester had a span of nearly twenty meters, multiple mouths full of whirling metal blades that could shred them beyond recognition almost as quickly, if not as efficiently, as the disposal unit they had seen back at the slaughterhouse.

"Whatever you do, don't fall down!"

The roar of multiple engines and clashing blades filled the air, and they had to shout to make themselves heard as they slowed, hesitating, trying to decide which gap offered the best opportunity. But there was no time to deliberate. Avery pointed abruptly and set off at the best speed he could manage, while Dona kept pace with him, eventually moved ahead, her longer legs and better muscle tone overcoming her fatigue.

To his great relief, they were able to slip past the nearest machine with considerable room to spare, and by cutting back behind it escaped any immediate danger.

"Won't they turn back?"

He shook his head. "I doubt it. They're probably following a preset pattern. As far as they're concerned, we don't exist, and even if Torgeson monitors their video feed, it's not likely he can get them turned around in time to catch us. He must have been desperate to try this, but I suppose he really didn't have anything to lose. If it had worked, we'd no longer be a problem, just a pair of tourists who wandered onto private property and met with a tragic accident. If we escape, we still can't prove he was trying to kill us."

They slowed to a walk once it was clear that the harvesters weren't going to wheel about and take up the pursuit, and when they reached the next field, they saw a line of trees not far ahead, rising above a low wall of parasoy.

Their clothing was matted to their bodies, damp with perspiration, and they were coated from head to foot with particles of grain, fragments of leaves, mud stains, and other debris they'd picked up on their travels. Avery had never felt this dirty in his entire life. His throat was so dry that it hurt and he felt the vague sense of unreality that usually meant one or more of his implants had been triggered. The roar of the harvesters had faded as the machines completed their recent maneuver and turned northeast, moving back toward the farm complex in a staggered line.

But there was another sound, a faint, irregular hum that grew louder with each passing second. It came from somewhere toward the east. Dona half turned, puzzled, but Avery had recognized the distinctive thrum almost immediately.

"Time to run again. We have to get to the trees, and quickly."

"But what is it?"

"Hanifer, most likely. That's security's lifter. There's a funny vibration in its engine. Remember from the other day? Torgeson must have called for reinforcements. The harvesters were probably meant to slow us down rather than stop us. They're clumsy and easy to avoid, but the lifter will have a human aboard, and weapons."

It was close, so close that Avery wasn't sure they could reach concealment within the trees before they were spotted. The bullet shaped craft was moving slowly in their direction, hovering level with the treetops, moving back and forth in a search pattern as it advanced, obviously searching for them. Apparently their progress had been underestimated because the lifter was north of their position, systematically examining one field after another.

"They think we're still hiding somewhere out there." Avery was quite unnecessarily whispering; there was no chance they could be overheard from that distance, but it was an instinctive caution. "I think we'll be all right so long as she doesn't double back and catch us out in the open."

"There's got to be a way we can get clear of all this." She

didn't sound as though she meant just their current surroundings. "I don't really relish spending the rest of my life as a fugitive."

"Neither do I. Our immediate problem is to survive the day. Tomorrow is another matter."

"Wonderfully optimistic man you are."

"It's part of my charm." He felt an improbable smile tugging at the corners of his mouth and realized that, even though he was trembling with fear, he was also perversely enjoying the sensation. He felt more vividly alive than he had in years.

The forest provided ample cover for as long as it lasted, but they couldn't remain under the heavy interweave of branches indefinitely. Sooner or later the searchers would realize their quarry had escaped the net cast for them, and certainly they were well enough organized to have alternative plans.

They avoided the public paths except to cross them, staying within the forest until they reached its easternmost edge. The land was better cultivated from that point on, with small islands of vegetation circumscribed by the threads of scenic lanes and more prosaic service roads that looped inefficiently around the resort area and village.

Avery and Tharmody made their way from one bit of cover to the next, crossing the open spaces hastily, stopping for increasingly frequent rests as time passed. The sound of the lifter remained intermittently audible but usually at a considerable distance. Twice they rushed to cover when it moved back in their direction, once lying in concealment while a long shadow moved slowly past, the vehicle itself almost directly above them. A small clear brook crossed their path a short while later and they both crouched, drinking unreservedly from its water. It was cool and sweet and helped restore their flagging strength.

Dona splashed some of the water onto her face and let it trickle down her neck. "I still don't know where we're going. Don't you think they'll be waiting at your cottage?"

"Maybe. We'll need to reconnoiter. I'm hoping that they'll hesitate before confronting us there. Their resources can't be unlimited either. Remember, there may be as few as four people involved, and for all we know, Damien has returned to Park City or taken himself off to some other secret retreat. He can't spend all his time in Haven, after all. Torgeson is presumably handling the harvesters, Hanifer is in the lifter. That still leaves this Noric, whoever he is."

"Noric Klanth. I recognized his voice. When we were working on the cottage control systems, Senator Damien hired him to help with some of the hardware. He's a talented technician, although he'd be hopelessly out of date on more advanced worlds. He did most of the physical installation while I argued with the software. I liked him. He lost his arm when he was a kid, hitching a ride on one of those." She gestured back toward the retreating line of harvesters. "He and a friend dared one another to walk out over the intake vents and he lost his balance."

Avery remembered the man he'd seen with Hanifer and Torgeson following the fight at Soothers, the man with the artificial arm. "Does he wear a prosthesis?"

"Of course. This isn't a frontier world, you know. The hospital facilities in Park City are excellent."

"We're going to have to keep our guard up even if it looks like we're safe. They won't just drop things because we've slipped through the net." Avery was surprised to discover that his fear was largely gone, most likely worn down by exhaustion. "With other vacationers in the area, they'll have to be careful. If there's any sign of uninvited company at my place, we'll try yours. The Senator's, I mean."

"I don't know if I like this. We might be walking right into a trap. Maybe we should just go straight into the village proper."

"And do what when we get there? Sooner or later, we'll have to leave. It's better if we don't give them any more time to anticipate us than is absolutely necessary."

Dona thought about it, but short of setting off cross-country without supplies or any hope of locating a useful destination, there was little else they could do. It would take days to reach the closest settlement on foot, and once they were outside Haven's immediate vicinity, the ecology would be almost exclusively native. They wouldn't even be able to forage for food.

They passed three young children running down one of the lanes but saw no one else up and about in the resort area. The recent rain had brought fresh color to the flowering shrubs of various sizes, shapes, and colors, some of them native and some imported. Bell vines and other creepers snaked through the branches and had woven themselves into a series of canopies which effectively concealed them from any overflight, which didn't matter greatly since the security lifter's thrumming engine sounds had gradually diminished and finally become inaudible.

"I don't see anything unusual."

Avery nodded slowly. "Neither do I, but I don't think they'd be sitting out front waving a flag to announce their presence."

"Do you always get sarcastic when you're playing the bold adventurer?"

"I don't know," and he grinned, enjoying the enhanced adrenaline flow even though he knew his implants would wake up if it continued for long. "I've never played the part before, except while composing. It feels rather good, actually. Real emotion beats the synthesized version any day. I'm beginning to wonder what people see in my rather bland imitations." He dropped the banter. "They might be inside, waiting for us."

"That's not likely. I helped the Senator set up the private security system for all the cottages in this area. State of the art, high integrity, automatic intruder alerts. Even a professional would need several minutes to neutralize the defensive system and turn off the alarms, and the audios are loud enough we'd have heard them way back in the fields. As far as I know, the Senator and I are the only two people with access to every cottage. I suppose it's possible that Damien brought in another technician and added his local cronies to all of the access lists, but I'd be surprised if that was the case. Why would he bother? The chances against anyone stumbling onto this little intrigue were pretty staggeringly high in the first place, and I think they've been off balance ever since. Why else would a couple of amateurs like us have gotten so far?"

"Your lack of faith in our ability isn't very inspiring, but I concede your point. Let's see if we can spot anything out of the ordinary."

They moved carefully through the underbrush, covered three sides of the building closely and studied the remaining one for long minutes, but saw no evidence that they were not alone.

"I say we chance it."

Avery pretended surprise. "Feeling brave?"

"No, I'm tired of hiding in the darkness like a crust beetle, and I itch in too many places to scratch. This skulking about is in basic conflict with my life style. I want to be clean, and I want a cold drink and something solid in my stomach. Even my brain hurts. If we're going to do something, let's do it now."

"All right, but from the rear. The front way's too exposed."

"There's a better chance of witnesses out front."

Avery glanced toward the facing cottage. Except for one brief glimpse of the occupant several days earlier, he had no proof that it was even tenanted, let alone that anyone would be able to see or care about what happened across the way. "Not enough to matter. Let's go."

Avery felt naked as they sprinted across the last few meters of open space to the rear of the cottage. The rear door slid aside obediently when he thumbed the lock, hadn't finished its cycle before they had both stumbled inside. The lights came on immediately and he quickly keyed the security system up to maximum. "I don't think they'll try anything here, frankly. Too difficult to keep things quiet this close to civilization." But he was talking to reassure himself rather than out of any real conviction.

He moved quickly from room to room, reassuring himself that they were alone. His few possessions all appeared to be exactly as he had left them and there was no sign at all that the cottage had been entered during his absence. Somewhat reassured, he returned to the rear entrance.

Dona was already half undressed, her discarded blouse and shoes tossed casually aside. "I don't know about you, but my first priority is to feel like a human being again. Can I borrow something to wear after I clean up? We look to be about the same size."

Avery had never been uncomfortable with nudity. As a child he had lived in a society where water was so scarce and valuable that family members and even acquaintances often bathed together to reduce consumption. On Aragon he'd been a frequent patron of lakeside beaches because the sight of all that water in one place was awe inspiring. So it made no logical sense that the sight of Dona Tharmody, only half naked, her flesh streaked with dirt and sweat, should be so immediately, painfully arousing.

"Come on," she called out, not even glancing in his direction. "You can't think creatively and sweat at the same time. It's a proven fact. Cleanliness first, serious planning afterward."

They progressed from washing each other in the primitive shower stall to making love in the bedroom with a lack of awkwardness or pretension that Avery found refreshing and exciting. Dona approached even this with a persistent dry humor that puzzled him at first, but once he got past his initial nervousness, things went remarkably well. Unavoidably he thought of Kim, her lean slender body and her absolutely serious demeanor even at the most passionate of moments, but he felt only a very faint twinge of regret and guilt. The undercurrent of danger had heightened his senses and, despite the long period of abstinence, he conducted himself with respectable skill and consideration. When they were finally lying quietly side by side, Avery fell into a reverie that persisted until Dona finally nudged his hip.

"Where'd you go?"

"Me? Oh, I was just wondering how I got myself locked into the life I've been living."

"Don't start feeling sorry for yourself. There are billions of people who would kill for the kind of success you've enjoyed. I'm sure you've already accumulated enough credit to live comfortably for the rest of your life, and even if you continue working, you don't have to deal with obnoxious customers, overbearing employers, bureaucratic tyrants, or any of that nonsense. Some people would consider that an ideal job. Look at me, I not only have to argue with my employers, but with their damned equipment as well."

"Maybe. But I have no close friends, no family, and at the moment not even a home to go back to. I can't return to Aragon, you know. My doctors insist that further exposure to the virus in its native state would be risky. And now I'm even having second thoughts about my choice of career. Hardly evidence of personal self-satisfaction and a fulfilling career."

"So what? There are rough spots in everyone's life. Some day I'll show you my virtual scars. At least you're alive and," she reached over and tapped his thigh, "sound of body if not of mind."

"For the moment anyway." His face darkened. "Dona, I'm sorry I dragged you into this mess. Really. I should have realized how dangerous it was and kept things to myself."

"Don't be ridiculous." She leaned back, stretching her arms high above her head, and despite the exertions they'd just completed, Avery found himself growing interested again, forced himself to look elsewhere. "I could have walked away if I'd wanted to, let the matter drop. I don't know exactly why I didn't, if you want the truth. Maybe I just got bored. Maybe I'm insatiably, even suicidally, nosy. But even if I could pull up stakes and leave, I wouldn't do it." She stared at him levelly and curled her lip. "Particularly not now."

"Then we need to come up with a plan. If we just keep floundering around in the dark, we'll end up reacting without getting anywhere. I think we shook them up today. They wouldn't have responded so dramatically otherwise. How do we keep them off balance?" He rose from the bed, rummaged through the closet, found simple sets of clothing for the two of them, baggy slacks, comfortable blouses. He tossed hers onto the bed, started dressing himself.

"We need some protection."

"What kind of protection? Bodyguards? You know anyone with a private army for rent?"

"That's not what I had in mind. We need insurance. How about recording everything we know or suspect and giving it to someone to hold as a guarantee of our safety? Charles Laszlow isn't as powerful as the Senator, but he has enough influence that they won't be able to act against him without raising a stink that would be heard all over this sector."

"Good melodrama, I suppose. But we don't know very much, at least nothing that couldn't be explained away. Laszlow might help if we approached him, but I suspect he'd demand to know a lot more than we've been able to discover so far. I'm reluctant to involve him until we understand things better ourselves. If we went public, sent a story to the comnet news services, what would that accomplish? A virtual dramatist subject to hallucinations sees a body that immediately disappears without a trace. He and a friend overhear, or claim to have overheard, vague threats against their lives while trespassing on private property and eavesdropping on their unwitting host. Following their discovery, they are attacked, in a manner of speaking, by harvesting machines but escape unscathed. They believe Senator Karl Damien is implicated and secretly present in the village, even though everyone knows the man isn't even on Meadow. Do you think anyone would believe us if we said all that without offering any proof?"

"Yeah, I guess you're right. You'd be under a doctor's care and I'd be lucky if I wasn't right there with you."

Avery was suddenly thoughtful. "You know, now that I

think about it, I don't see that we present any real threat. I mean, we don't have any information that would hurt them, at least nothing that we can prove. The best I could manage would be to cast doubt on Hanifer's professionalism, for not following up on my report, and for all I know, she'd insist I never called her in the first place. I don't even have a witness to prove that much. If you hadn't overheard Torgeson's threats, I'm not sure you'd believe me. You weren't convinced before then, were you?"

"No," she admitted, "but I wanted to be. Maybe we know something that we don't know we know."

"Right, or maybe they think we know something that we don't know we know, and know we think something that they think we ought not to know."

She grinned. "You know what I think?"

"Haven't the faintest idea."

"I think we need something to drink."

Avery had finished dressing so he offered to fetch the refreshments, walked barefoot from the bedroom to the kitchen, where he drew two chilled and mildly fermented fruit mixes from the dispenser, still trying to decide what options were available to them. The only person on Meadow they knew well enough to approach with this was Charles Laszlow. There was no reason to assume Laszlow was anything other than what he appeared, a wealthy, politically active former executive with a moderately well developed social conscience, but Avery had reached the point where he suspected everyone. Laszlow came from a background where there were specific policies and courses of action to be followed in any given situation, which made it easy to respond to a crisis, but which also encouraged conformity and discouraged imagination. He would want to notify the authorities and initiate a formal investigation, but there was so much they didn't know or couldn't substantiate that Avery doubted the authorities would take them seriously. All they would accomplish would be to show their hand prematurely.

And foolhardy though it might be, Avery was disinclined to turn things over to another party even if he thought he could convince anyone that he was telling the truth. This had become a personal issue for him. He was tired of being ignored and outmaneuvered and made to look foolish, and if that meant he had to take some chances in order to become a player rather than a playing piece, then that was a risk he was prepared to take. He just hoped that Dona was walking into this with her eyes as open as his own.

His attention had drifted and he was standing there staring down blindly at the two drinks when she joined him, also barefoot. "There you are. I could have died of thirst back there and you'd never have noticed. Is something wrong?"

"What? Oh! Sorry. I was just thinking about something and lost track of what I was doing." He picked up one of the glasses and offered it to her. "Extra sour, the way you ordered it."

She had just raised her arm to accept the drink when a deep, male voice came from the direction of the back door.

"Would you mind making one of those for me as well? It's been a long day, and it's not nearly over yet."

Avery spun around so fast that he almost dropped the glass he was holding, and Dona stepped back with a low cry of dismay. A tall figure stood in the arch of the corridor, apparently alone, hands clasped behind his back, the expression on his face serious but unthreatening.

It was Senator Karl Damien.

Chapter Eleven

❋ ❋ ❋

After a moment of such absolute shock that Avery could easily have believed his heart had stopped beating, he felt a surge of intense rage so pure that there was no room left for fear. Temporary though his tenancy might be, this was his home and the uninvited presence of another was so outrageous a breach of protocol that all thoughts of his own personal welfare were momentarily subordinated.

"What are you doing here?" He hadn't even realized that he had clenched his fists and was advancing toward Senator Damien until the other man raised his own hands placatingly.

"Please. I'm not here to harm you, either of you. Quite the contrary, as a matter of fact. I'm here to help, if you'll allow me."

Unwilling to be lulled so easily, Avery slowed his advance but didn't drop his guard. "How did you know we were here?"

Damien sighed. "I instructed the AI to notify me when you returned. You must know by now that I own this cottage. It should have been obvious when you reviewed the village survey."

Avery blinked with surprise. How had Damien known that he'd looked at the survey? Was Churienko part of the conspiracy as well? This reminder that the Senator had an unknown number of allies caused him to look past the other man into the other room, but the lights were off and he couldn't see anything beyond the small illuminated area just inside the doorway.

Damien correctly interpolated his fears. "I'm quite alone. I give you my personal assurance that you're in no immediate danger, at least not from me and my associates."

Although there was no obvious reason for the man to lie, Avery was not ready to trust him. "I'm sure you'll pardon us if we're a bit skeptical. During the past few days, I've been threatened and intimidated, and today the two of us had to run for our lives. I trust you won't insult our intelligence by pretending that none of that had anything to do with you."

"No, I think we're past the point of cover stories or bluster. It's time to drop the playacting and get things out in the open. I suppose you'd find this difficult to believe of any politician, but subtle intrigues and back room plotting have never held any real appeal for me. We've misjudged you both and made a bad situation worse, and I'm here to try to straighten things out, at least as far as I can." He paused, nodded to Tharmody. "I'm sorry if I'm tarnishing my image with you, Dona, but this hasn't been entirely my fault, although ultimately I'm responsible for everything that has happened."

"Including murder?" Her voice was cool, tinged with contempt.

Damien sighed. "This is all very complicated and for a variety of reasons, I probably won't be able to answer all your questions, at least not to your satisfaction. Do you suppose I might have a cold drink first though? I haven't had a particularly pleasant day either."

After a momentary hesitation, Avery decided it could do no harm, and a few minutes later the three were sitting in the front room. Dona curled up in the grasp of a morphing chair with her legs beneath her body while Avery and Damien sat more conventionally, across from each other, surreptitiously taking each other's measure.

It was Damien who finally broke the silence. "I want you to know from the outset that, despite appearances to the contrary, you've never been in any real danger. Certain steps were taken to discourage you both, sometimes with my foreknowledge, sometimes under general guidelines I had approved. I have been urged to take more stringent steps but I have given strict instructions to the contrary. Still, whatever unpleasantness you experienced was at my instigation or performed in my name, and I hope you won't hold those actions against people who were only acting out of loyalty."

"I've never considered being chased across a field by a robot threshing machine a particularly safe way to spend a morning." Dona sounded more indignant than frightened. "If you're telling the truth, then your friends are either incompetent or they're ignoring your instructions."

"Well, you did rather catch Kier by surprise, and he reacted without thinking things through. He's a hard man and sometimes lacks judgment. But I hardly think you would have had any difficulty eluding the harvesters. Their top speed isn't much more than a fast walk. The idea was to cut your line of retreat so that Hanifer would have time to intercept you. They were tentatively planning to arrest you both for breaking and entering, which might have taken you out of circulation for a while, but it would only have complicated things even further in the long run. Kier's a good man, hard working, but narrowly focused and unimaginative. Lydia was already having second thoughts while she was on her way out to look for you, but she's been on edge ever since this all started and not at her best. The strain has been wearing for all of us."

"You'll have to excuse me if I don't have a lot of sympathy. And frankly I doubt there was much hesitation in their minds about what to do with us." Avery leaned forward, watching to see if Damien would flinch. He didn't. "Suppose we told you that we overheard Torgeson and another man plotting to kill us, me anyway, just before we were spotted out at the farm. He sure didn't sound very indecisive to me."

Damien appeared genuinely surprised, then confused. "You must have misunderstood something. Kier Torgeson talks a good fight, and he wouldn't be above calling you out and breaking both your arms, but he's not the kind of man who'd take another's life lightly. And he knows how I feel about such things."

"Maybe you don't know him as well as you think you do, Senator. What we heard was unambiguous." He turned toward Dona, who nodded her own confirmation.

"He sounded seriously pissed off."

Damien was either very distressed or an excellent actor. "I can't believe that. No, I'm not doubting your word that you heard something, but there must be some other explanation . . ." His voice trailed off and there was silence while he reorganized his thoughts. "Let's forget that for the time being. I'll deal with it before the night is through, I promise you, and firmly enough to keep you safe."

There was an uncomfortable silence during which Avery and Tharmody exchanged cryptic looks, trying to gauge each other's reaction. If Damien was aware of the byplay, and it was hard to believe he wasn't, he chose to ignore it.

"Look," he said at last. "You stumbled into something that you shouldn't have, that you don't understand, a situation which could potentially cause more harm than you can possibly imagine. I don't suppose you'd accept my personal assurance that there is no good you can do by pursuing matters, and potentially a great deal of harm?"

Avery licked his lips. It appeared that he was being offered a way out. The temptation to seek an accommodation was strong but not compelling. "There are a lot of things I could overlook, Senator. Murder isn't one of them."

The older man sighed. "Murder? Are you sure that's what it was? Suppose I told you it was a natural death?"

Avery felt a rush of elation, recognizing the tacit admission that a dead body did in fact exist, or at least had existed. No matter how firmly he had believed it before, it still helped to hear it confirmed.

"Is it the custom in Haven to spirit away the bodies of those who die naturally and later deny that they ever existed?"

Damien seemed to be considering the question seriously. "The circumstances in this instance were unusual," he replied after a long pause. "I won't fence with you. The man whose body you stumbled upon was in fact killed by someone working on my behalf, or at least what they believed to be my behalf. If I'd had some warning, the outcome might have been different, but it's too late now to agonize over what might have been. Certainly the man was no friend of mine, and arguably we're all better off with him gone, but I won't try to justify what was done. On the other hand, I won't betray someone whose only motive was to protect me."

"Was it Torgeson?"

The Senator shook his head, but without specifically denying the allegation. "I won't tell you who was responsible. I'm sorry, but that must remain my secret. Suffice it to say that the deed was and is my responsibility. If it weren't for me, he'd still be alive, and my friend would have committed no crime."

"Who was he then? A political rival? An old enemy? Someone whose continued existence was inconvenient to your career?" Avery felt anger rising in place of the fear he'd felt only moments earlier.

Damien was thoughtful for a few seconds, then responded calmly. "In a sense, all of those answers are correct. But the truth is a lot bigger than that, and more complicated."

"And the truth is . . . ?"

"It's something you don't need to know, and won't hear from me. Not right now, anyway."

"Senator Damien, if you're trying to convince me that I should drop this matter and pretend none of it ever happened, you're not doing a very good job. I know your reputation as a debater. Surely you can be more persuasive than that."

"Would you prefer that I concoct some plausible set of lies?"

"I'd prefer the truth."

"I'm telling you the truth. Not the entire truth, I admit. There are some things I will not, cannot say. I'm treading a tightrope just being here; officially, I'm eleven light years from Meadow preparing for the next session of the Senate. There are issues involved that are so important, individual lives are of comparatively little significance. Including my own." Damien seemed suddenly weary. He slumped in the seat and raised his left hand to knead his forehead, his voice thin with strain, and it seemed that he was speaking to himself rather than to Avery. "He shouldn't have died, not that way, but I can't honestly say I'm sorry he's gone. His life was a disaster from beginning to end, and he probably endured as much pain as he inflicted on others, perhaps more." His voice had started to rise, but he regained control of himself. "But it's done now and I can't change that fact. I've never been one to look back at mistakes. What's important is always what we have yet to do."

"So what *are* you going to do?" It was the first time Tharmody had spoken in a while.

"I'm going to explain as much about the situation as I can, and hope I can convince you to give me the benefit of the doubt. First of all, whether you believe me or not, I say again your lives are not in jeopardy. Before I leave here tonight, I'll speak to Kier Torgeson and make it clear to him how I feel about the matter and dissuade him from doing anything precipitous, although I still think you misunderstood whatever it was that you heard. I want no more deaths on my conscience. Second, by whoever's hand and for whatever reason, there's a man dead, and dead because of me, because of who I am. When the time is right, I'll acknowledge that fact and deal with the consequences. I don't have any right to expect you to believe me, or to agree with me, but there are certain issues at risk right now that overshadow even murder."

"I find that rather hard to accept." She sounded angry as well as skeptical.

Damien shook his head. "To be frank, so do I. I've had to rethink a lot of the things I believed in recently, and I haven't enjoyed some of the conclusions I've reached."

"You seem to have triumphed over your conscience."

"You're judging me without all the facts, but I won't argue the point. At the very least, I'm guilty of conspiring to conceal a murder. Perhaps I'm here now because I need to confess to someone. You must realize that I could have let the two of you continue to flounder around aimlessly trying to uncover evidence that doesn't exist. Believe me, you won't learn anything further that we don't want you to know. If it hadn't been for spectacularly bad timing, the body would have been disposed of quietly and this whole crisis would never have arisen."

"You must feel pretty confident to admit all this to us," said Avery. "But why bother if we have no chance of uncovering the truth?"

"I have a great deal of respect for Dona," he nodded in her direction, "and no reason to think any less of you. I had hoped we could come to some sort of truce, at least temporarily."

"And if we refuse?"

"Then I suppose I'll just have to work around you. Without hard evidence, what harm can you do? I don't mean to be patronizing, but you're both offworlders without personal power or influence here. You, Mr. Avery, enjoy a certain popular notoriety and might be able to attract some attention, but that would inevitably lead to an examination of your recent medical history. If you managed to convince one of the news services to repeat your story, my office would simply issue brief, puzzled denials and express sympathy for your ailment."

Avery maintained a neutral expression but he'd already come to very much the same conclusion.

Damien sat up suddenly. "Speaking of which, may I use your com for a moment?"

The sudden question caught Avery by surprise, but he recovered quickly. "Of course. After all, it's really yours, isn't it?"

Damien refused to rise to the bait, but he did rise to his feet, moved directly to the unit, touched the power icon, and turned on the privacy field before making his call. Avery took advantage of his preoccupation to lean toward Dona, keeping his voice low. "What do you think is going on? What he said about our not being able to cause him more than a minor inconvenience is probably true."

She shrugged dramatically. "Beats me. He seems to be leveling with us, but he's a politician. Counterfeit integrity is almost second nature. I think he's told part of the truth, but he's holding back all the important bits. And I wouldn't be so sure that he's quite as invulnerable as he claims. It doesn't take much of a scandal to sway public opinion."

"He claims that we're in no danger. I wish I could believe that."

She smiled broadly. "If it's true, then we're free to investigate anything we like, aren't we?"

"If he's telling the truth. Are we going to risk our lives on the assumption that he's a man of his word? That's what it may amount to."

"Can we get into worse trouble than we have already?"

He thought about it. "As a matter of fact, yes, we can. I seem to have discovered a positive talent for it lately."

"I think he told one lie, though. He was looking right at me and then, suddenly, his eyes moved away."

Avery's eyebrows rose. "When was that?"

"When he said we couldn't do any harm. I think he's very much afraid that we will."

They both lapsed into a thoughtful silence that lasted until Damien broke the connection and rejoined them, not taking a seat this time. His mouth was twisted into what was almost an attractive smile, although his eyes remained guarded and fatigued.

"You do seem to have a talent for being in the right place at the wrong time." He looked back and forth between them. "Kier's a good man, but pigheaded. Ever since his wife died, he's tried to be both father and mother to Dini, his only daughter. She's run off with one of the local boys, not Kier's first choice either, although I doubt any of them would be good enough to measure up to his standards. He's all torn up inside about it and he's made threats against the boy as well. But it was mostly frustration and depression talking. He's not above taking the boy out behind the barn and roughing him up, but that's as far as it would go. He may think he could actually kill someone in cold blood, but when faced with the actual task, I doubt he'd be able to carry through. In any case, I have promised to reveal everything I know publicly if anything happens to either of you, so I don't think you'll have any further problems with Kier or his friends."

"But you're not denying that Torgeson is capable of violence?"

"No, I'm not. All of us are capable of violence, even you. I do say that Kier would never follow through, no matter how dangerous he may have sounded. He was a wild youth and got into a lot of minor trouble in his day, and his temper is shorter now than it was then. If he had the chance, he'd deal harshly with young Karnov because his daughter means the world to him and no man would ever be good enough in his eyes. Hopefully, it will never come to that. Some of us have known where the two of them have been hiding almost from the moment they ran off, and we've carefully steered Kier in the wrong direction. Once he's had time to adjust to the way things are, it will be safe for the kids to come back, or not, as they choose."

"So where do we go from here?"

Damien shrugged noncommittally. "I've done as much as I can to ease your fears. I hope I've been more successful than it appears, but there's nothing more I can say to reassure you. Either you'll believe me and disengage yourselves from my affairs or you'll persevere to no purpose. Naturally we'll continue to be interested in your activities, but you're both perfectly free to come and go as you wish. If I meant you any harm, this conversation wouldn't even be taking place. It might not be convenient if you just disappeared, but if I was the monster you have been assuming, I could easily have arranged a tragic accident. I'm not trying to frighten you; that wasn't a threat, just an observation."

Avery glanced at Dona, whose face was unreadable. "We'll take what you've said under advisement." Damien nodded, but was clearly less than satisfied.

Damien left the cottage a short time later, walking off into the distance with a steady, confident stride. Avery watched from the window until the tall figure had disappeared behind a copse of flowering trees.

"What do you think of that?"

Dona was slow to respond. "If our lives weren't at stake, I'd be inclined to trust him. I don't always agree with Damien but he has always seemed to be a man of principle. Even Charles admits to a grudging respect for the man, and they're bitter opponents, if not enemies. I think he's more vulnerable than he let on, that he came here tonight to see if he could dissuade us by the power of his personality."

"I had much the same impression, although I still think he'd have us killed if he thought it was necessary. He might agonize over it later, genuinely regret the necessity, but he wouldn't fail to act if he thought we were a danger to whatever really matters to him." He dropped limply into a chair, turning recent events over in his mind as though they were parts of an intricate box puzzle, searching for the key that would reveal its hidden secrets. "So long as we're no threat, I don't think he'll act against us. But if we actually learn something potentially incriminating . . ." His voice drifted off.

"Do we keep on then, or drop it?"

"What do you want to do?"

She pursed her lips. "I don't like unsolved mysteries and I don't like being bullied, even when it's done ever so gently."

"Nor do I. So what's next?"

"I think it's time to talk to Charles again. There are a few questions we need to ask. He's not going to like having only part of the story, but I still don't think we should tell him everything. We'll need to decide in advance just how much we want him to know."

She didn't return to the Senator's cottage that night, and the following morning they walked together to the village center and caught the lifterbus to Park City. The only other passengers were an elderly woman who fell asleep a few minutes into the trip, and a young man who had already plugged into the entertainment console before they were airborne.

Charles Laszlow was waiting at the entrance to his property when they arrived. He greeted them with a cheery wave, waited patiently while Avery instructed the vehicle to wait for their return.

"I see you both made it this time. Welcome, Dona. It's been quite a while since we've seen one another." They embraced briefly but sufficiently familiarly that Avery wondered just how close their friendship had been. Dona had mentioned meeting Laszlow shortly after her arrival on

Meadow, indicated they'd spent a good deal of time together before drifting apart. Jealousy was an unfamiliar emotion for Avery, and he wasn't certain how to deal with it.

"You're looking good, Charles. Lost that weight you were always complaining about, I notice."

Laszlow positively preened. "Glad it's obvious. I worked at it hard enough. Come on up to the house."

They followed his lead, Avery watching for the Nerudi. "Are your guests still here?"

Laszlow was momentarily puzzled. "Oh, yes, of course, the Nerudi. They've been here so long, I think of them more as family rather than as visitors. Let's go around the back way. They've created quite a remarkable reconstruction of one of their villages, on a considerably smaller scale, of course. I tried to convince them to live in the house, but they refused. Too much of a cultural gap to leap all at once, I suppose."

"I wouldn't want to intrude. Didn't you say there was some ceremony involved before we could meet them?"

"Right, but a quick tour won't matter, and in any case I believe they're out in the garden. Even if they've returned, they won't recognize you as fellow intelligent beings since you haven't been introduced, so effectively this visit will never have taken place."

"Formally, maybe, but they'll still know."

Laszlow shook his head. "You're imposing human values where they don't apply. We've had observation posts among the Nerudi for years, clandestine at first, but openly since the company was forced to acknowledge their existence. The Nerudi ignored us completely, for generations in fact, until a research team finally managed to correctly interpret and initiate the ritual of acknowledgment, and during that time they never made any effort to conceal their activities. I'm not sure they even have the concept of privacy. We still only understand their culture in very general ways. Obviously the Nerudi don't ignore the physical presence of strangers and run into them, but they do seem to recognize our behavior and judge us as people only after the necessary social customs have been satisfied. It's actually rather useful at times. Strangers can often observe where acquaintances would be tactfully ushered away."

Avery still felt uneasy, but he followed Tharmody and Laszlow around the side of the villa to a large cleared space, one end of which had been visible from inside during his last visit. At the opposite end, huddled under a stand of tall trees, stood a scene from another world.

"They don't have buildings the way humans do, not even primitive ones," explained Laszlow. "The markers aren't meant to be permanent, because they have no real concept of land ownership. The land just is, like the sky and the air and the oceans. They do have personal property, but it only becomes theirs once they have contributed to its shaping. Freshly harvested breadfruit is community property, but if you cut one in half, it belongs to you."

None of Meadow's natives were present at the moment, but Avery still felt like an intruder. The Nerudi had marked off rough rectangles of ground with elaborately carved poles varying from one to three meters in length, each embedded in the ground to provide rough borders. Feathery fabric was occasionally draped from one to another, but not on a large enough scale to provide any real barrier. A tightly woven cloth canopy had been erected over the entire encampment. There were three depressions in the ground, each lined with thickly interwoven leaves and branches to form a sort of mattress. Small piles of artifacts were scattered about: long-bladed knives with jeweled or carved handles, intricately woven baskets, ceramic pieces, carved wood, other items Avery couldn't readily identify.

"Do they always leave things lying out like this?"

"Generally. Weather isn't a particularly serious concern, and Nerudi make things to last. No real roof, you notice? Just a sunshade. It was a while before I could convince my friends to come inside, and I think they're still uneasy when they have a barrier between themselves and the sky."

"What about theft? I mean, there's presumably no question of that here, but it must be a real problem in their larger settlements."

Laszlow grunted. "There aren't much in the way of permanent communities among the Nerudi, but I understand what you mean. As far as we can determine, theft is completely unknown among the natives. They have a highly intricate sense of private property that we are only beginning to understand, but the very idea of taking anything without permission seems to be literally unthinkable among them. The highest honor you can afford a Neroo is to present a gift, but it's not something one does lightly. Gifts cannot be refused, not for any reason, and the recipient must protect that object for the rest of his or her life. In most cases it is also necessary to reciprocate with something of equal value." He gestured toward the scattered piles of varicolored objects. "You see there everything these three Nerudi own, everything they have accumulated in their lives. To accidentally misplace even the most insignificant object would be a terribly shameful thing, possibly requiring ceremonial suicide."

"What would happen if I gave one of them something he couldn't move, like a lifter? Or your villa?"

"I imagine they'd be forced to remain in its immediate

vicinity for the rest of their lives. No, that's an exaggeration. The Nerudi can go out hunting or exploring, within certain limits, without lugging everything along. But they can't abandon anything. Presenting such an impractical gift would be a terrible breach of custom. No Nerudi would ever do such a thing to another, because of the requirements of possession and reciprocity. Every gift must be balanced with another. Fortunately, we've convinced them that personal services can serve that purpose when dealing with our kind or I could never have brought Tavarasan and the others here. They pay for my gifts of food by maintaining the grounds, keeping my house in order, and performing certain other services."

As interesting as all this might be, Avery was preoccupied with the real purpose of their visit. "We need to speak to you about . . . the matter I touched on last time."

Laszlow nodded, his expression carefully neutral. "I assumed something of that nature. Are you in a position to tell me what's going on now? I confess I've wondered about it a great deal these past five days."

He and Dona had argued that very point the previous evening, settling on a compromise that would probably make Laszlow more curious than ever. "More than I did before, anyway, though I'm afraid we still can't be entirely frank."

"Well, that's something, I suppose. Why don't we go inside? We'll have to fend for ourselves, I'm afraid. Tavarasan and the others are involved in some protracted ceremony of inlooking, whatever that might be."

It wasn't long before they were seated comfortably indoors, drinking a spicy concoction Laszlow had recommended. After making polite noises, Avery launched his rehearsed, abridged summary.

"Several days ago, a man disappeared in Haven under mysterious circumstances. By chance, I witnessed part of what happened and tried to report it, but couldn't get the local authorities to act."

"Lydia Hanifer," Laszlow interrupted. "Hence your earlier visit. Go on."

Avery drew a deep breath, choosing his words carefully. "We have reason to believe that a number of people are involved in covering up the incident, including a very powerful rival of yours, Senator Karl Damien."

Laszlow blinked, then sat back, scratching his chin through his beard. "Senator Damien isn't on Meadow at the moment. He's at a private caucus on Ozymandias."

"Is he?" Avery let the two words hover a few seconds, refusing to elaborate. It didn't take long for Laszlow to catch on.

"So that's the way it is. Owning your own starship does provide some obvious advantages, doesn't it? And you think Damien is responsible for this man's disappearance?"

"For the moment, let's just say he's involved. We can't prove any of this, you must realize, or we'd have gone straight to the authorities in Park City. And we really don't know much more than we're telling you." Except that the man was dead, not missing, and murdered by one of Damien's associates.

"The missing man, who is he?"

"We don't know his identity. Hanifer never filed a report or made any attempt to find out who he was, and it doesn't appear that he's local."

Laszlow didn't reply, stood instead and began pacing slowly around the room. Avery glanced at Tharmody, who merely lifted her eyebrows and returned to her drink. After an uncomfortably long silence, their host returned to his seat.

"All right, I suppose I'm going to have to trust the two of you. Karl Damien and I have been political enemies for many years now; the Nerudi citizenship question is only the most recent of many points of difference between us. I assume you're not naive enough to believe that we restrain our animosity to the government center here or the Senate. For years I've kept unofficial track of what Damien's been up to and I have no doubt he devotes the same attention to me. One of the reasons I live so far outside the city is that it provides some protection from prying eyes and ears.

"Damien's a careful man, goes out of his way to avoid anything that might make him look bad in the public eye, even when a perfectly legal personal gain was involved. I think his opinions are often ill conceived, but I would be very surprised to learn that he'd done anything dishonest. If his priorities were a little different, I might even be able to like him, and to a certain extent I do admire him. But I have to accept reality and I'm afraid we're fated to be adversaries." He stood up abruptly, slid an input grid for the comnet out of its recessed compartment, and began entering information through the keypad. "I want you to look at something. Wait a second. There!"

It was the image of a man, a bit fuzzy, and at first Avery thought it was a hologram of Senator Damien himself. But then he noticed the differences, primarily in the lower part of the face, the smaller jaw, flatter cheeks. And then he remembered.

"It's him," he said quietly. "That's the man I saw, the man who disappeared."

Dona rose and moved to Laszlow's side, studying the projection from close at hand. "Who is he? I've never seen him before. He looks a little bit like the Senator."

"His name's Kurt Royce. Comes from some place called

Tempus originally, an undeveloped world, just a mining colony for the most part, and the exclusive property of the Damien family since its discovery. I hate to disappoint you but I don't know much about Royce, and not from lack of trying. He's had at least three meetings with Damien, all private, and we had no reason to pay any particular attention to him until recently. The meetings we know about took place elsewhere, twice on Grendel, once on Ozymandias. I was aware that Royce was on Meadow but since I assumed that the Senator was not, we weren't paying much attention to him. We became interested in him when we noticed that after each of their meetings, the Senator would almost immediately take an unscheduled vacation. When we tried to track Royce's movements, we found out that he'd also left the planet, although not on a commercial transport."

"He went along on Damien's private ship?"

"In all likelihood, although it's possible that he had other means of avoiding detection."

"So what made you think this was the man I saw?"

"Senator Damien leads a very open life and doesn't have many obvious secrets. We have Royce flagged because he represents a possible weakness and, frankly, one that we hoped one day to exploit if possible. When you told me that Damien is in fact still on Meadow, the possibility of a clandestine meeting with Royce occurred to me immediately. When did you last see him?"

Avery thought back, counting days. "It was nine days ago, early in the morning, shortly after sunrise. I'm sorry but I don't know the local calendar very well."

Laszlow touched the keypad and read the screen. "That was two days after Royce arrived in Park City. He came in on the *Heart of Darkness*." Laszlow nodded to himself, as though confirming something he'd already suspected. "Royce went to Damien's office directly from the spaceport, and was told that the Senator was not available."

"He was visiting Debussy that day," interposed Tharmody.

"Who's Debussy?" asked Avery.

"Not who, where. Debussy is the permanent mission to the Nerudi, more a research outpost than anything else, although it serves some of the functions of an embassy as well. I know because I was waiting for him to get back before the two of us could go to Haven and deal with his AI."

Laszlow nodded. "Royce is apparently not a patient man. He created a disturbance at Damien's office and stormed off. Tried to hire someone to take him to Debussy, without any success, of course. You need a special government permit to travel to Nerudi territory. He even tried to buy a sea skimmer outright. Royce apparently controls a great deal of credit."

"Apparently? Why not query his file? That ought to give you an idea."

"That's another reason why we're interested in Mr. Royce. After his first visit with Damien, one of my agents ran a routine background query. He got a null return."

Avery frowned. "I don't understand."

"It couldn't find any records," explained Dona. "It happens a lot with offworlders. Unless there's some reason to transfer their data, if their visit isn't for an extended period of time because of a work assignment like mine, or an extended vacation like yours, personal files aren't transferred."

"At the time," Laszlow continued, "it didn't seem important enough to be worth pursuing. The same thing happened following their second meeting. After the third, I directed an inquiry to Tempus, his home of record. Kurt Royce was listed there as a native, now expatriated. All but the most basic information was expunged from his file when he emigrated. When his name showed up on the arrivals log in Park City, it triggered a watchdog program. I ran a query the same day, and came up with some interesting results. No such person was currently on Meadow according to the comnet. Someone had prevented his name from passing through the interface between the port authority and planetary records management."

"How is that possible?"

Laszlow sighed. "I'm afraid the comnet isn't as foolproof as most people believe. If you have credit to spare and know the right people, you can acquire a shielded account. Most of the time, it's not worth it. A negative reply to a query is often significant in itself. But it's not unheard of."

"Royce couldn't get to the Nerudi territory so he came to Haven to wait for Damien to return."

"Apparently, although I have only your word for that. No one seems to have kept track of his movements. We don't even know precisely when he left, though there's good reason to believe he set out shortly after failing to find the transport he wanted. There's no record of his having taken lodging in Park City, but he did rent a small lifter."

"Which means he reached Haven the day before I saw him."

"So it would appear. But he hasn't been seen since, and neither has his lifter. We even ran a trace on his emergency beacon, but it doesn't respond. Someone has deactivated it."

"Which means not only has he vanished, but as far as the authorities are concerned, he wasn't here in the first place. I don't understand that. I mean, he had to register with customs and immigration when he arrived. Don't they keep track of offworlders?"

"Sure, and eventually someone might even start wondering what happened to Royce. Unless someone else in authority alters the records to show that he left, or died of natural causes, or never arrived in the first place."

"It sounds like you're telling us that we're in over our heads and there's nothing we can do."

"You are in over your heads, as far as I can see, and unless you're ready to tell me what's going on, I'm not sure there's anything you can do. If Karl Damien has been involved in some criminal act, and you have evidence to support that charge, I urge you in no uncertain terms to report it to the proper authorities, or let me do it for you. There's a woman working in the governor's office, Audrey Lisleton, who won't hesitate to act against Damien. If you don't feel you can talk to me, I urge you to look her up. She'll listen to you in confidence."

Avery noted the name, but without much hope. They still had no evidence. Something else was bothering him about the entire situation, something he couldn't rationalize or even articulate. Once again, he felt like a chess piece, a pawn caught between two opposing forces he could sense but not name. And as much as he wished to cast Damien in the role of the black player, he couldn't do it.

"We'll think about it."

Laszlow's shoulders slumped. "I hoped you'd be more sensible, but then I don't know everything that's happened. All I can do then is wish you both the best of luck, and hope you figure out the right thing to do before it's too late. If my suspicions are right, and it's more than just a missing man you're worried about, you're both potentially in a great deal of danger. If something unfortunately happened to either of you, I would not like to think that I stood by and refrained from acting."

Chapter Twelve

❋ ❋ ❋

Avery and Tharmody did not immediately return to Haven. Instead they spent the next two days in Park City. There was no immediate call for Dona's professional services and she was more than happy to act as tour guide, but admitted the city itself had little to offer that he could not have found elsewhere in greater abundance and on a larger scale. "Until they resolve the colony's uncertain future, there's not much chance of attracting outside investment. Most of the visitors are scientists, not entrepreneurs."

That first night, he had suggested that they call to arrange temporary lodging for him at one of the transient hostelries, but Dona would not hear of it.

"There's plenty of room at my place. You can even have your own bed. There's an extra room I had intended to turn into an office, but I never got around to it, and probably never will. It's a little messy but we can fix that easily enough." Even that limited effort had proven unnecessary; the master bedroom was quite large enough to accommodate two.

During what Avery later thought of as vacation from his vacation, he very consciously attempted to put the matter of missing bodies and interplanetary conspiracies out of his mind, though not entirely successfully. Dona proved to be a delightful distraction; her energetic approach to their friendship and physical intimacy was a refreshing contrast to his previous romantic experiences.

They spent a morning at one of the beaches along the northern coast, walking the shoreline rather than swimming or sunbathing, watching sand snakes scurry out of their way and occasional waveriders spreading their diaphanous wings to suck up the sunlight, enjoying each other's company without feeling a need to fill the silence with meaningless conversation. There were a few fancy tourist spots and restaurants in Park City, but nothing out of the ordinary, and they chose instead to patronize less familiar, out-of-the-way places that catered primarily to the local inhabitants rather than the transient population.

But on the third day, Avery realized that he was becoming restless. That morning, he was sitting in the front room of Dona's apartment when she startled him by placing her hand on his shoulder.

"You want to go back, don't you?"

He looked up into her face and nodded. "Yes, I'm afraid I do. Sorry to bring all this to an end, but I can't let it go. I won't be able to rest until I know what happened. I'll stay in touch though."

She nodded. "You're right about that. I'm going with you. I've already notified the agency that I'm taking some vacation time." She grinned at him. "I assume you won't mind having a roommate for a few more days."

"Not at all. Are you sure you want to get involved any further than you already are?"

"You're not the only one who can be stubborn. There's a flight out to Haven scheduled later today."

He raised his eyebrows. "Did you memorize the schedule for amusement or have you been a few steps ahead of me?"

"I'm always a few steps ahead of you." She winked and started to turn away.

"How much later today? Do we have to rush?"

"No, there's plenty of time. Did you have something in particular in mind?"

"As a matter of fact, I did."

Dona and Avery reached Haven late that same afternoon and went directly to his cottage. There was nothing to indicate that there had been any intruders during their absence, but Avery wasn't surprised by that. They were supposed to believe that they posed no further threat and were therefore beneath consideration. Dona unpacked while he checked the com, which had a short queue of unread messages including a financial statement from his trust management system, advertisements, a brief query from his outpatient coordinator, and a public service announcement about an upsurge in cochinitus cases on the west coast, whatever that might be.

"Anything interesting?" Dona had changed into short pants and a billowy blouse in deference to the heat outside. Although technically it was autumn on Meadow, the seasons varied very little and it had been unusually warm for the past several days.

"My investments have been performing much better lately, and I only have a few days left before the import fees on personal flitters go up ten percent."

"You don't sound particularly thrilled by either item."

Avery shrugged. "I don't spend the income on my investments now." His face abruptly cracked into a smile. "Of course, I haven't really been trying."

She ignored his banter. "So what do we do now that we're here?"

Avery glanced at the nearest window. It was almost dusk, but the sky was clear. "Would you object to taking a longish walk? Down to the village, I mean."

"You have a plan?"

"Not really. But I don't want them to think they've scared me into hiding. Maybe some opportunity to cause trouble will come our way."

"Oh, trouble. I like the sound of that. Let's go."

For a change, he actually saw some of his neighbors out and about. A young couple with strikingly oval eyes and the palest complexions Avery had ever seen nodded politely from where they sat in the front yard of a nearby cottage. A short time later, two dark skinned women jogged by, and they exchanged nods with an elderly man wearing the ceremonial sarong of the Sikhara aristocracy just before they reached the village proper, where they encountered a group of almost a dozen children, probably Haveners, who burst raucously from behind a building, playing some mysterious game that engaged their attention so fully they almost ran down the two adults before chasing each other off amidst a thunder of giggling.

"It's hard to believe this isn't just another normal town," Dona said softly.

"Maybe it is," Avery answered after a moment. "Maybe we're just seeing things with unusual clarity. Maybe every community has its hidden secrets, not necessarily murders, but intrigues, blackmail, extortion, scandals, whatever. Individually, we try to project a calm, competent, reassuring image of ourselves, hiding what goes on inside: the petty hatreds, jealousies, anger, and weakness, even the occasional crime. Why should it surprise us if communities function in much the same way, concealing shared sins?"

"Are we waxing philosophical this evening or what?"

He grinned, tapped the side of his head with a forefinger. "The active mind is always looking for explanations," he announced loftily. "While lesser minds merely accept things as they appear."

"Well, this particular lesser mind is more interested in accepting something cool to drink than the secrets of the universe, at least at this specific moment."

So he led the way to Soothers.

Apparently the heat was bothering more than just Tharmody, because Soothers was more crowded than he had ever seen it before. All of the tables were occupied, people standing about in small, noisy clusters crowded the main serving area, and the building's environmental control system was losing the battle to keep things comfortable. Dona and Avery had to place their heads close together in order to hear one another.

"Since you're not using your credit as fast as it accumulates, I suggest we try one of the expensive tourist spots for a change," Dona suggested. "I don't think we're going to find anyplace to sit here."

"Unfortunately, I think you're right." But just as they were turning toward the door, a hand gripped his left arm tightly and a familiar voice cut through the din.

"Mr. Avery! I thought that was you! How was your trip to the city?"

It was Tanya Churienko, her face flushed with the heat. Avery nodded pleasantly, tried to introduce Dona, but the din was overwhelming. "Let's step outside!" he managed at last, and the three spilled out onto the street, where it was only marginally hotter than it had been within but much quieter. Avery introduced the two women, who touched palms amicably.

"We were just going to go look for someplace less

crowded to get a cool drink. Would you like to join us?"

"As a matter of fact, I would. And please call me Tanya."

"All right, and I'm Wes and this is Dona. Now the important question is where should we go?"

But they had no better luck at either of the two tourist centers, both of which were unusually crowded. They did manage to get served at the Starloft, but the environmental system wasn't working properly there either. The air was cool but it was too dry and tasted stale. Churienko began sneezing and invited them back to her home.

"I'm afraid I don't have all the luxuries you'll find offworld, but it should be comfortable enough and I'm sure I can arrange something cool to drink."

His first inclination had been to decline the invitation, but then he remembered her position in the community. It would certainly be difficult for anything significant to be going on without her being aware of it. He wondered if she'd been watching for them, had attached herself specifically to find out what they were up to, but then decided that it didn't matter.

Her house was larger than he expected: half the size of Laszlow's villa, a sprawling, vaguely unbalanced structure on a full acre lot. The door opened obediently when she touched the access pad and she ushered them into a small foyer from which three doors led to inner rooms. The lights had come up automatically as they entered, and both Tharmody and Avery were startled by what was revealed.

"You'll have to excuse the clutter, but living by myself, I've been able to indulge my passion for these things." She led the way into the leftmost room which, like the others, was filled with a bewildering collection of items, mounted on walls, in stasis cases, on pedestals and shelves, in racks and display cases. It was a riot of color and shapes: ceremonial masks, spears, carvings in wood and stone, porcelain, jewel-encrusted cups and plates, what appeared to be primitive musical instruments including a harp and a set of brass horns of varying sizes and shapes. They could only guess at the purpose of some of the artifacts that surrounded them.

"You must have been collecting these for years." Dona was standing beneath an elaborate case filled with blown-glass figures, prisms, jewelry, and ornate hand mirrors. Avery glanced in that direction and noticed the elaborate necklace with the sharply pronged ornamentation that Churienko had been wearing when they first met.

"Actually, most of what you see here has been in my family for generations; I can't really afford to add much, although I do find a piece advertised from time to time that doesn't break my budget. They all have a common origin, though. Everything you see here comes from Earth, most of it predating the age of expansion."

Avery was impressed, made no effort to conceal it, and noticed that despite her disclaimer, Churienko was pleased by his reaction. "If they're all authentic, what you have here must represent a not insignificant amount of credit."

"Theoretically, yes. But not in practice. What can I get you to drink?"

Avery and Tharmody both asked for a fruit drink popular on Meadow, and Churienko brought them large, chilled glasses a moment later. For herself, she'd brought a smaller glass of some pale liquid which she sipped tentatively.

"A generation ago, during the height of the nostalgia craze, my parents could have sold this all for enough to become rather spectacularly wealthy. Technically, the value of the individual pieces remains the same or higher today, but even if I was willing to part with any of this, and I'm not, the problem is that there are no longer very many avid collectors, and those like myself who remain can occasionally pick up underpriced pieces from all those who invested during the fad and later lost interest."

Avery thought of his own youth on Parchmont, realized that except for a few holos he hadn't looked at in over a decade, he had no physical possessions by which to remember his home world. He'd sold the Avery holdings shortly before leaving the desert planet, without any trace of regret, and had never looked back until now.

"Have you ever been there? Earth, I mean?"

She shook her head. "I've never even thought about it. What I want of Earth is here with me."

"I've been there," said Dona, surprising the other two. "Went with my older brother a few years ago. Lots of museums but otherwise it looks a lot like everyplace else. Once I got over the initial thrill of actually being on the birthplace of humanity, I was bored, as a matter of fact."

Avery had never been to Earth, although he had planned the trip on more than one occasion. He had never actually followed through, probably because he knew that the reality would never live up to the image in his mind, and he'd been disenchanted often enough in the past that he didn't want to risk losing another illusion.

They made small talk long enough to finish their drinks and start on a second round. Churienko seemed relaxed and friendly and Avery decided his earlier inclination to like her had been justified. They were amicably arguing the advantages and disadvantages of living in such isolated circumstances when Avery mentioned the elopement of Torgeson's daughter and suggested that internal pressures would eventually erode the community's cohesion.

"Oh, haven't you heard? But then how could you have? Dini and Nils are back, showed up two mornings ago."

"Who found them?" Avery suppressed an image of Torgeson throwing the younger man into the maw of a harvester.

"No one. They came back on their own. Best thing that could have happened, actually, particularly considering the circumstances. Nils is lucky to have gotten off with nothing more serious than a few bruises and a headache."

Avery nodded. "Kier Torgeson must have been in a charitable mood."

Churienko laughed shortly. "It wasn't Kier who did it, although I'm sure he'd have liked to. Dini did the damage herself. I guess after a couple of days alone with Nils, she decided that life with her father wasn't quite as bad as she'd originally thought. Neither of them is saying much about it, and it's none of my business either, but it looks like she lost her patience with him and he said or did something she didn't care for. She brought him back to his father's place and left him there without a word of explanation, but Nils has already told everyone who will listen that she's as crazy as her father and twice as mean. When Kier hears that, if he hasn't already, it'll put him in a good mood for the rest of the season."

"Will her father take her back then after all that?"

"Certainly he will. Dotes on her, he does. You'd never suspect it to hear them go at each other the way they do, but there's a strong bond of affection between father and daughter. Family ties are a lot stronger in places like Haven than in the cities. When we're unhappy with a situation, we do something about it, and don't hold grudges afterwards. Wouldn't surprise me if Nils ended up working for Kier, now that he's clearly not going to spirit Dini away to Park City."

They spent a pleasant, relaxed evening with Tanya

Churienko, who gave them a guided tour of the ground floor of her home, pointing out her favorite objects, which included a Zulu war shield, an ancient personal computer which was considerably larger than the master control module of a modern starship, and a collection of children's stories actually printed on paper, which she carefully removed from a sealed cube so that she could show them the old fashioned, two dimensional colored illustrations scattered through the text.

It was dark outside when they finally took their leave, Churienko walking partway back to the village with them before saying goodbye.

"I like her," admitted Dona. "I don't think I've ever met anyone before who was so completely satisfied with the life they were leading."

Avery, who had been wondering why such an intelligent, interesting person would hide herself away in Haven, suddenly saw things from a new perspective. After all, he had abandoned his small, inward-looking community on Parchmont and then the more cosmopolitan cultures of Galatea, Myrmidon, Versailles, and New Andover, each of which he'd sampled briefly, to make a new home for himself on a newly-opened agricultural world. Tanya wasn't the only person to prefer a quiet backwater to the hectic lifestyle found on the developed worlds.

The following morning, Dona and Avery held a strategy session, reviewing every bit of information they had in their possession, and were dismayed to discover how little they really knew. Another visit to the Torgeson farm would be unnecessarily dangerous, and it was unlikely that anything incriminating would remain for them to find even if they took the risk.

They checked Noric Klanth's personal data and learned that he supported himself repairing equipment in Haven and occasionally elsewhere, was married with two young children, and had been arrested once as a youth after being caught vandalizing some of the vacation cottages. He lived not far from Kier Torgeson. Dona shrugged and crossed his name off as well. "Unless you want to kidnap and torture him for information," she said lightly, "I can't think of any opportunity there."

"I think we'll pass on that."

Dona tried to query the name Kurt Royce. Not surprisingly, she found nothing that didn't agree with what Laszlow had told them. Officially, Karl Damien was still on Ozymandias, or at least not on Meadow, but they had no idea where he really was. He'd had more than enough time to leave again, but there were no records of his coming and going in the port logs. Someone was covering for him, because even if he used a skiff and avoided the official spaceport, his orbital insertion would have been monitored and logged. His local office claimed to have no certain knowledge of his forthcoming movements. If Damien was still on Meadow, there was little chance they could find him unless he chose to reveal himself.

"We need a break," Dona said at last. "There's not enough here to work with. Unless we can find something they've overlooked, some mistake they've not noticed or not covered up adequately, we're never going to know what really happened."

Avery pursed his lips. "There might be one weak link in the chain. I can think of one Havener who might be willing to talk out of turn."

She raised an eyebrow. "You don't mean Tanya?"

"No, Tanya's as loyal as they come. If she's a party to

any of what's going on, we'll never hear it from her lips. I had Nils Karnov in mind."

She hesitated a second before recognizing the name. "The kid who ran off with Torgeson's daughter? Why would he say anything?"

"I don't know that he would, but he's got a loose tongue and no reason to like Kier Torgeson. I doubt that anyone would trust him with anything confidential and it might be a waste of time, but we don't have any other ideas. Unless you're holding out on me?"

She shook her head. "How do we approach him?"

"Ideally, I'd like to ply him with drink. He has a weakness for it. But even if we could catch him alone at Soothers, we'd be seen and that would tip off the opposition. I don't know if that would matter, but I'd rather keep them in the dark. Or at least the dim."

Neither of them could think of any way to approach Karnov directly, and after coming up with a string of totally implausible scenarios, they finally gave up, although the possibility was filed for future reference.

"I don't know about you, Dona, but my brain hurts. I don't want to let this thing go, but I don't want it to become an obsession either. Maybe if we don't try so hard, let our subconscious minds mull over what we've talked about, something will occur to us later."

"All right. So what do we do instead?"

"How about some sightseeing?"

Haven sat near the base of a wedge-shaped triangle of land that jutted out of the southern coast into the salt water ocean. Steep cliffs and an unfriendly shore with virtually no natural beaches made the shoreline unsuitable for a seaport. It was scenic enough to attract sightseers, but not enough to justify development. Although it was much too far to walk, there was a rental company in Arcadia, just east of Haven, which would send a lifter over on autopilot to pick them up.

Dona wasn't hard to convince. Unfortunately, the hatchet-faced young man whose face appeared on the com told them with genuine or well-feigned sympathy that all of his lifters were committed for the day. Disappointed, Avery almost broke the connection before reconsidering, then reserved one for the following morning.

"So what do we do instead?"

She leaned back in her chair and grinned mischievously. "Maybe we could just lie around the house for a while."

And that's what they did.

It rained briefly that night, accompanied by mild thunder and distant lightning, the first of either Avery had seen since arriving on Meadow. The morning was clear and bright, but the ground was wet enough to steam humidly and the soil felt spongy under their feet. They started toward the village at first light, both carrying stasis packs that contained their lunch and a variety of liquids. The lifter was sitting in the center of the village landing strip just past the security office, bearing a garish company logo. Avery noticed that the security lifter was nowhere in sight.

"I wonder where Hanifer is off to so early in the morning?"

"Stop that." Dona punched his shoulder. "Remember, no investigating today."

A woman he'd never met before turned away from her companion to greet them when they stepped inside. "You must be Mr. Avery. That lifter over there claims it's waiting for you."

Dona blinked and looked startled, then nodded to the young man who stood watching them, his expression clearly hostile. "How have you been, Nils? Still working for the Solitude Corporation?"

Nils Karnov averted his eyes but answered calmly. "Not lately. They've been using local help."

Avery had managed to cover his own surprise with difficulty. "Yes, I'm Avery. Is there a landing fee or something I need to worry about?"

She shook her head. "None whatsoever. I'm just supposed to make sure that you know enough to avoid the restricted areas." She glanced at the lifter. "Waste of time, actually. You couldn't reach them in one of these anyway. Are you going far?"

"Just sightseeing. We don't have any particular destination in mind."

She made a few suggestions, seemed honestly interested in helping. The boy never said a word, but he was obviously listening to the conversation. Avery felt that he might be wasting an opportunity, but he couldn't think of any way to exploit the situation.

A few minutes later, they were sitting in the lifter, which waited patiently while they decided which of several suggested routes along the coast looked to be the most promising. When they finally punched in the appropriate code, it rose slowly into the air and started south out of the city. The sound shielding wasn't first class and they had to raise their voices to be heard, but the ride was smooth and the interior had been well maintained.

Unlike the security lifter, theirs was quite limited. They were only a few meters above ground level, and when Avery tried to nudge it toward rougher terrain, a warning tone buzzed and the lifter informed them pedantically that destabilization could cause personal injury as well as damage to the equipment, which would of course be charged to Avery's account. They were therefore confined to the roads and grassland and waterways, all of which were safe if rather boring. The countryside gradually changed from farmland and forest to a flatter contour covered with stubbly grass and low, ragged bushes. Avery became lost in his thoughts and Tharmody put her head back and fell asleep.

Although he tried to relax and enjoy himself, Avery couldn't stop thinking about Karl Damien. The man was an admitted murderer, or at least an accomplice, and was apparently engaged in an ambitious political effort to deprive the Nerudi of their rights to their own planet. Nevertheless, Avery could not help feeling drawn to the Senator, who had seemed honestly distressed. He knew that there had to be something significant about Damien's mysterious comings and goings; it took considerable effort to cover up arrivals and departures, no matter how important and powerful a person you might be. What was the connection between Damien and Haven? Why was he pretending to be on Ozymandias while secretly visiting a small village? Was the Nerudi question pivotal or just a side issue? And if it was important, how did Haven come into the picture, since there had never been Nerudi anywhere near the small community? The local residents might have some strong feelings about the matter, but there didn't seem to be much of immediate concern to them. No one had seriously proposed abandoning the planet and dismantling the colony; it was too late for that. The flow of investment credit had been dramatically reduced, but most Haveners seemed disinclined to welcome the change in their lifestyles that would necessarily follow major development of the area. Would they be willing to overcome their disinclination to sell their land if the price was high enough? Possibly. But even if

Meadow was opened up to unrestricted exploitation, there was no reason why Haven in particular would be a prime site. Better than ninety percent of the subcontinent was unclaimed and largely unexplored except by orbital survey. Avery had no answers, not even plausible guesses, but he had an instinctive feeling that he was fumbling around the edges of the solution.

He made a mental list of key names.

Haven. Damien. Royce. Nerudi. Torgeson. Hanifer. There were lines of contact from Damien to and among all of the others, except that there were no Nerudi in Haven, and only Damien was connected to Royce. Might Royce have been on Meadow previously? It was possible. Laszlow hadn't said so, but then he wasn't interested in Royce except when the man was interacting with Damien. It was entirely possible that Royce had visited previously, may even have come to Haven any number of times. Was Royce connected to the Nerudi somehow? Did he perhaps know something that would make a difference in the decision about their future? If there was no direct link between Royce and the Nerudi, then the motive for his death must lie elsewhere. And why was Damien concealing his presence in Haven? Obviously Royce presented some kind of threat to the Senator, either to his agenda or his career. Was it a question of blackmail?

He tried to form a working hypothesis, a scenario that would fit all the facts. Kurt Royce had come to Meadow looking for Damien, who was, or at least claimed to be, unavailable. Royce had then arranged transportation to Haven, presumably believing that Damien would eventually return to the village, a not unrealistic expectation given his usual habits. Royce may or may not have known about Damien's more clandestine visits. Shortly after arriving and probably before he managed to see the Senator, Royce was killed by one of Damien's allies, probably Torgeson or Hanifer, and the body disposed of in a rather thorough fashion. His death might have been deliberate; it might be that an effort at intimidation had gone too far. If Avery hadn't been in the right place at the wrong time, the entire matter could have been smoothed over as though it had never occurred. The body had presumably been destroyed and it didn't look like anyone was going to come looking for Royce.

It all seemed to fit, but even if he was right, how much of it could he prove? There was a record of Royce arriving on Meadow and leaving in the lifter he'd purchased, but no more than that, and it would be easy enough to suppress any investigation at least in the short term. If necessary, Damien could claim to have taken Royce offworld in his private ship. The rented lifter could be accounted for in various ways. Avery thought the easiest would be to disable it in such a way that it looked as though Royce had sent it back on autopilot and that it had failed along the way.

The convolutions were giving him a headache. Leave it for a while, he told himself. Talk it over with Dona later. She might spot something that he was overlooking.

He turned to stare out at the passing landscape, in time to see a dark shape moving just beyond a thin line of scrawny trees. It was a small lifter, too distant to identify, moving parallel to their course and near the limit of their vision. Avery tensed, unwilling to dismiss this as another coincidence. It had to be Hanifer. He'd noticed that the security lifter was gone when they'd left that morning. Obviously she could have known they'd reserved one of their own and followed them, trying to decide what they were up to. But why waste her time? Today's trip had nothing to do with Damien or Royce. That much should have been obvious. A routine precaution? It didn't make any sense. There had to be some other explanation.

A few seconds later, he lost sight of the other vehicle as they reached a more heavily forested area and although he watched for several minutes afterward, he never spotted the sleek bullet shape again. When Dona shook herself awake, he didn't mention it, unwilling to alarm her unnecessarily. It was, after all, entirely possible that the other vehicle carried innocent tourists, and in any case there was nothing they could do about it. So instead he summarized his latest theory.

"It sounds right, and I'd like to think that the Senator is protecting his people rather than masterminding a crime spree," she said at last. "If I knew what Royce's business with Damien really was, I might have a different attitude."

The landscape was suddenly open again, the last line of trees disappearing behind them. The hardy native grass grew only in tentative patches scattered across increasingly rocky soil. A fuzzy, greenish red growth covered the shady portions of the rocks, which were otherwise bare to the elements. A line of low but sharply cut hills appeared ahead and the lifter shifted to a less direct course as it avoided natural obstacles. A few minutes later they passed through a breach in the line of hills and slowed. The lifter hovered for a second, then set down in a level spot that looked artificial, although it was not paved.

"We have reached our programmed destination. Awaiting instructions."

Avery keyed the vehicle to wait for their return and stepped outside. The sun was still quite warm but a brisk, salty wind blew steadily, occasionally gusting so enthusiastically that they were forced to turn their heads away.

"Quite a change," Dona remarked. "It only gets like this on the north coast when there's a big storm coming, or what passes for a big storm on Meadow."

At one end of the parking area a small kiosk displayed a large holographic map of the area and a printed copy was dispensed automatically when Avery touched an icon on the panel. A variety of hiking trails were clearly marked, with a legend underneath describing the advantages and disadvantages of each.

"Do we want scenic or challenging?"

Dona suppressed a yawn. "Scenic, I think. I'm not up to much in the way of challenging today."

"You should have slept longer last night."

"Whose fault is that?"

"You didn't have any complaints at the time."

She grinned at him. "Who's complaining?"

They chose a winding but gradual trail that led out to the cliff face and down, cutting back and forth as it descended toward the water. When they reached the first crest and Avery saw the ocean stretching to the horizon in three directions, he was struck by its beauty. Even after visiting a half dozen planets, the sight of so much water in one place never failed to mesmerize him.

They fell into a companionable silence as they followed the rough path by spotting glittering markers that had been placed strategically along the way. There were several routes that intersected the one they had chosen, some leading more directly to the narrow beach, others offering greater degrees of physical challenge or promising vantage points for better viewing. Only a limited number of hardy plants grew in this area, all native, but there was a greater diversity of insect life as well as some higher forms roughly analogous to birds, which swept down from the higher altitudes, then rose slowly on rising air currents. The largest was no bigger than Avery's clenched fist.

They reached the base of the cliff just before mid-day, sat on a relatively dry promontory above the crashing surf while they ate the simple meal they'd brought with them. Tourist attraction or not, this was a wild, remote place and they hadn't seen any evidence of other humans, not even a footprint. If it hadn't been for the trail markers, Avery might have thought that they were in virgin territory. The wind was so brisk that they sat with their backs to the ocean while they ate, and Avery could feel salt crackling as it dried on his exposed arms and face.

With considerably lighter packs, they reluctantly stirred themselves to move a while later. "It's going to be tougher going back up," said Dona, shading her eyes to study the face of the cliff towering above their heads.

"We can take a shorter route back, but it'll be steeper."

"I'm in no hurry."

They might have been better off taking the more direct trail, because it wound its way up a deeply cut scar that offered considerable cover. As it was, they had just climbed above a jutting knob of bleached white stone when the attack came.

Chapter Thirteen

❋ ❋ ❋

It was a chance misstep that saved Dona, who was at that moment a few steps ahead of Avery. She had paused and was in the process of turning to say something to him when a stone rolled under one foot and she pitched forward, arms instinctively extended to break her fall. A brief stream of flechettes passed just above her head as she stumbled to her knees, shattering against the rock wall beside her. Avery froze in shock, staring stupidly at the two distant figures rising from behind a low rock ridge upslope, their faces sheathed to hide their identity, both carrying military style weapons. They started forward immediately, picking their way carefully, apparently too worried about their own footing to fire for the second or two that it took him to realize his danger and drop behind cover. Dona had been quicker off the mark and had scuttled behind a wall of earth.

"Dona, are you all right?"

"Yes." She was lying motionless a meter away, sheltered behind a low, flat ledge of shale. Her voice cracked with tension. "Who's shooting at us?"

"Can't tell, they're too far off and their faces are covered. But they're heading this way. We have to get out of here fast. Keep your head down and crawl back here. I don't think they'll be able to see us once we're a few meters back down the cliff. We have to find a way to throw them off our trail." He felt a sudden giddiness and knew that the increase in his adrenaline flow had triggered an implant. His sudden relative calmness was artificially induced, but he was still pleased not to have given in to panic. "I don't suppose you brought a wristcom with you?"

"Of course not. That would be too easy."

"It probably doesn't matter. It would take at least an hour for help to arrive. Let's go now!"

They moved quickly down the slope, leaving the marked path and following a natural ravine until there was a break in the rock wall. Taking care not to make any unnecessary noise, they started to move parallel to the cliff face, occasionally glancing back upslope. Unfortunately, the same heavy cover that concealed them from their attackers made it equally impossible for them to determine just how close the pursuit might be. The need to make as little noise as possible slowed them, and the occasional sound of movement from above and behind did nothing to soothe their frayed nerves. They continued roughly horizontally along the cliff face, occasionally rising or descending.

Twice they were forced to spring across relatively exposed areas where not even the native plant life could get a foothold. On each occasion, Avery felt the hairs rise on the back of his neck and expected to feel the sudden pain of a flechette, but fortunately their enemies were apparently unable to take advantage of their exposure. After several minutes, they came around one swell of rock to find themselves facing a much wider ledge. A fairly thick patch of two-meter-high brush provided cover, stretching for a fair distance ahead, and disappearing around the next curve of the cliff face. It looked almost as though a giant shovel had scooped out a chunk of the mountain at some time in the distant past. The sea breeze had picked up and the foliage was being whipped back and forth enthusiastically, so there was a good chance that the signs of their passing would be camouflaged. For the first time, they heard the other parties calling to one another, too remote to hear individual words, too close to allow them much time to consider their options.

They pushed forward, ignoring the tiny scratches that were inevitable given the tough, thorny branches and close quarters. In some places the growth was so thick that the lower branches had died and rotted off, and here they were occasionally able to crawl through extensive natural tunnels, while desiccated branches crackled and crumpled to dust, and made much better time than when they were forced to press through the tight mesh of living branches. On the other hand, it was hard to stay properly oriented and Avery was terrified that they'd somehow reversed course and might be moving directly toward the assassins. When they finally reached the last of the covered ground, he was relieved to see that they'd followed a reasonably straight course, but dismayed by the necessity of crossing the considerably more exposed terrain that lay beyond.

"Any suggestions?" Avery viewed the scoured stretch of open ground with distrust. There were occasional clusters of eroding rock interrupting the smooth expanse, but they were widely scattered and provided only intermittent concealment.

Dona moved closer to him, whispering, "It doesn't look promising, but the idea of sitting here waiting for them to find us is even less appealing. What's that shadow over there?"

Avery followed her pointing finger, noticed the feature

she was referring to, a dark stripe further along the side of the cliff. "I don't know. Some kind of depression. It might be just a shallow curve or a crack in the rock."

"Or it might be deep enough to provide cover while we look for another way up." She glanced toward the top of the cliff, but the crest was concealed at this point by a series of jutting tiers draped with vines and more of the chaotic brush.

They broke from their cover and sprinted across the bare rock, hoping their pursuers were searching in the wrong direction. An excited shout from somewhere behind and slightly below them dashed that hope. At least one of the pair had overshot the point where they had left the trail and descended too far down the slope; the other didn't answer and for all they knew, was preparing to fire at them even now. Avery didn't look back, but he expected to feel the sting of flechettes ripping into his back at any second, was mildly surprised that it hadn't happened by the time they rounded the exposed rock face and found themselves looking out across a series of deeply cut chasms and rock falls.

"I don't see any way up." He leaned against the facing rock and tried to regain his breath, rubbing idly at a painful stitch in his right side. "And it looks like we're running out of ledge."

Dona tried to grin but it ended up being a grimace. "You want to go back then?"

He shook his head unnecessarily. "We'll have to hope that the passageway opens up somewhere."

It was slower going from that point onward, a random tumble of stone rather than a carefully chosen trail. Worse, there was a lot of loose sand which acted as a lubricant, making the footing treacherous and nerve-wracking. Avery continued to worry that they might be heading into a dead end. Already the two facing walls were noticeably closer than at the entrance, and they angled even more sharply inward further along. Enough light penetrated for them to be able to pick out their footing, but cloaks of shadow were draped from the walls on either side. Although their attackers were no longer shouting to one another, Avery had heard rocks sliding to their rear, and was certain they hadn't abandoned the pursuit.

He was breathing heavily when they crested the second rise, and might have paused for breath had it not been for a rather dramatic reminder of their situation. A fresh stream of flechettes, fortunately very far off target, lacerated a stone column to their left. Avery and Tharmody half jumped, half fell over the lip to the sheltered side, scraping and banging elbows and shins in their desperation to put something solid between themselves and their pursuers. Avery gestured for his companion to stay where she was, then crawled back up and carefully poked his head over the lip. For the first time he had a fairly clear look at the twosome, one wearing a bright yellow coverall, the other a similar garment in faded gray, as they struggled up a steep slope near the entrance to this crevice.

He slid back down under cover. "They don't seem to be giving up."

"I noticed that," she answered with weary sarcasm. "I think we're more likely to collapse than they are. Neither of us is particularly athletic and we've spent the morning wearing ourselves out while they were just sitting waiting for us."

"Yeah, but we've got more of an incentive to keep going. Let's move."

The next slope was easier, not as steep and with plenty

of handholds, but the one that followed was so daunting they were briefly afraid that they wouldn't be able to scale it. As they had feared, the walls were closing in rapidly, and the rock surfaces were much too smooth and steep for them to climb. But even if they were heading into a dead end, they had no real alternative but to go on.

They were helping each other over another spur of rock when they heard renewed shouting from behind. Avery turned and saw that their lead was growing shorter. The two assassins were close together and moving forward with swift, deadly purpose. As he watched, the one in yellow stumbled, windmilled both arms, then fell heavily and slid awkwardly for several meters before coming to rest. Avery felt a burst of elation and hoped that the fall had been serious enough to end the pursuit. He watched as the figure in gray climbed carefully down to render assistance and felt his spirits drop a moment later when it was obvious that both figures were advancing toward them again, although the one in yellow seemed to be favoring his or her right leg. Avery and Tharmody cut short their rest and clambered over the spine of the next ridge, descending the opposite side.

They found themselves confronting a surprisingly smooth concave slope, so they sat on the lip and slid most of the way down on their backsides, using outstretched arms and legs to maintain a semblance of balance. The walls loomed so close on either side that Avery felt a twinge of claustrophobia. The rock surface was shiny and wet, but the ground beneath their feet was dry, well above the reach of the planet's weak tides. At the foot of the slope, the ground was chalky and cracked in crazed patterns, and when they ran across the surface small puffs of dust erupted beneath their feet. Just beyond was a smooth hummock twice their height, and when they tried to climb it the sand shifted treacherously under their feet, providing no purchase. After three abortive tries, Dona led the way through a narrow gap between the sand and the nearest rock wall. It was so close that they had to slide through part of the narrow passage on their stomachs and when they emerged on the opposite side, they were both coated with dirt from head to foot.

"You really know how to show a girl a good time," she said brightly, but there was fatigue in her voice. They both knew that they couldn't maintain this pace for much longer.

Just ahead, the two walls merged, but not, fortunately, into a solid barrier. The cliff face here reminded Avery of a rotting corpse, a comparison he chose not to dwell upon. There were several shallow caves of various sizes and shapes, and occasional craggy trees that grew horizontally out of the hollowed spaces and then spread their branches like spiderwebs. Long streamers of thick, rust colored moss carpeted some of the exposed surfaces and hung down from projecting stones above their heads, dropping in layers toward the ground. In a few places, water trickled from draining pools somewhere higher, perhaps on the plateau above.

"Looks like we're climbing," Dona said briefly. "No way we can fit through there." She nodded toward a narrow slit beyond which they could hear waves crashing against the shore.

It was fairly easy at first, at least compared to their frantic scramble up the ravine. The hillside was as porous as the inside of a sponge, providing not only a number of ways to move steadily upward, but also intermittent concealment from anyone approaching from below. They were able to peer down from time to time and locate the others, yellow obviously struggling to keep up, gray moving much more easily. Avery kept an eye open for anything he could use as a makeshift missile, but the cliffs were sedimentary stone that crumbled rather than fractured, and what loose stone existed was too small and sandy to be useful.

Fighting exhaustion, Avery and Tharmody continued to climb, occasionally backtracking when they ran into dead ends or ledges so narrow they didn't dare risk using them. Fortunately, where the pockmarked cliff itself didn't hide them, the hanging moss did, and by the time they were forced to risk exposing themselves, gray and yellow were both inside the lower convolutions of the cliff and could not see them.

They were staggering when they finally emerged into full sunlight, on what they at first thought was the summit. It was a cruel disappointment to realize they were instead on a lower ledge, although a large one, roughly oval shaped. The area ahead of them was ringed with sheer walls that looked to be virtually unscalable. The ledge itself consisted of broken, but fairly clear ground on the exposed side, facing the ocean. Irregular mounds of broken rock marked the spreading collapse of the cliff side, dotting the ledge with piles of crumbling rubble.

Avery nearly wept with fatigue and frustration. "Wasn't this a lot shorter on the way down?"

"Wisecracks are my job. You're supposed to provide the serious suggestions."

He looked around, saw lots of rock, a few plants, nothing promising. He moved to the lip of the cliff and stared down. He could hear movement, but saw nothing. The broken stone offered plenty of ammunition now, but he lacked a target. "Can't even drop rocks on them," he complained testily.

"We could jump off and deprive them of the satisfaction of killing us."

"I'll take that under advisement. Come on, there has to be a way up." But the closer they got, the lower their hopes slumped. The impregnability of the cliff ahead was so complete that it seemed artificial.

"Maybe we can sneak down past them somehow?" Dona didn't sound particularly optimistic.

Avery suddenly had a thought. "I have an idea. It's not much of one, but it'll have to do."

When gray and yellow reached the rocky shelf, they moved boldly, clearly confident that their quarry carried no weapons. From his hiding place in the shelter of a small knob of splintered stone, Avery watched closely, trying to anticipate which way the twosome would move next. He was delighted to see that yellow, the taller of the two, was in evident pain, even sat briefly on a flat piece of rock to massage an injured ankle. They were close enough for him to have seen their faces if they hadn't worn privacy hoods. Judging by their body mass, both were probably men. One wore his hair in a short braid and the other was completely bald.

Gray started toward the cliff wall, obviously assuming that Avery and Tharmody had taken cover within the piles of debris around its base, but yellow called out for him to wait, and they had a brief conference in voices too low for Avery to eavesdrop. He felt an annoying cramp in his right thigh, but didn't dare shift position, fearing he might dislodge a stone and give away his location. The two voices became more animated as they disagreed about how to proceed. A sudden gust of wind disturbed the loose sand, creating tiny whirlwinds that died down after a few seconds.

The respite didn't last long. One or the other prevailed

and they were in motion again, moving in a direction that would bring them quite close to the pile of rocks behind which Avery crouched. He couldn't delay any longer, gathered his courage and rose, his arm moving in a short arc as he launched a fist-sized stone directly toward gray's head, dropping back quickly to grab the next from his small pile of ammunition.

There was a shout but no answering fire and he edged carefully to a new position, then popped up suddenly. As he cocked his arm he spotted Tharmody emerging from cover, tossing a missile of her own before dropping back out of sight. Yellow raised his weapon, an ugly looking military style flechette pistol, waiting for her to show herself again, while gray stood to one side, rubbing his shoulder. Avery threw another stone, crouched and rolled, rearmed himself and stood up.

Gray raised his weapon and fired while yellow danced back to avoid Tharmody's throw, jostling his partner's arm. The stream of tiny projectiles went wide of their mark. Avery's aim was improving and yellow had to move so quickly to avoid being struck in the face that he lost his footing and went sprawling for the second time that day. Almost at the same moment, Tharmody launched another missile that struck gray squarely on the side of his head. He twisted and fell to one side, his arms windmilling ineffectually for balance, and his head struck an abutting rock with an audible thud.

Avery crouched and took a stone in each hand, then stood up warily, just in time to see yellow fire at Tharmody. Desperately, he threw with both arms but his aim was off and in any case his efforts would have been too late. Dona raised both hands to her head and fell backward. Enraged and dismayed, Avery reached for fresh ammunition but lost his own balance and fell, scrambling frantically for purchase, and only managing to make things worse. He was barely able to throw his arms in front of his face before the ground came up and hit him hard in the ribs, driving the air from his lungs.

Although he never actually lost consciousness, a few minutes passed before Avery took interest in anything except the effort to breathe. The image of yellow stalking him with a raised weapon finally provided enough incentive for him to make an effort to rise. It was utter agony when he finally found the strength to roll over, then rise to hands and knees. A little voice at the back of his head was screaming that he needed to move faster or he'd be dead, but his implants were trying to calm him down and that just made him more lethargic.

It was very quiet, he realized. He could hear the wind, the distant sound of surf, and his own madly beating heart. It was a point of some interest that he was still alive, and he wondered if that last desperate throw had somehow disabled the man in yellow. He emerged from cover cautiously and saw only the prone body of the gray man Tharmody had felled, his broken skull lying in a pool of blood which had already begun to dry. Her throw hadn't killed him, at least not directly. He'd fallen against a spur of jagged rock that had struck him in the temple.

The other man had disappeared as though he had never existed.

Although he dreaded what he might find, Avery worked his way around to where Dona had been hiding. She was lying on her back, one arm thrown across her face, and the ground and surrounding rocks were also stained with blood. He was convinced that she was dead, but when he approached more closely, saw that she was still breathing.

Gently, he lifted her arm and examined the bloody wound, was relieved to find that it was a shallow but ugly furrow across her scalp. She'd been hit by at least three flechettes, one of which was still embedded in her flesh, although it had entered at a shallow angle. Although his shirt was torn and dirty, he made a makeshift bandage, held it pressed closely against her head until he was sure that clotting blood had stanched the worst of the flow.

He shifted her to what he hoped was a more comfortable position out of the direct sunlight, then cautiously returned to the corpse. It was the second he'd touched in recent days, but this time he felt no sympathy for the dead. Avery crouched and removed the privacy hood, examined what was left of the man's face. He was a complete stranger and was of a racial type with which Avery wasn't familiar. Certainly not a Havener. Suppressing his distaste for the task, he went through the man's pockets, finding nothing except a spare clip for a flechette pistol. That inspired him to look for the fallen man's weapon, but it was nowhere to be found.

Nor was there any sign at all of the man in yellow. He had vanished as completely as had Kurt Royce.

He returned to Dona, who seemed to be breathing somewhat more easily, although she was still unconscious. Avery had no idea what to do next. Even if he could somehow manage to carry her back down the cliff and up one of the trails, which was unlikely in itself, he was afraid that he would do her further injury in the process. The sheer walls that surrounded them offered no hope of an easier escape. Just moving her limp form to a flatter stretch of ground took several minutes, and he abandoned any plan to carry her further. The most sensible course of action was probably to make the climb by himself, call for help from the lifter, then wait to guide rescuers back to the scene. But what if the missing assassin was lying in wait somewhere below? And for that matter, if Damien and/or his friends had decided that it was time to dispose of a minor but irritating risk, whoever answered the distress call might be less than friendly.

He was still trying to decide what to do when a lifter roared past the summit directly overhead and turned east. Almost immediately a second, much louder one followed a nearly identical path, and Avery recognized the unmistakable signature of Hanifer's maladjusted vehicle even before he spotted the security insignia on the side. Was Hanifer involved in the attack?

From the distance, a hollow boom coincided with a puff of oily black smoke and a flash so short-lived it hardly registered. The security ship jerked to one side as its defenses detonated the incoming missile, then spun into a spiraling dive to the left, leveled off, and shot up from below. The lead ship cut right in a desperate attempt to evade the attack, but the heavier armament of the security ship overwhelmed it easily. A fusillade of small projectiles struck the smaller craft, which swerved seaward, smoke pouring out of its rear quarter, then dropped its nose and fell so quickly it might almost have been an intentional dive. There was a spew of foam at the point of impact, which fell back onto an unblemished patch of open water. The security lifter hovered over the spot for a moment or two, then slowly began to turn, running parallel to the shoreline.

Avery felt that he should make some attempt to find cover. He and Dona were out in the open and couldn't possibly be missed by an overflight. But he was tired of running and unwilling to leave Dona. He made no effort to attract attention, but sat quietly cradling her head while the lifter approached, hovered briefly overhead, then dropped cautiously onto the only part of the ledge clear enough and wide enough, just barely, to accommodate the craft.

As he had expected, Lydia Hanifer jumped down from the pilot's seat, and came briskly toward him. She had a weapon on her hip but none in her hands.

"Mr. Avery, are you all right?" She sounded genuinely concerned, to his surprise, and squatted down to examine Dona. When she reached toward the unconscious woman's bandaged head, he instinctively raised his own arm to ward her off.

She let her arm fall back. "I have a medkit with me. Wait while I get it." She displayed neither surprise nor anger at his interference.

Avery still didn't trust her, but he relaxed slightly when she returned carrying a large medical bag, though he watched closely while she replaced his makeshift bandage with a more professional pressure pack. "Painkiller and parabiotics," she explained, firing a pressure injection into the side of Dona's neck. "We can store the rear seats in the cargo area so we can lay her down comfortably. Would you give me a hand moving them?"

Avery stirred himself to help her, finally breaking his silence. "Who were they? The men who attacked us."

"They? I only saw one person." She sounded honestly surprised. "He ignored my order to identify himself and had an illegal missile launcher mounted on his vehicle. I would really like to know what has been going on here, and since I'm obviously not going to be able to question the man who fired at me, I hope you'll help clear up the situation." Her tone had grown more serious and demanding.

"There's another one lying over behind those rocks." He gestured vaguely. "Dead. They were trying to kill us."

Hanifer glanced in the direction indicated, then back, and he noticed a change in her expression. "You're a man of many surprises, Mr. Avery. I would not have thought you capable of taking another life."

"It was luck rather than skill," he admitted. "But we were pretty desperate." He refrained from telling Hanifer that it was Tharmody who had killed gray. "So, you have no idea who they were?"

"I was hoping that you could tell me. Why would someone go to such great effort to kill you? Have you been making a habit of interfering in other people's affairs?"

His head was starting to hurt despite the implants and he wanted very much to lie down and close his eyes for a while. This was all becoming very confused. Hanifer was one of Damien's people, yet she had just killed one of their assailants. To cover up the botched attempt perhaps? That made no sense. She was in a perfect position to make sure that it succeeded, could even have dumped their bodies so far out to sea that they'd never be found. For that matter, why had yellow not finished off both Avery and Tharmody when he had the chance? Why retreat at the point of victory? Something was not making sense here.

"I don't understand any of this," he admitted wearily. Then one thought did occur to him. "Why were you following us if you didn't know we were in trouble? Do you routinely check up on tourists who go rock climbing?" Or just the ones who know you're an accessory to murder, he added silently.

"As a matter of fact, I had no idea you were anywhere in the area until a short while ago. A geological survey team spotted a lifter traveling in this direction earlier today, a lifter which crossed one of their test sites despite the warning markers and cost them several hours' work. One of the team members wrote down the serial number on its tail, which coincided with that of a similar vehicle, which was stolen from a storage garage in Park City yesterday. Its homing beacon had been disabled and it wasn't responding to recall transmissions. That is why I was in the vicinity. I found the lifter not far from here, parked beside a second vehicle, which to my considerable surprise had been rented by you."

"But why were they trying to kill us?" Avery shook his head, more confused than ever. "They attacked from ambush. We had nothing worth stealing, and I've never seen either of them before."

Hanifer's face was professionally calm and serious. "That's an excellent question which we will have to discuss in more detail later. But first, I suggest we get the young lady more skilled medical attention than I can provide."

Avery fell into a doze in his seat as they flew back to Haven, his body reacting to the excessive medications administered by his implants during the past few hours. Hanifer assured him that a recall order would be broadcast to retrieve the rented lifter.

He didn't waken until they were settling to the ground. A medical team immediately eased Tharmody's inert form out of the rear compartment. Avery hastily climbed down and attempted to go to her side, but he was deflected by Hanifer who stepped forward to intercept him.

"She's in good hands and I don't think there's any real danger. I'll need a statement from you for my report."

"It'll have to wait." He tried to brush past her but she caught his forearm.

"There's nothing you can do now. No further harm will come to her; you have my word."

Avery didn't flinch, pulled his arm free with a steady

pressure. "No offense, but I'm not taking anyone's word for anything until I have some answers. I'll be happy to tell you what happened today, if you really care to hear it, but only after I know that Dona's all right."

For a second, Hanifer seemed ready to argue the point, but she relaxed slightly and nodded. "Very well. Under the circumstances, I'll await your convenience. Please don't put it off any longer than is necessary. You might forget some detail of importance."

Haven's aid station might not be state of the art, but it was more than adequate to deal with what proved not to be life-threatening damage. "The damage is mostly superficial and she'll make a full recovery," the technician advised him, "but she's going to wake up with a pretty bad headache. We'll keep her overnight because there's a chance she suffered a concussion, but I think you'll find her up and around in the morning."

Relieved, Avery almost collapsed on his way to the security office. He sat on a bench in a small park until he felt more in control, then went to see Hanifer in a somewhat improved state of mind.

The security office was surprisingly small, with most of the rear three quarters of the building blocked off by opaque walls and a single, reinforced door. Hanifer was sitting at a data console, and she blanked the screen with a gesture as soon as she saw him.

"Please make yourself comfortable." She indicated a seat near her own. "How is your friend?"

"She'll be okay. What do you want from me? I need to bathe and change clothes." He didn't sit down.

Hanifer sighed, drummed her fingers against the keypad of the console. "Mr. Avery, I know that you feel you've been treated badly since you've been here . . ."

"Now there's an understatement," he interrupted.

". . . and I'll admit to you frankly that you're justified in your resentment. But I have two deaths to explain, an injured woman under medical care, a stolen lifter destroyed, what appears to have been a double murder attempt by persons unknown and now deceased, and who knows what other complications." She slammed her hand palm down on the desk, and her face hardened. "Whatever you may think of me personally, I am responsible for the administration of security in Haven and its environs and I take those responsibilities very seriously. Now would you please sit down and allow me to record your statement?"

It was an order, not a request, and Avery acquiesced, still resentful but cooperative when Hanifer turned on the holographic recorder and asked him to give a chronological narration of what happened, starting from the moment they left Haven. He did so, remembering his own brief sighting of a lifter near their route, relating everything as objectively and in as much detail as he could remember. When he was done, Hanifer hesitated a moment, then asked him a few details about the events on the plateau.

"And you have no idea why the second man didn't kill you while you lay stunned?"

"None whatsoever." It had bothered him then and it bothered him now. "Maybe when we killed his friend, we spooked him. Have you identified them yet?"

Her voice and face were expressionless. "We've recovered and identified the body of the man you killed. He's a former Intercorp security guard, fired for misconduct. A salvage team is still trying to find the other body but the currents are very strong along that stretch of coast. Earlier you said that they avoided firing at you on at least two occasions when you were exposed?"

He nodded. "But when they first spotted us, they nearly killed Dona. It was only luck that she escaped. Twice in fact. The burst that finally hit her might easily have killed her." He felt a flash of anger.

"But they didn't fire at the two of you when you were together in the ravine?"

Avery thought about it and suddenly understood what Hanifer was getting at. "Are you suggesting that they were after Dona and not me? That it was just a coincidence that I was there? There have been too many damned coincidences around here lately, if that's what you're implying."

"If that were the case, they would have fired at both of you indiscriminately, not just at her. This wasn't a chance encounter. These men followed the two of you, they had a specific mission in mind, and it seems to have involved the death of your companion, but significantly, it also appears that they were being very careful not to kill you."

He was still silently puzzling that out in his mind when Hanifer turned off the recorder, asked to be excused for a moment, and disappeared through the heavy door into another room. When she returned, he started to ask a question, but she waved it aside.

"I've just spoken to Senator Damien, who would like very much to talk to you about this incident. If you're willing, I'll fly you to where he's presently staying."

Although he was mildly surprised to learn that the Senator was still on Meadow, Avery's first impulse was to refuse, but then he realized this might be the break for which he had been waiting. "All right, but only if you take me home first. I always feel at a disadvantage when I'm filthy." Hanifer sighed, but didn't argue with him.

The cottage to which they flew later that afternoon was

set in the center of a broad forested area on the east side of Haven. It was larger than most of those allotted to tourists, and was flanked by two landing areas, one of which held a late-model private lifter. The building was well maintained but obviously not of recent construction. This was particularly interesting since he was virtually certain that it had not appeared on the survey he'd viewed only a few days previously. He knew theoretically how easy it would be to edit the recording and conceal its existence, but it had never occurred to him that the information contained in government archives might be corrupt. In retrospect, he was surprised at how naive he'd been.

Damien greeted him at the door, dressed casually, his voice warm but his eyes alert and probing. "Come inside, please. We have a great deal to talk about." He nodded familiarly to Hanifer, who did not follow as they entered.

The interior was decorated in a surprisingly simple fashion, most of the furniture static, some apparently handmade, judging by its irregularities. The walls were covered with still paintings, primarily landscapes, and Avery had the distinct impression that these were original pieces of art, probably very old. The only anachronistic item was an exceptionally large data console and communications terminal, with a display that indicated it had direct offworld capability. From here, Damien could communicate with orbiting ships, perhaps even nearby star systems, without boosting his signal through the main complex in Park City.

"Can I offer you something to drink?"

Avery declined, but accepted the offer of a chair. The shower had been refreshing, but his calves and feet were still sore. "I'm told you wanted to see me?"

Damien nodded, settled into another seat and crossed

his legs. "Your experiences today were distressing, but potentially enlightening."

"You know what happened then?"

"I've seen the report you made to Lydia."

Avery felt mild indignation. "I thought security reports were confidential."

"They are. Only government officials can review them. As it happens, I'm an officer of the government and have access. Meadow is still a ward of the Concourse, ruled more or less directly by the Senate through its various agents, primarily the governor, of course, but any Senator or Delegate has quasi-legal authority here."

"I don't suppose you have an explanation for what happened?"

"Not exactly, not yet, although I think I have a pretty good idea. You and Dona have not abandoned your investigation, I take it?"

Avery stared levelly into Damien's eyes, neither confirming nor denying the charge.

"It's self-evident, actually. It would appear that you have somehow managed to convince someone that I am vulnerable, and unfortunately they tried to use you as leverage against me. We've identified the man whose body was retrieved from the cliffs. His name is Edvarik Thrombold, nominally a citizen of Bullpen, who arrived on Meadow several days ago in the company of another man, Luther Tchuka, a native Meadower who spends much of his time elsewhere. Both men are former Intercorp employees, and both are currently employed by a subsidiary of Intercorp as project expediters, which is often a euphemism used to cover unorthodox or even illegal activities."

Avery made no effort to disguise his confusion. "How is Intercorp involved in this?"

"That is something I was hoping you could tell me. I had been assuming that your story was sufficiently vague and uncorroborated that no one would take you seriously even if you found someone willing to listen. Obviously, I was wrong. My guess is that this unknown party believes you know even more than you've let on, and the attempt on Dona's life was designed to frighten you either into going public or at a minimum into revealing more than you have already. Very few people have been involved enough to realize both how much and how little information you possess, but there are issues here that might convince the less scrupulous to sacrifice a few lives if they thought it would prove helpful to their cause."

The casual condescension angered Avery. "You don't seem to suffer from an excess of scruples yourself, Senator. And perhaps I know more than you think I do."

Damien flushed but his voice remained calm. "Or perhaps you think you have more knowledge than is in fact the case. An active imagination is no doubt a valuable tool while creating virtual dramas, but often a source of frustration and wasted effort in the real world."

Avery leaned forward aggressively, never suspecting that the provocation might be deliberate. "You haven't kept us entirely in the dark, Senator. I know the name of the dead man now." He settled back, waiting for Damien to react.

The Senator smiled humorlessly. "Do you indeed?"

"His name was Kurt Royce," Avery said evenly. "An occasional acquaintance of yours, I believe."

Damien nodded and his smile didn't slip, but he did stand up, clasp his hands behind his back, and begin pacing the room. "Interesting. I assume that information came from Charles Laszlow? Don't bother to deny it; he's the only man on Meadow with the motive and resources to acquire such information, and I remember now that Dona mentioned knowing him."

Avery was concerned that he might have let too much slip, cursed himself for being so quick to speak without thinking. Damien was still pacing thoughtfully and, after a few seconds, he spoke again, his voice as calm as before.

"I admit that you've proven more resourceful than I expected, but you're mistaken about the identity of the murdered man. He wasn't Kurt Royce, although he was traveling under that name at the time. It was only one of several identities he's used."

Feeling completely out of his depth, Avery abandoned caution. "All right, then who was he? Why was he here? And why was he killed?"

Damien sighed. "I'm beginning to believe you'll keep asking those questions until you get an acceptable answer. I admire your tenacity, if not your judgment. All right then, the man who identified himself as Kurt Royce was on Meadow specifically to make life difficult for me. He hoped to fatally damage the initiative to place the Nerudi in a protectorate status, and he was killed more or less because of that fact."

"But not by your hand, you said."

"Not directly, no, but I am still responsible. It was done in my name, to protect me."

"Then who was he really?" Avery was dismayed to hear a plaintive note in his voice, but he had to know the answer. "Whose body did I find in that clearing?"

Damien hesitated only a second before answering. "Why, it was the real Karl Damien, of course."

Chapter Fourteen

❋ ❋ ❋

Avery stood with his mouth open, unable to think of anything to say. Damien ignored him and continued as though he hadn't said anything out of the ordinary.

"My advisors would be quite distressed to hear of this conversation, but frankly I'm tired of all the subterfuge, and once this Nerudi business is over and done with, one way or the other, I think it's going to be time for me to retire from public life." His voice was suddenly filled with strain. "What I've told you has been a closely held secret for a long time."

"You know I won't be satisfied until I have the whole story," he said slowly.

"No, I wouldn't expect you to. I'm going to follow my instincts for a change and tell you the truth. Or most of it anyway. I warn you that you'll be accepting some heavy responsibility if you agree to hear me out."

Avery thought about it. "I can't promise not to pursue the matter further. You can't buy my silence with information. You'll have to convince me."

"Fair enough. I have to start a good long time ago." Damien began to pace.

"Nguyen Minh and Gretta Damien, my parents, were rarities among their kind. Sexual and familial liaisons among the mercantile empires are almost always plotted cold-bloodedly. They're tactical maneuvers, temporary or permanent alliances to secure trading advantages or new sources of credit. They're almost invariably fueled by politics rather than emotion. My parents scandalized their families and their associates by falling in love, and deciding to marry against the recommendations of their respective staffs. Fortunately, Gretta was a financial genius. She diversified their combined investments until they were no longer dependent upon the financial health of a single cartel, controlling instead significant minority holdings in so many different organizations that only their AIs knew the true extent of their fortune. Once their personal independence was secured, Nguyen and Gretta decided to have a child.

"Karl Damien was born on Callipygia Prime slightly more than fifty standard years ago, a fairly easy birth, following a rigorously monitored pregnancy. The infant was everything his parents could have asked for: a potential leader, highly intelligent, no physical defects, no genetic flaws."

"Wasn't there some kind of disaster on Callipygia? The name's familiar."

Damien nodded. "A solar collection satellite was damaged by a stray meteorite that also took out the emergency self-destruct unit. The backup system kicked in, but not before the capital city took a direct hit from a focused beam. Twenty thousand dead and three times that many injured, including Karl Damien and his parents. Nguyen's injuries were superficial. Karl and his mother weren't as lucky. They saved her life, although she lost the use of both legs and had to wear a prosthetic sheath for the rest of her life. She was also rendered physically incapable of bearing another child, even ex utero, and suffered bouts of deep depression until the day she died.

"Karl's injuries were both more and less serious. His skull was fractured and he lost both eyes, but those injuries could be repaired with implants and fusion surgery. Unfortunately, there was also damage to the brain and it was initially considered unlikely that Karl would ever regain consciousness. Nguyen waited while Gretta underwent a lengthy period of treatment and rehabilitation before breaking the news. After the initial shock had worn off, she calmly announced what she intended to do, and would listen to no arguments to the contrary. Karl was the only child that would ever be born of her body and Gretta was not willing to accept his loss. If Karl's body and mind could never be normal, he would survive in another fashion." He paused, as though considering whether or not to continue. "She had him cloned, and the clone was raised in his place, while Karl was moved to a secret facility devoted to his care. I am that clone. The trauma to his head resulted in significant changes to his physical appearance or we'd have been identical."

It took Avery a few seconds before he was able to speak. "Obviously the situation changed. Damien, the original Damien, made some kind of miraculous recovery."

Damien nodded. "Our parents arranged for the most advanced treatment possible and during his sixth year, he regained consciousness, although he remained paralyzed. Nerve replacement therapy restored his ability to speak and eventually provided limited mobility. Once he was conscious, it was much easier to repair the remaining physical damage, put the machine of his body back into working order. It was not so easy to restore his mind.

"As you might expect, my brother's personality was abnormal. He was not told his true identity, but rather that he was the only child of a couple who had perished in the same disaster that injured him. Evan and Luwanda Royce really existed, although they were childless when they died. My mother wanted to acknowledge her true son, but my father was more cautious. When the original Damien's mental problems began to surface—fits of irrational petulance, violent mood swings, occasional convulsions—he persuaded her to continue the masquerade. Eventually they disengaged themselves emotionally, devoted their efforts to my upbringing with an almost manic fervor. I think in Mother's case, it was guilt rather than affection that drove her, and the chronic depression that eventually killed her was almost certainly related. I wasn't told the truth about the original Karl Damien until much later, shortly before my mother's death in fact. She explained everything then and made me promise that I would carry on with the family obligation, never realizing that I might be unwise enough to tell my brother the truth."

"That must have been a difficult conversation."

"The first of many. If I had stopped to think, I might have realized I was not acting rationally, that the discovery that I was a clone and not what I'd thought myself to be had distorted my judgment. I went to see him almost immediately following her death, ignored the doctors and their psychological profiles and behavioral projections and insisted on meeting my brother. Before the day was through, I had told him everything and set the wheels in motion to liberate him from what seemed to me a virtual prison." He stopped pacing and clenched both hands behind his neck.

"I didn't realize how badly I had blundered for a long time. After arranging for Karl to have access to a significant part of the family fortune, I threw myself into politics. I suppose that it was dishonest of me not to reveal that I was not born through conventional means, but I'm sure you know that the unreasoning prejudice against clones would have ended my career before it had started, and I believe I've done more good than harm. Free of restraints and with considerable wealth at his disposal, Kurt traveled extensively, eventually leaving the Concourse entirely."

"But he came back."

"More than once, as a matter of fact. On the first occasion, he was in a state of near collapse. He accosted me in the street, disheveled and drawn, shouting obscenities at the top of his voice, accusing me of so many patently absurd crimes that no one paid any attention to his claims that I was a clone. I arranged for him to be confined and treated, and three years passed before he was a free man again. I was advised against allowing him to leave, but I still felt a degree of obligation to him which I cannot begin to describe. It probably would have been better if he'd remained institutionalized for the rest of his life, but I insisted he be given his freedom and regrets cannot change things now. He agreed to remain silent about his true identity, and as far as I know, he has never told anyone. Or at least he hadn't before this last visit to Meadow."

"Royce was blackmailing you." As soon as he spoke, Avery was struck by the absurdity of it. Damien had already given Royce more money than he could spend. Why would he attempt to extort more?

"That's what Charles Laszlow hinted, I suppose. He's a man of many surprises; I often wish he were my ally instead of my opponent. He's a brilliant tactician, but unscrupulous and so caught up in his own pursuits that he often loses his perspective. What he told you was basically true, but Karl wasn't blackmailing me. Why should he? He had virtually unlimited resources, no obligations. The only thing I couldn't give him was my reputation. When Kurt's mind was stable, he was calm and reasonable, but occasionally he'd lapse into extended introspective periods during which he would become hostile, sometimes violent. During those periods, he would fix upon me as his enemy, as the person who had deprived him of his birthright, and he would come looking for me. The moods were frequently short-lived and he would recover long before he was in a position to cause a scandal. But not always. On one occasion, he arrived in a particularly foul mood just as I was in the midst of a rather bitter and close fought re-election campaign. Any hint of the truth would have shifted the balance. In a moment of weakness, I had Karl subdued and transported to one of the border worlds where he was safely out of the way until after the election. By then, his fit of fury had passed and he couldn't even remember how he'd gotten there or what his intentions had been."

"But he still wasn't cured?"

"No. Just two standard years ago there was another incident, although it came at a less critical time. Karl was waiting for me when I arrived at my house on Ozymandias. Outwardly at least he seemed more in control of himself, but the festering hatred was barely concealed. I was tempted to have him locked away permanently, but I was also weary of the entire business. He threatened to return when the time was right and destroy me, my career anyway. Then he left and I never saw him again."

"He came to Meadow looking for you, though."

"Yes. Yes, he did. But he never found me. I wasn't available, so he paid a few bribes and discovered a few holes in my personal security system. Among other things, he learned the reason I spend so much time in Haven."

"Which is . . . ?"

"Which is irrelevant just now. You'll have to allow me a few personal secrets. I give you my word, my reasons for visiting here are and always have been honorable."

Avery hesitated, then accepted the statement, at least conditionally. "All right. Go on."

"Kurt acquired a lifter and came looking for me. Somehow he had learned of one of my indiscretions, and arranged a meeting during which he made some threats to a person close to me. The individual concerned was alarmed, decided to do whatever was necessary to protect my reputation, and most of the rest you already know."

"How much of this could be proved if it were made public?"

"Enough to cause a stir, probably not enough to destroy me if I denied everything. But I won't deny it. I'll do my best to shield my friend, even if that means accepting responsibility myself. This has all forced me to shift resources from important issues in order to maintain a shield around myself and others, and I'm frankly weary of it all. I won't help you to destroy me and my work, but neither will I oppose you in this matter any longer."

The conversation had not been at all what Avery expected, and he wasn't sure that he was satisfied. It was still possible that Damien was a superb liar with a quick mind, but he had sounded sincere.

"There's one thing I still don't understand."

"And that is . . . ?"

"Who tried to kill us today, or at least tried to kill Dona? If Intercorp is involved, even at second hand, how did they find out about all this and what's their agenda?"

Damien's face expressed surprise. "Aren't you being a bit naive? It was Charles Laszlow, of course. He's the primary agent for Intercorp on Meadow."

Avery blinked. "But Laszlow doesn't work for Intercorp. He resigned under a cloud according to . . ." His voice trailed off.

"You're beginning to see the light, I gather. Intercorp sponsors a number of unofficial employees, including the men who attacked you. Laszlow's resignation was a sham designed to conceal a covert operation to reclaim Meadow for the company. Intercorp wouldn't have invested so much credit to oppose the Nerudi Protection Initiative if they didn't expect a lucrative return somewhere down the line."

"But how will that help them? If they win and the Nerudi become full citizens, they'll have the same rights as humans on Meadow."

"Granted, but the Nerudi aren't human, and their culture is not designed to work in tandem with the laws of the Concourse. They conform to certain compulsory behavior patterns that put them at a distinct disadvantage. The exchange of gifts, for example, is analogous to a religious rite. It's an absolute obligation."

"I know a bit about that." Avery summarized what Laszlow had told him, that each gift required a complementary one and that no gift could ever be abandoned.

"That's essentially correct," Damien admitted. "We don't yet understand how they measure relative values, of course. The worth of certain objects seems to fluctuate while others remain fixed, and sometimes the context in which the exchange is made adds another variable. We're being very tentative in our approaches to the Nerudi, because we don't want to traumatize their culture more than necessary. But there is at least one physical property in their world whose value is always the same, because it has no value at all. Land."

"Laszlow mentioned that the Nerudi don't recognize ownership of real estate."

"That's right, because you can't take it with you. The soil itself may have value, I suppose, but the physical coordinates of a place, the space, is valueless because it's owned in common by everyone."

A few puzzle pieces were beginning to fall into place, and Avery chose his next question very carefully. "What happens if a new gift is introduced into the system? How does its value get measured?"

"Very astute. I think we have underestimated you, Laszlow as well as myself. We don't know the exact answer to that question, but we think Intercorp has a better idea than we do. They were studying the Nerudi for generations before the Senate asserted its authority, and while in theory all of their records were turned over to us, there are suggestive gaps in some of the documentation. We do know that the person who introduces the concept of a new gift has a lot to say in the assignment of its value. If a craftsman or inventor develops something unprecedented, I imagine they're in the best position to estimate how much effort was involved in its creation."

"So Intercorp could introduce some innocuous and not particularly valuable item into the Nerudi economy."

Damien nodded. "They've apparently decided that it would be possible to convince Nerudi to accept the possibility of exchanging land. Given a free hand, they could literally buy the entire planet."

"But wouldn't there be a terrific scandal once word leaked out?"

"Oh yes. There'd be an uproar and even a chance that the deal would ultimately be reversed, although I suspect Intercorp could drag out the proceedings for long enough to make back their investment many times over. Destroying the Nerudi in the process, of course. If they didn't die out, they'd be forced to adapt, and their culture would never recover."

"And as a protectorate?"

"Legally they'd be a sovereign nation, except that all of their dealings with offworlders and local humans would be monitored by a government agency. Hopefully we will eventually be able to work out some way that the two species can interact more directly, but at their present state of development, contact would be minimized and carefully controlled."

"All right, I believe you." Avery felt a great surge of relief. "And I won't betray you either. I can't say I'm happy about helping cover up a murder, but given the facts as I know them, the alternative is worse. So where does that leave us?"

Damien also seemed relieved. "I'm leaving tomorrow to prepare for the next session of the Senate. We're ready to bring the Nerudi question to a vote, and it looks like we have enough support to carry the measure."

"But what about Laszlow?"

"He'll sputter and fume when his side loses, but he's a pragmatist. Once it's obvious he can't make his career, or a personal fortune, at the expense of the Nerudi, he'll lose all interest in them and Meadow and move on. Intercorp may take him back officially, or they may be disappointed enough to make his feigned departure into a real one. I entertain hopes of the latter."

"But what about those two killers he sent after us? Can't you have him arrested? You said you knew he was responsible."

"Knowing and proving aren't the same thing. But I do

think it prudent that we do something to protect the two of you. I doubt he'll try again, but if he realizes how far into the corner he's been pushed, he might become desperate enough to do something foolish."

"So what do you suggest? Armed guards? Protective custody?"

"Nothing so extreme. With your permission, I propose that my staff announce publicly that Wes Avery, prominent virtual dramatist, has taken a temporary consulting position on the personal staff of Senator Karl Damien. I'd suggest the same for Dona, but she already has an employment contract."

"I don't understand how that will help."

"Laszlow is an intelligent man. He'll interpret that as meaning you've come over to our side, that we've convinced you your best interests include a change of allegiance. Most likely he'll think we bribed you. But I also suggest that you remain in Haven for the duration of your stay on Meadow, or at least until after the Senate has acted. Lydia has a direct feed from here," he gestured toward the elaborate data console, "and now that we're forewarned, we can keep close track of anyone approaching the village. If Laszlow sends a backup team, we'll know about it well in advance."

They talked for a while longer, but Avery could tell that the Senator was distracted and allowed himself to be dismissed. There was so much to think about that he wanted time to digest it all. Hanifer silently brought him back to his own cottage, and left him with a glance that might almost have been friendly. He called to check on Dona, but she'd just been given a sedative. He, on the other hand, needed nothing artificial to aid him in falling asleep.

* * * * *

The following morning, Dona was feeling well enough to demand that he come see her and explain just how they had managed to stay alive. "The medtechs keep telling me not to worry about it and stay calm, but how can I stay calm until I know?" Avery pulled himself together and did as she requested, and once he was certain they were alone, repeated as much of his conversation with Damien as he could remember. Dona shook her head in obvious shock when Laszlow was implicated, but eventually admitted that she believed Damien's version of events.

"I suppose I shouldn't be surprised. Charles always was a bit cold-blooded. He was good company when we first met; we disagreed about a lot of issues but he never seemed to take them personally. Now I guess that's because he didn't really care about anything that didn't affect him personally. Too bad; he's a brilliant guy."

Six days later, Dona returned to Park City and her job, the same day the Executive Council of the Concourse Senate voted by a comfortable margin to award protectorate status to the Nerudi for a period to consist of no less than one hundred standard years, to be automatically renewed for a like period at that time unless there was compelling evidence supporting a change in their status.

The following day, Senator Karl Damien announced that at the end of his present term of office, he would be resigning his seat in the Senate in order to pursue undisclosed personal interests.

Chapter Fifteen

❋ ❋ ❋

Wes Avery did not leave Meadow several weeks later, as he had originally planned. When the lease on the cottage ran out, he moved to an apartment in Park City within walking distance of Dona's small house. The capital was in great turmoil. At the extremes, dire forebodings of doom about the future of humankind on Meadow stood in contrast to pious platitudes about the sanctity of alien cultures. The vast majority seemed happy that, with the Senate's decision to declare Meadow a protectorate, at least the ambiguous future had taken on some form. Avery and Dona noted the highly charged atmosphere, but were not directly affected. Neither of them would be around long enough to see any real changes on Meadow, and they were in any case too involved with each other to pay much attention. The next few weeks were among the happiest of their lives.

It was Avery who first realized there was something wrong, and Dona who spoke it aloud.

"You're thinking about leaving, aren't you? Meadow, I mean."

They were sitting on the rooftop balcony of his apartment building, which had been decorated in a not particularly accurate rendition of a coniferous forest. Avery hesitated for a second, then nodded his head. "It's time for me to go. I need to work again, Dona. What's happened to us here has given me an entirely new perspective. I want to develop it while it's fresh in my mind and in my senses, while I still have the edge."

"You have your equipment with you."

"What I have with me is a simple, portable recorder used to sketch in impressions and convert them into rough code. It doesn't have the capacity for an intricate, multi-layered artificial reality. You have meaningful things to do here, but all I can do is pretend to be doing serious work or wander around the city sightseeing. Maybe it's because I've been so close to death recently, but I'm constantly aware of how short life is and how much I'd like to achieve before it's over."

"There's a starliner due in three days."

"I know. You could come with me."

She shook her head immediately. "No, my contract doesn't end for almost another local year."

"I could buy it out. You could work for me. I've had a new studio built on Caliban and the house is much too large for a single person."

"There's no way I'm going to call you 'boss.' I like our relationship just as it is. On the other hand, I'd always planned to take an extended vacation when my contract ends and I've never been to Caliban. Do you think you'd be up to entertaining a long-term guest? Maybe I'll look around for a new job while I'm there."

Avery grinned and gave her what he hoped was a suggestive wink. "I think something might be arranged."

They spent as much of their remaining time together as possible, but there was no sense of desperation about it. Each felt confident that their friendship would survive the separation, and Avery was already thinking ahead to their new lives on Caliban. When their final morning together dawned, they said their goodbyes at her home and left separately, she to her assignment at the city's data facility, he for the spaceport.

His equipment and personal possessions had been sent ahead to be loaded aboard the shuttle before liftoff. Avery sat in the passenger lounge and reflected upon the changes he'd undergone since arriving here. Although he had no regrets about leaving Meadow behind, an important but no longer relevant part of his life, he knew that the course of his future had been altered here, that what he had learned through his experiences—primarily about himself—would change the way he dealt with his work, with other people, and with the universe at large. To say nothing of his relationship with Dona Tharmody.

Avery was in fact so caught up in his thoughts that the security guard was forced to address him twice before he realized he had company. He glanced up to see a man and a woman, both wearing the official security sash, their expressions carefully neutral.

"Excuse the interruption, Mr. Avery, but we must ask you to come with us." The man's voice was flat, emotionless.

Avery shifted in his seat but made no move to stand. There were a handful of other passengers scattered about the lounge, all of whom were pretending that they hadn't overheard anything while simultaneously listening to every word. "What's this all about?"

They exchanged looks and this time it was the woman who spoke. "I'm sure everything will be explained to you later. Our instructions are just to provide you with an escort."

"An escort to where?"

The man looked uncomfortable and more than slightly impatient, but the woman just shook her head. "We're not at liberty to tell you that, I'm afraid. It would really be much better if you just came along quietly and waited for an explanation from the appropriate authorities."

Briefly, Avery considered refusing, or at least asking what the consequences would be if he did refuse. After a short but intense inner struggle, he decided to cooperate, up to a point.

"I'm supposed to be leaving on the shuttle. Is this likely to force a change in my plans?"

"I'm afraid that information was not part of our instructions. We really don't know much more about this than you do."

He was skeptical, but short of attempting to physically elude or overcome two seasoned and probably armed security officers, Avery could see no real alternative to cooperation. "All right, I suppose there's nothing else to be done."

Although they made no attempt to physically restrain him, Avery noticed that they moved to strategic positions, the man slightly forward and to his right, the woman a half step behind to his left. He followed as they led him out of the lounge, back through the embarkation area, and through a sliding door marked "Authorized Personnel Only." Beyond was a featureless corridor lined with numbered doors.

They walked the length of the corridor in silence, then paused as the man pressed a sequence of icons on a secured doorway, presumably an entrance code. The barrier shushed obediently to one side and they continued, this time out into a large equipment bay, one wall of which was currently open to the landing field.

"If you'll take a seat, please." The woman was pointing

to a small, open-topped groundcar. Avery obediently climbed in and the man sat beside him, while the woman moved up front and entered a destination code.

Once outside the building, Avery craned his head and spotted two orbital shuttles sitting on well-maintained launch pads to his right. One was in the process of being fueled, presumably in anticipation of its imminent liftoff to rendezvous with the *Advent of Dawn*, on which he still hoped to travel to Nova Brasilia in time to catch a luxury liner back to Caliban. Cargo robots were moving around its base, placing baggage, supplies, and freight on liftpads for stowage. It would still be some time before passengers were allowed to board, and Avery wondered if he'd be returned in time. He was feeling a mild sense of alarm, but no panic. His capacity for panic had burned out some time ago.

At first he thought the shuttle was their destination; the groundcar's course only diverged by a few degrees. But as the distance narrowed, the gap widened, and they passed to the left of the slender ship without slowing. There was a line of enormous warehouses beyond the shuttles, storage depots for the once thriving export business. Most of these were empty now, he guessed; changes in supply and demand had reduced the planet's offworld agribusiness significantly.

They passed between two of the silent buildings, and emerged onto a broader landing field which had clearly not been maintained as well as the first. In the far right corner, the sleek shape of a shuttle, smaller but much more modern than the commercial craft, pointed challengingly at the sky. The groundcar turned in that direction.

"Is that where we're headed? The shuttle?"

The woman didn't turn her head and the man pointedly ignored the question, but the answer was obvious. They crossed the intervening distance quickly, and the groundcar stopped only a few meters from the passenger ramp. Avery stood up immediately but his two companions remained seated.

"This is as far as we go."

"Will you wait here until I return?"

"We have no further instructions regarding you. I'm sure arrangements have been made."

As he had more than half expected, Avery was greeted at the top of the ramp by Senator Karl Damien.

"Nice to see you again. Please excuse the cloak and dagger tactics, but I'm trying to keep knowledge of my presence on Meadow as narrowly held as possible."

"That hasn't been a problem for you in the past, but I understand your concern. I did hear about the assassination attempt."

"Very amateurish, and not nearly as dangerous as the comnet would have you believe." The two would-be assassins had been killed by Damien's bodyguards so quickly that they hadn't even fired a shot.

"I assume they were agents of Intercorp."

"No, not at all. Once the initiative had definitely passed, this was no longer an issue for them. An assassination attempt would have been an unnecessary expense, particularly given the announcement of my retirement. The possibility that they might have been implicated would have represented an unjustifiable financial risk. No, it appears to have been the work of a small group of intense but misguided individuals who still don't accept that the Nerudi are not human and that granting them citizenship at this point in their development would ultimately destroy them as a people."

Avery glanced around. He had followed Damien into a

surprisingly large room furnished with old style furniture that looked to be antique. "So why are you on Meadow this time, and why am I here?"

Damien laughed. "The answer to the first part of your question is that I am here on secret but official business, to consult with the local governor about implementation of the provisions of the initiative. As to the second part, well, I felt that under the circumstances, I owed you a favor, and since I'm due to lift off myself, I thought I might be allowed to ferry you up to the *Advent of Dawn*."

Avery thought about refusing. Although he'd ultimately decided that Damien was the lesser of two evils, he still resented the way he'd been treated and couldn't forget that Damien had used his prestige and personal power to conceal the murder of another human being. "I appreciate the gesture, but it's unnecessary. I'd be perfectly happy to take the commercial shuttle."

Damien nodded, to himself rather than his guest. "I rather thought that would be your reaction. I suppose if I were in your place, if I'd been chased by killers and threatened and generally treated as a nuisance, I might feel the same way."

It sounded petty and Avery hastily tried to correct the other man's impression. "That's not it at all, Senator. While I understand that there were issues involved which may have required extraordinary measures, the fact is that you have condoned, actually subverted, the law you supposedly represent. There's a murderer in Haven, after all, a murderer who goes unpunished because of your protection."

Damien sighed, but didn't deny the charge. "Tell me, would you? What is the purpose of law? Any law?"

Wary, Avery thought about his response before voicing

it. "To maintain order, to provide protection for citizens and institutions, to ensure that there's a system of justice."

"Ah, justice. You believe in justice then?"

"Of course."

"Laws are the creation of imperfect beings, and they are as circumscribed and limited as are the people who shape them. At best, they're a guideline for behavior, not an absolute. Surely you don't argue that every law is just, or that a just law is equally applicable in all circumstances?"

"Senator, I am willing to concede that you're a better debater than I am. But we're talking about murder here. I believe in the sanctity of intelligent life."

Damien's face changed and he suddenly looked much older. "Have you ever wondered why I spend so much time on Meadow, specifically in Haven?"

Avery had and he said so. "You've been criticized on the comnet for the amount of official time you've spent here, and they don't even know about the secret visits."

"You're very fond of Dona Tharmody, are you not?"

He was surprised at the sudden change of subject. "What does that have to do with any of this?"

"I have similar feelings for someone on Meadow, a Havener, a woman who has allowed me to escape the pressures, obligations, and frustrations of my life. If it were my choice, I'd acknowledge her part in my career immediately, and give her much of the credit for supporting me through some very trying times."

This wasn't at all what Avery had expected. "I don't understand. Why would you go to such great pains to conceal that? If anything, I would think it would help to make you seem more human, more accessible to your constituents I mean."

"I'm bowing to the wishes of the woman involved, whose

name must remain my secret. She's a Havener, through and through, refuses to leave her home, although I've offered to take her on a personal tour of the Concourse." His smile was tentative, self-deprecating. "I've long since given up trying to persuade her. It's been one of my rare personal defeats, a lesson in itself."

"But why keep it such a secret? Even if she did remain here in Haven?"

"Precisely because of that. One of the reasons I have my own starship is to enable me to travel without publicizing my movements. Even in quieter times, I am forced to employ a small army of public relations experts, bodyguards, and general staff workers to keep myself insulated from angry citizens, the comnet, interested private interests, even assassins and nut cases. If our relationship were known, she would lose her privacy, and it's quite possible that Haven itself would be permanently altered."

"All right, I can see that."

"When my brother, the man you think of as Kurt Royce, was unable to find me, he traveled to Haven because he knew that I spent a great deal of time there, wouldn't be likely to leave Meadow without paying a visit. Somehow he had managed to find out the purpose of my visits, or at least strongly suspected it. He called on my friend and, in the course of their conversation, implied pretty clearly that his purpose in coming to Meadow was to destroy my reputation for once and for all. I don't know that he would have followed through this time, and actually I rather doubt it. He enjoyed being able to dangle exposure over my head too thoroughly to ever deprive himself of that power by using it."

"So she killed him."

"She offered to take him to my concealed cottage, for a

meeting. While he was waiting, she remembered a present I had given her. It was meant to deliver poison to an unsuspecting victim, but she filled it with a powerful tranquilizer instead. She had intended simply to incapacitate him and enlist Lydia Hanifer's aid until they could reach me for instructions. Unfortunately the tranquilizer was designed for a larger body mass and a different biochemistry and my brother died almost immediately. She called Lydia, who sent me a message and asked Kier Torgeson to remove the body. The rest of what happened you pretty much know already."

A long silence followed before Avery finally sighed and relaxed. "All right, I'm trying to put myself in your position, and I suppose I might react in much the same way. But what she did was still wrong."

"I know that, and so does she. When she found out who Kurt Royce really was, she was so upset that I was concerned that she might take her own life. No matter what I do now to help her, the guilt will never go away. Once I've left office, I'll be taking up residence in Haven. It may even be possible to normalize our relationship once the attention of the comnet has turned toward fresh prey."

"So he wasn't killed on your instructions."

"No, not on my instructions, but it was still because of me and I accept whatever blame is involved. As I said, I even provided the murder weapon, an ancient artifact from Earth, an assassin's weapon disguised as a piece of jewelry. The tranquilizer was for Kier Torgeson; she routinely delivers small parcels from Park City to the outlying farms."

Avery blinked, hoped that his face had not betrayed his sudden realization that he knew the identity of the murderer. The chance of there being two collectors of ancient relics in Haven was too low to admit any other explanation.

Tanya Churienko was Senator Damien's lover, he realized, and also Kurt Royce's murderer, or executioner. He remembered the elaborate fanged necklace he'd seen the night he visited her home.

"All right," he said finally. "No more questions. I suppose there are situations in which the usual rules don't apply." Avery allowed himself to smile. "One way or another, you've certainly made this a memorable visit for me, Senator."

"I hope, with the passage of time, your memories will be more pleasant than otherwise."

Avery thought about the way he felt now and the way he'd felt when he'd first arrived on Meadow, and he thought about Dona Tharmody as well. "As a matter of fact, they already are."

About the Author

❋ ❋ ❋

Don D'Ammassa is the author of three previous novels, *Blood Beast*, *Servants of Chaos*, and *Scarab*, as well as over a hundred short stories that have appeared in *Analog*, *Isaac Asimov's Science Fiction*, and other magazines and anthologies. He has been a book reviewer for *Science Fiction Chronicle* for twenty-five years, and is currently writing full time.